...about her
greatest desires...

More . . .

Princess
in Love

JULIANNE MacLEAN

St. Martin's Paperbacks

This is a work of fiction. All of the characters, organizations, and events portrayed in this novel are either products of the author's imagination or are used fictitiously.

PRINCESS IN LOVE

Copyright © 2012 by Julianne MacLean.

All rights reserved.

For information address St. Martin's Press, 175 Fifth Avenue, New York, NY 10010.

ISBN: 978-0-312-55279-4

Printed in the United States of America

St. Martin's Paperbacks edition / November 2012

St. Martin's Paperbacks are published by St. Martin's Press, 175 Fifth Avenue, New York, NY 10010.

10 9 8 7 6 5 4 3 2 1

Prologue

She'd always known life did not follow a straight or predictable path—it was riddled with unexpected twists, turns, and steep inclines—but never had Rose Sebastian understood that fact as well as she did on the day her world turned upside down and her heart was smashed to pieces.

As the uniformed guard led her down a steep set of spiraling stone steps that seemed to go on forever into a hellishly dark dungeon in the very guts of the earth, Rose wondered if she would ever look back on these events and understand why it all happened the way it did. Would she ever let go of the regret? Would she ever be grateful for the cruel lessons that had been forced upon her?

The guard continued down a long stone corridor with torches blazing in wall sconces. The hay-strewn floor was wet beneath her feet. She had never ventured this deeply into Briggin's Prison before. How medieval it seemed. The air was cold and damp and made her body shiver.

At last they reached the cell at the end of the corridor, and the guard lifted the bar on the heavy oaken door. It creaked open on rusty iron hinges.

"He's in here, Your Highness. Shall I accompany you, or do you wish me to wait outside?"

Rose hesitated. Of course the guard must wait outside, for there were intimate matters to discuss with the prisoner.

The prisoner. Dear God, what if she lost her temper and struck him? Or worse, what if she took one look at him and desire still burned, despite everything he had done?

"Wait outside, please," she firmly replied, moving toward the threshold. "Shut the door behind me and bar it. I will knock twice to signal when I am through with him."

She handed the guard a ten-pound note—a small price to pay for his silence—then took a deep breath and steeled her nerves as she entered the prison cell.

The door slammed shut behind her, and she jumped at the sound of it—like a judge's gavel—while her gaze fell upon the man she had come here to confront.

He was already standing in the center of the cell as if he had known it was she outside the door. *She,* who had once adored him. Trusted him. Desired him.

He wore the same fashionable clothing from a few short hours ago when he was arrested in the palace courtyard and dragged away for high treason and attempted murder.

For he had tried to kill her beloved brother, the king.

Her heart squeezed like a wrathful fist in her chest, and for a moment she couldn't breathe.

"You seem surprised to see me," Rose said, lifting her chin and resisting any urge to rush forward into his arms and beg to hear that he was safe and unharmed, for his welfare did not matter. She should not care about that. He deserved to rot down here with the rest of the rats, and she hoped he would.

"Yes," he replied. "And no, because all I've done since they dragged me here was pray you would come to me. I could think of nothing else."

Rose scoffed. "There it is again. The flattery and seduction. Did you imagine I would learn of your peril and try to rescue you? Did you think I would drop to my brother's feet and beg him to set you free because I had fallen in love with you? Even after what you did to my family and how you used me?"

He stepped forward, but she held up a hand. "Stay where you are, sir. I know everything. My brother told me of your plot to replace him on the throne. I know how you came to the palace to win the queen's affections. I know that your father has been planning your marriage to her since the day you were born so that you would one day rule this country at her side. You have been deceiving us all, and for that reason I came here to tell you that anything I felt for you in the past is annihilated. Nothing I said remains true any longer for I was misled, and I certainly have no intention of helping you escape your sentence, whatever it may be."

He shook his head in disbelief. "You're lying. If you felt nothing for me, why did you come here? If I did not matter to you, you would simply watch my head roll."

Her fury erupted again, for he was not wrong. She was not indifferent, but damn him for recognizing it. Damn him for pointing it out.

The chill of the prison cell seeped into her bones, and she rubbed at her arms. "I will never forgive you," she said.

He stared at her. "Yes you will, Rose, because you know I am innocent."

She felt nauseous suddenly. A part of her wanted to weep at the loss of him. Another part of her wanted to strike him and shake him senseless until he confessed that he had treated her wrongly and that he was sorry. That he regretted all the lies and betrayals, and that this was all just a bad dream.

"I know no such thing," she replied nevertheless. "My brother was poisoned with arsenic just like my father, who is now dead. You of all people know how much I loved my father. Yet you, as a devout Royalist, were behind the plot to kill him."

He made a fist at his side. "No, I knew nothing of that, just as I knew nothing of the attempt on Randolph's life. I love you, Rose. You know that. You know I would never do anything to hurt you."

He tried to move closer again, and what was left of her heart split in two. He was still the most beautiful man she had ever known, and despite all her cool, contemptuous bravado, she could never forget the passion they shared, how his touch had ignited her whole world into a boundless realm of happiness.

But she must push those memories aside, for she was devastated by his betrayal and by the total destruction of her first love.

How could she have been so foolish? How could she not have seen the truth? How would she ever recover from this?

"Please," he said, spreading his arms wide in open surrender. "Tell Randolph I had nothing to do with the arsenic. I confess I was raised as a Royalist, and yes . . . my father wanted to remove your family from the throne and I was involved in that. But since the day we met on that muddy road in England, Rose, I have cared less and less for politics and thrones. I fell in love with you. You know it in your heart." He inhaled deeply. "Speak to Randolph on my behalf. Tell him I am sincere. I knew nothing of the attempt on his life or your father's murder. Treason, yes . . . I am guilty of that. I was part of the plot to take back the throne, at least in the beginning, but I am no killer."

Her heart was beating so fast she feared she might faint, but it was not like before, when her heart raced simply because Leopold Hunt, Marquess of Cavanaugh, entered a room. This was different. Everything had changed. She was not the same naive girl she was six months ago. The trust was gone. She must smother all that remained of her foolish infatuation.

"It will fall on the court to determine whether or not you are a killer," she told him. "I cannot help you in that regard, for clearly I am incapable of sensible judgments where you are concerned."

"That is not true."

A part of her wanted to believe him, but she clung to

the dark shadow of contempt that had taken over her soul.

"Yes it is," she replied, "for you were the worst mistake of my life."

All the color drained from his face—as if she had thrust a knife into his belly.

"I pray you will not feel that way forever," he said.

She laughed bitterly. "Why? So there might be a chance for us? Or perhaps you hope my feelings might change in time to reduce your sentence?"

"It has nothing to do with that."

For a flashing instant, her thoughts flew back to that muddy road in England when the world was a different place and she still believed in heroes and fairy tales.

She quickly pounded the life out of that memory and kicked it into a deep grave.

"If I must repeat myself, I will," she replied. "I want nothing more to do with you, Leopold. I want to forget what happened between us and move on with my life. I wish you luck in the trial, but I will not be here to witness it, for I will be leaving Petersbourg as soon as possible. I intend to marry the archduke of Austria, as planned."

"Rose, wait . . ."

Again, he took a step closer but she swung around, fearful that he might touch her, hold her, weaken her resolve. She rushed to the door and rapped hard against it with a tight fist. "Guard!"

The bar lifted and the door opened. Rose rushed out.

"Is everything all right, Your Highness?" the guard asked, looking more than a little concerned.

"I am fine," she lied.

While she struggled to resist the treacherous urge to change her mind and return to Leopold's side, the door slammed shut behind her.

Suddenly, to her utter shame and chagrin, she wondered what would happen if she spoke to Randolph on Leopold's behalf. Would he show mercy? Life in prison perhaps, instead of death?

No. No! She would do nothing of the sort! She was a Sebastian and had a duty to fulfill. Her brother's new monarchy had only just begun. She must remain strong, serve her beloved country, and marry the future emperor of Austria.

She would forget about Leopold Hunt, and she would be more sensible from this day forward. She would not spend another moment wondering how this unthinkable heartache had come to pass, nor would she wonder what she could have done differently to avoid it.

What was done was done. He was dead to her now.

It was time to leave Petersbourg.

PART I

England

Six months earlier

Chapter One

June 22, 1814

"What is happening? Dear Lord, we are all going to die!"

The coach swerved ominously like a snake's tail behind the frightened team of horses. With terrifying violence, Rose was tossed out of her seat and thrown against the side door.

"We are not going to die!" she shouted to the dowager Duchess of Pembroke. It seemed a rather silly assertion, however, spoken from the floor of the coach when she was blind as a bat because her bonnet had fallen forward over her face.

She tugged it back and groped at the seat cushions to remove herself from the floor, when suddenly the coach veered sharply again in the opposite direction. She shot across the interior like a cannonball and slammed into the window.

"Oh, my word!" the duchess cried. "Are you hurt?"

The coach was still careening left and right. Rose

scrambled to her knees and reached for something—
anything—to hold on to for she had no wish to go flying through the air a third time.

"I am well enough," she replied, though she'd landed
hard on her wrist and it was throbbing painfully. "And
you, Your Grace? Are you hurt?"

A cacophony of shouts and hollers began outside
the coach as the team was brought under control and
the coach at last drew to a halt. Everything went suddenly still and blessedly quiet.

"What happened?" the dowager asked in a daze.

Rose struggled to her feet and tasted blood on her
lower lip. It was already beginning to swell.

"I am not certain," she replied, "but we at least seem
to be out of harm's way."

She was just climbing onto the seat when the coach
door flew open. "Everything all right in here?" the driver
asked with wide eyes. The dowager's footman appeared
in the open doorway beside him.

"Yes, I believe so," Rose replied, though she was aching all over and the dowager was white as a sheet.

"My apologies," he said. "We hit a slippery patch and
one of the horses kicked another before they all went
stark raving mad. We're lucky we didn't flip over and
roll down the hillside."

"Lucky indeed," the dowager replied with notable
sarcasm.

Rose leaned her head back against the seat and shut
her eyes. *Thank God we are all safe.*

Quickly recovering her senses, she sat forward.
"What about you, Samson? And Charles? Unscathed, I
hope?"

"Yes, ma'am," Samson replied. "Just a little shook up, is all. It was quite a ride. I thought we were done for."

Perhaps it was the fragile state of her nerves, or a sudden burst of euphoria at having cheated death, but Rose found herself laughing.

"I believe we are in agreement there, Mr. Samson. If only you could have seen me! I've never been airborne before today, and I am quite certain I do not wish to repeat the experience."

Samson's shoulders relaxed and he bent forward with relief. "Indeed, madam. I saw my life pass before my eyes. It made me realize I didn't eat nearly enough cakes and pies."

She laughed uproariously, despite the fact that her lip was throbbing and she was having some trouble moving her wrist without considerable pain.

The dowager shook her head at them. "You young people are half mad! We all nearly met our maker just now, and you are laughing!" Then she, too, joined them with a smile. "But I daresay there are times one must appreciate being spared from near-fatal disaster. We are still breathing, and that is what matters."

A short while later, they were all standing outside the coach staring at the rear wheel that was up to its axle in a puddle of sticky muck, while the wind gusted across the rolling green hills and whipped at the ladies' skirts.

Samson had tried with considerable effort to motivate the horses to pull, but the coach simply would not budge.

"Whatever shall we do?" the dowager asked. "It will soon be dark. We cannot remain here all night."

"Have no fear, Your Grace," Samson replied. "We

will unhitch one of the horses and send Charles to fetch help. He'll be back before we know it."

The men set to work to prepare a horse to ride, while the ladies returned to the coach. An hour later, it was pitch-dark outside, and they were still waiting.

"How much longer do you think it will be?" the dowager asked as a few raindrops went *plop* on the roof.

Seconds later, a thunderous downpour began.

Rose looked up. "Oh dear. Poor Samson. He'll drown out there. I must invite him to wait inside with us."

She opened the door and poked her head out into the driving rain. "Mr. Samson! Please come inside! I insist!"

"Thank you kindly, madam, but I am fine here at my post. Must keep an eye out for help when it arrives."

"No, you most certainly are not fine out there, and you have done your duty a dozen times over. Come down here at once, or I will drag you out of that seat myself."

The wind shook the coach while raindrops, hard as pellets, pummelled the rooftop. At last, Mr. Samson surrendered and joined them inside. He was soaking wet and shivering as he took a seat across from Rose and the duchess.

"How much longer do you suspect it will be before help arrives?" the dowager asked. "I am beginning to believe we may be stranded here all night. What a shame. Don't you have tickets for the play at Covent Garden tomorrow evening?"

"Wait a moment . . ." Rose cupped a hand to her ear. "Listen. Do you hear that? A vehicle is approaching."

Samson peered out the dark window. "It is too soon for Charles to return. It must be someone else."

"Oh dear Lord, save us," the duchess said. "What misfortune will befall us next?"

"What do you mean?" Rose asked.

The duchess sighed heavily. "What sort of bad character travels anywhere on a night like this? A highwayman, no doubt. I suspect we are about to be robbed."

Rose scoffed. "I am sure that is not the case."

Though her skin was prickling. She had witnessed far too much violence in her life not to feel some unease in a situation such as this, for she was a princess from a country that was still raw from the wounds of a revolution that deposed the former king and put her own father—a military general—on the throne in his place.

Though it happened twenty years ago when she was barely old enough to toddle, she would never forget the night an assassin sneaked into her father's bedchamber while she was sitting on his lap in front of the fire. The man had brandished a knife that gleamed dangerously in the firelight. Absolutely terrorized, Rose had watched her father strangle the villain to his death.

She felt that same paralyzing fear now and tried to tell herself it was not rational. This was not Petersbourg where her father's enemies still gathered secretly to plot an overthrow of the New Regime. She and her brothers were in England on a diplomatic visit.

There were no enemy Royalists here. She was quite safe, except for the wind and the rain, of course, but surely the passengers in the approaching vehicle would offer assistance and everything would be fine. In an hour or two, she and the duchess would be enjoying a hot meal while sipping tea in a cozy inn.

As the vehicle rumbled to a halt behind them and the horses shook noisily in the harness, Rose clasped her hands together on her lap to hide the fact that they were trembling.

Samson opened the door and got out. A strong gust of wind blew into the coach and the door slammed shut behind him.

Voices shouted over the roar of the storm. Good Lord, what was happening? Was Samson all right?

Rose slid across the seat to look out the window and nearly swallowed her tongue when the door flew open again and she found herself staring up at a tall man in a top hat and black overcoat, holding himself steady against the wind. It was too dark to make out his face, and the terror she experienced in that moment was more piercing than the panic she'd felt when the coach nearly flipped over and toppled down the hillside.

"Your Royal Highness!" the man shouted, and she was taken aback by the familiarity in his tone. "May I join you inside?"

Before waiting for an answer, the stranger swung his large frame into the vehicle, removed his hat, and sat down on the facing seat.

As the golden lamplight reached his face, Rose sucked in a breath of surprise.

"Lord Cavanaugh? Good heavens, what are *you* doing here?"

"I am here to rescue you, of course," he replied with a magnificent smile that melted all her fears about highwaymen, but reminded her that she and Lord Cavanaugh had once flirted shamelessly in Petersbourg.

Although as soon as her heart had become involved, he had rejected her. Quite cruelly in fact.

Her pride was still bruised by those events, but she would die a thousand deaths before she'd let him see it.

"My word," she replied, sounding completely cool and collected, not the least bit unruffled. "How is this possible? Did you somehow learn we were stranded? I was not even aware you were in England."

Removing his black leather gloves, he shook his head elegantly, and as usual her heart stumbled backward into that old infatuation that simply would not die, no matter how many times she tried to beat it into submission.

But how could she, when Leopold Hunt was the most darkly sensual and seductive man in the world? She'd been enamored of him since she was a young girl.

Damn him, and damn her stubborn attraction to him. She hated that he made her feel flustered. She thought she was over that by now. It had been two years, for pity's sake, and she had done very well since then, behaving with complete indifference toward him as if none of it mattered at all.

"If I had known," he said, "I assure you I would have come much sooner, so I must confess the truth. This is an utterly odd coincidence that causes me to wonder if there are higher forces at play. Of course I knew you and your brothers were visiting London, but what in the world are you doing *here,* Rose, on this remote country road?" His stunning blue eyes turned to the duchess, as if he realized only then that they were not completely alone. "My apologies for the intrusion, madam," he said with a frown. "We have not yet been introduced."

"I do beg your pardon," Rose quickly interjected.

What was wrong with her? Oh, but she knew the answer to that question. As soon as she recognized the impossibly gorgeous and charming Lord Cavanaugh, the rest of the world had simply disappeared. She had become distracted and forgotten about the duchess entirely.

In fact, she had forgotten about everything. The fierce gales. The stinging rain.

Most important, her recent engagement, which had not yet been announced.

"Your Grace," she said, "may I present Leopold Hunt, the Marquess of Cavanaugh and a great hero in the war against Napoleon. Lord Cavanaugh is an old friend of my brother's. They went to school together in Petersbourg." She gestured with a hand. "Lord Cavanaugh . . . the dowager Duchess of Pembroke."

"I am delighted, Your Grace," he replied. "What brings you both out on a night like this?"

How perfectly agreeably he behaved, as if the awkward, humiliating end to their affair had never occurred.

The coach shuddered in the wind, and another blast of rain struck the windowpanes.

Rose gave the duchess a sidelong glance. "We attended a charitable event in Bath but were late leaving town. We didn't expect to encounter such treacherous roads."

"Welcome to springtime in England," the duchess said with a chuckle.

Lord Cavanaugh raised an eyebrow. "Indeed. Well, then. I have already spoken to your driver, and I insist that you both join me in my coach. I, too, am on my way to London, but I've made arrangements to stay at the Crimson Flower Inn for the night. I can deliver you both there safely, and your good man Samson is transferring your bags to my vehicle as we speak. He promises to meet you in the morning to continue on your way, providing there is no damage to your vehicle, of course, in which case you shall ride the rest of the way with me."

Rose's pride reared up, and she wished she could reject Lord Cavanaugh's assistance, but the fact remained—they were stranded and in desperate need of help.

"We most gratefully accept," the duchess replied. "How fortunate for us that you came along when you did, Lord Cavanaugh. You are the hero of the day!"

He turned his arresting blue eyes to Rose. "Shall we?"

She managed a polite smile.

The next thing she knew, he was handing her up into his own well-appointed vehicle with warm bricks on the floor, lush velvet seats, and luxurious cushions with gold tassels thrown freely about. The light from a small carriage lamp filled the space with a warm glow, and it smelled cozy and inviting—like apples and cinnamon.

Cavanaugh climbed in and sat down across from her. Though he wore a heavy greatcoat, she could still make out the muscular contours of his body beneath it. Or perhaps she simply remembered all too well those particular details of his appearance—along with the rich chestnut color of his hair and the unruly manner in which it fell forward around his temples.

It was difficult not to stare at those long black lashes, which framed an intense pair of blue eyes—a rare and striking feature on a man. And that mouth . . . so full of confident sexuality.

He was a devastatingly handsome man by all accounts and she wondered if he had any notion of the power he possessed. Did he know that he could make a woman swoon and ruin her for life with a mere glance in her direction?

Oh, probably.

As Rose sat back in the seat and settled in, she wondered if his chance arrival and heroic chivalry was an event too good to be true, or if it was the worst possible thing that could ever happen—for she certainly did not wish to be tempted away from her fiancé. Not only was Archduke Joseph the future emperor of Austria, he was, by all accounts, utterly besotted with her and would never in a thousand years break her heart.

If only she could be more indifferent toward Lord Cavanaugh and his extraordinary charisma.

She feared this was going to be a bumpy ride.

Chapter Two

As the coach prepared to depart, Leopold sat across from Princess Rose and wondered irritably if this was some sort of test of his Royalist allegiances, for what the devil were the odds of running into a Sebastian on a deserted country road on a night like this, when he was on his way back to London to meet a Tremaine?

Rose of all people. *Rose.*

Discreetly he watched her while she arranged her skirts in the most enchanting manner and unbuttoned the top of her cloak to reveal her lavish bosom beneath. She should have looked ragged and weary after what she'd been through this evening, but somehow this rather remarkable princess always managed to appear delicious and fetching in pretty silks and ribbons and lace. One more gust of wind a few minutes ago, and he might have ended up in the ditch lamenting his damned inconvenient carnal desires.

For he had no business desiring a Sebastian.

The coach lurched forward unexpectedly, and Rose reached out to grab at something, as if she half expected to be tossed to the floor.

A rather unfortunate metaphor for her future, he supposed, which did not help his mood in the slightest.

Nevertheless, Leopold frowned as he watched her wrap a hand around her wrist and wince in pain.

"You're hurt," he observed.

"Not at all," she replied, which prompted the duchess to speak on her behalf.

"Princess Rose is very brave, Lord Cavanaugh, and too proud to describe how she was thrown about with such violence, it is a wonder she still lives."

His eyebrows drew together with concern. "You must see a doctor, then."

"I am sure that's not necessary," she casually replied. "It is a mild sprain, nothing more. I am perfectly well."

He sat back, unconvinced she was telling the truth. "We will send for a doctor nonetheless, as soon as we reach the inn. Best not to take chances."

"Quite right," the duchess said, while the coach picked up speed.

Rose lifted her compelling blue eyes to meet his, and despite their polite discourse when he entered her coach a few minutes ago, she was now regarding him with an unmistakable note of disdain.

He couldn't pretend not to understand why, for he remembered all too well how he had treated her so shabbily a few years back.

His thoughts meandered a bit further into the past . . . to that bright sunny day when they went riding together during a shooting party on his father's estate. The

Sebastian royals of the New Regime were the guests of honor, which had been a carefully plotted ruse to prove Leopold's loyalty to the crown and secure greater power for him in the Sebastian court.

Rose had just turned twenty, and he hadn't been able to keep his eyes—or his hands—off her, for she was an exquisite beauty with unparalleled intelligence and a boatload of charm to go along with it.

During the hunt, her brothers—the princes Randolph and Nicholas—had raced ahead with the hounds barking at their heels. Leopold and Rose chose to follow at a more leisurely pace and flirted up a storm while discussing books and theater and the latest gossip at court.

Rose was coquettish that day, and if he'd wanted to, he could have bedded her before the week was out, for there was an undeniable spark of attraction between them that exploded like cannon fire each time they met. She aroused him to a wicked degree, and he knew the feeling was mutual. They had been wildly attracted to each other, and despite the look she'd given him just now, he suspected not much had changed. And he still wanted to bed her, goddammit.

Growing increasingly sensitive to the heady scent of her perfume inside the close confines of the coach and the enticing curves of her appealing body, he turned his gaze to the window and reminded himself that nothing could ever come of it, for she was a Sebastian and he, a secret Royalist. One day he would help topple her usurping family from the throne of Petersbourg, and from that moment on, Rose would count him among the very worst of her enemies. And she had more than a few.

When he glanced back at her, he was still disturbingly aware of those soft, full lips and the captivating lavish bosom he remembered so well. The lust he once felt for her reared up quite violently, and he cursed this damnable weather for thrusting them together again.

It had not been part of the plan.

"Do tell us, Lord Cavanaugh," the duchess said. "What brings you to England? Are you part of the shipbuilding campaign to strengthen our allied navies?"

Rose tried not to stare too closely at Leopold as he lounged back casually in the seat like a gorgeous lion. "Not at this time, Your Grace, but I understand Prince Randolph is making excellent progress in that regard."

It was not lost on Rose that he hadn't answered the question, and though she wished she couldn't care less about his comings and goings, she rephrased it.

"Are you visiting acquaintances, my lord?"

His seductive blue eyes turned to her while the rain beat hard upon the roof.

"I've been traveling with my father for the past month," he replied. "He is journeying to Scotland tomorrow, but I shall return home to Petersbourg in the next day or so."

"Sailing out of London?" the duchess asked.

"Yes, that's correct." He then steered the conversation to the celebrations in France since Napoleon's capture. Thank heavens there was much to discuss on that front.

Later, as the coach rocked and swayed on its stormy path to the inn, the dowager's head began to nod and her eyes fluttered closed. Soon she was snoring softly.

Uncomfortably aware of the fact that she had just

lost the company of her chaperone, Rose glanced across at Lord Cavanaugh, who was resting a finger on his temple and watching her with those sly, devilish eyes.

"Don't look at me like that," she said, "as if we are alone here and I am something you find amusing."

"Amusing?" He shook his head as if baffled by her remark. "That is not the word I would choose." He casually began to unbutton his overcoat. "Do you not find it strange that we've bumped into each other like this? Honestly, what are the odds?"

"Very slim indeed," she replied. "I am beginning to wonder if it is some sort of punishment. Though I am not quite sure what I did to deserve it."

"Punishment." He sighed heavily. "Ah, Rose, I thought we were beyond that. It's been two years."

She shifted her body on the seat and rubbed at her aching wrist, which had begun to swell. "Has it truly been that long? I hadn't thought about it. I am happy to hear *you* are keeping track, though."

The dowager snorted and jumped, as if startled out of a bad dream. Then her eyes fell closed again.

Lord Cavanaugh leaned forward, weaved his fingers together, and rested his elbows on his knees. He regarded Rose carefully with narrowed eyes, as if he were studying her mood, trying to decipher her like a riddle.

As usual, she felt very exposed. He was too close, and she didn't want to smell the pleasing fragrance of his cologne, or look at those strong, manly hands, for they reminded her of the past.

"Can we not be friends?" he asked.

Her breaths were coming faster now, and she

swallowed hard over the urge to tell him what she *really* wanted him to do with his friendship.

"Does it even matter to you, Leopold? Because I don't believe it does. I think you want my approval only because we are stuck here together and there is no escaping the awkwardness of it. The whole country knows you do not accept defeat, and you want to have the upper hand again. As soon as I tell you that you are forgiven and I adore you, you will sit back in that seat, quite satisfied with your triumph, and you will stop working so hard to be charming."

In the very next instant, he sat back. "You never fail to astonish me."

"How so?"

He frowned. "I've never met a woman who speaks as candidly as you. You don't mince words. You say what you think."

She scoffed. "No, I assure you, Leopold, I do not. If I said what I really thought, you would be a great deal more than astonished."

His frankly sensual eyes studied her with admiration, and he leaned forward again. "I am sure you are quite right about that, but let us travel back a bit. I certainly don't think you adore me. Quite to the contrary, I believe you are very unhappy with me, and I cannot blame you. What happened between us two years ago was . . . it was . . ."

He paused, and she clenched her teeth in anger. For the love of God, she couldn't stomach any more of this unnecessary degradation.

Raising a hand and shaking her head, she said, "Please, Leopold. There is no need for us to discuss it. It was a long time ago and I am completely over it. I am very happy now. I no longer wish that you would become the man I once wished you to be."

He regarded her shrewdly. "Now *there* is an artful insult if I ever heard one."

"Not at all," she helpfully replied. "You are who you are, and two years ago I was simply mistaken in my impression of you." She waved a dismissing hand through the air. "I was very young."

He chuckled. "You were twenty. And what *was* your impression of me, exactly?"

He appeared quite genuinely curious.

Rose paused. If she were being honest, she would tell him she believed him to be the most handsome, compelling, and intelligent man she'd ever imagined could exist, and that she was certain they were destined to be together, and she wanted him to father her children—at least a half dozen of them.

But that romantic first impression had died a swift death when she showed her true feelings and he blatantly rejected her. For that reason, he did not deserve to hear such praise.

"I thought you were very charming," she simply said.

"There's that word again." He shook his head and waved a finger, as if he knew she was holding back and would have none of it.

She let out a frustrated breath. "What do you want me to say? That I fancied myself in love with you? That I thought you might feel the same way, and I was heartbroken when I realized it meant nothing to you? Or that I still dream of a proposal from you?"

His lips parted, and he was about to answer the question when the dowager snorted and started awake.

"Oh, I do beg your pardon," she said, sitting up. "Was I sleeping? Are we almost there?"

Leopold inclined his head at Rose, as if to say, *We are not done here.*

The coach slowed to a halt just then, and he peered out the window. "Your instincts are impeccable, madam," he said. "It appears we have arrived."

Chapter Three

The rain continued to fall and the wind howled over the shingled roof of the inn as Rose and the dowager dashed out of the coach and across the yard to the front door.

Inside the parlor—blessedly warm with the heat of a roaring fire in an enormous hearth—the innkeeper was waiting with a smile. Rose lowered the hood of her cloak and tried to ignore the pain in her wrist, which had swelled considerably over the past hour.

"Your Royal Highness, Your Grace . . ." The innkeeper bowed to them both. "Welcome. It is an honor to serve you this evening. I have your rooms prepared, if you will follow me this way."

He led them upstairs to two rooms, side by side, small but cozy and clean, with polished brass beds and freshly laundered sheets and quilts.

Rose took one look at the soft, dry bed and the brick fireplace, freshly kindled and waiting to be lit, and nearly wept with joy, for she was exhausted after the numerous charity events and speeches in Bath, followed by a near-fatal carriage accident, and the unexpected arrival of a man she would have preferred never to see again.

She ran her tongue over her swollen lip and held her wrist close to her chest. Lord Cavanaugh had insisted she be seen by a doctor, and though she'd put on a brave face, she was beginning to feel grateful for that. It would be best to ensure she hadn't broken anything, or at the very least, to be prescribed something to numb the pain.

"The maid will be up shortly with hot water and fresh linens," the innkeeper said. "Would you like supper trays sent up, or would you prefer to join the marquess in the private dining room?"

Rose was about to select the supper tray, but the dowager was quicker to respond. "We would be delighted to join the marquess. Please thank him for arranging our accommodations and tell him we will be downstairs directly."

The innkeeper bowed and retreated.

"What a charming gentleman," the dowager said, as she stood in Rose's doorway and glanced about the room, which was identical to her own.

"Are you referring to the innkeeper or the marquess?" Rose asked.

"Why, the marquess, of course," the dowager replied. "How lucky we were to be rescued by such a man. I daresay we must toast to our good fortune. Now if you will excuse me, I must dress for dinner. I am positively famished."

Rose smiled in agreement, rubbed a hand over her throbbing wrist, and shut her door with a frown.

* * *

Two hours later, after they dined on a moist and mouth-watering main course of lamb with spiced gravy, roasted potatoes, and carrots dripping in cinnamon butter, their private table in the back room was cleared for dessert. By that time, Rose was feeling no pain in her wrist on account of the sumptuous full-bodied wine that had accompanied the meal.

While Lord Cavanaugh described his treacherous voyage across the North Sea on his way to England, a sweet apple brandy was served to the table, along with raspberry cream cakes and sugared plums.

The dowager's cheeks were, by now, beyond rosy, for she had enjoyed the wine a little too much and became unmindful of her obligation to be a strict and moral chaperone. During dinner she permitted Rose's glass to be refilled more than once, and Rose soon found herself laughing openly with the marquess about the infamous kitchen incident of 1811—when her father's dog escaped into the palace courtyard with a giant block of cheese in his jaws, and the cook chased after him with a rolling pin, tripped over her skirts, and fell tumbling into the reflecting pond.

The dog was forced to sleep in the wine cellar that night, while the cook, unfortunately, was dismissed. Though it was not such a sad occasion when all was said and done, for that particular cook possessed no sense of humor. The dog certainly didn't mourn the loss of her.

For that brief period of time at the table during dessert, Rose managed to forget about her awkward history with Leopold, and simply enjoyed herself. Soon she began to wonder if it might be possible for them to be friends after all. She was engaged to another man now, which provided a certain protection from Cavanaugh's attentions and attractiveness. If she could move past the humiliation of his rejection and accept him for what he truly was—a dangerously charming flirt who was too handsome for his own good—it might very well be possible. For she certainly did enjoy his conversation. Nothing about that had changed, and she doubted it ever would.

Eventually she found herself relaxing in her chair while quietly observing him talk to the dowager about her beloved Italian Gardens at Pembroke Palace.

It was probably a mistake to enjoy watching him like that, but the delicious aroma of the apple brandy, mixed with the spicy warmth of it as it touched her lips, put Rose in a reflective mood.

A carriage pulled up outside the window just then, and a man got out. Leopold stood up and pulled a white lace curtain aside. "That must be the doctor."

A moment later, the door to their private dining room swung open and the doctor was shown in. He was an older gentleman with white hair and spectacles.

Rose set down her cup. Introductions were made, and the doctor joined them at the table. He ordered a glass of claret and conversed with them for a few minutes before inquiring about Rose's accident.

"I am sure it is nothing," she explained as she rubbed at her arm.

He peered at her over the tops of his spectacles. "May I?"

"Of course."

He adjusted his spectacles on the tip of his nose, then turned her arm this way and that while pressing on her wrist bone with the pad of his thumb. "Any pain here?" he asked.

"No."

"Here?"

"No."

"Does it hurt when I bend it like this?" He flexed her hand and straightened her wrist.

"Ouch. Yes. That is quite painful."

The doctor removed his spectacles and sat back in his chair. "Well, madam, I do not believe anything is broken, but you did some damage. It is as you thought, a mild sprain, and you are sure to experience some discomfort over the next few days. I should like to wrap it if you don't object, to provide you with some support and comfort. Try not to move it more than absolutely necessary and it should heal quickly. You will be right as rain before you know it."

Rose smiled at him. "That is a relief, I must say. Thank you, Doctor."

He opened his leather bag and withdrew a rolled-up bandage along with a small bottle. "I suspect you may have some trouble sleeping tonight, but a few drops of this before you retire will help ease any discomfort." He handed it to her.

"Thank you," she replied.

He began to wrap her wrist.

A short while later, Leopold escorted him to the door and thanked him for venturing out on such a terrible night, then returned to the table and sat down.

"That was good of you to send for him," Rose said.

Leopold shook his head as if it were nothing. "Say no more about it. I am honored to be of service."

He picked up his brandy and swirled it around in the glass before tipping it back and finishing it.

Rose watched the movement of his throat and couldn't seem to pull her gaze away from his beautiful mouth as he swept his tongue across his lips to taste the last few drops.

For a moment, she felt as if she were floating in a dream, yet she wanted desperately to shake herself awake.

Thankfully, the dowager gathered up her gloves just then and stood.

"What a delightful evening it has been," she said. "You have been most generous and hospitable, my lord."

Cavanaugh stood and bowed to her. "The pleasure was all mine, and please rest peacefully this evening knowing that I have sent assistance to your coachman. In the morning, we will evaluate the condition of your vehicle and make a decision about the rest of your travel arrangements. Needless to say, I am at your service and would be delighted to escort you the rest of the way to London, if need be."

He kissed the dowager's hand. She smiled blushingly, then left the room and waited at the stairs for Rose to join her.

Rose held out her good hand and Leopold bent forward to kiss it. His lips lingered hotly upon her knuckles, and a delicious pulse of awareness skirted down the length of her body.

"Join me for another drink after the duchess has retired," he suggested as his seductive eyes lifted. "I will wait for you."

Clinging to her good sense, she pulled her hand free. "That is not possible, my lord. I must bid you good night."

As she passed him on her way to the door, he spoke in a low voice that was edged in command. "But there are things that must be said."

More than a little shaken by the request, Rose hurried to her room before she agreed to do something she might later regret.

Chapter Four

Leopold sat before the fire in the private dining room for two solid hours waiting for Rose to return. When she did not come, his mood turned increasingly foul. He attempted to drown it out by finishing what was left of the brandy and berating himself for wanting her—when she was the one woman in the world he should not want and could not have.

It shouldn't matter that she was over him. He should, in fact, be pleased about that. Nor should he care if she was still angry about his detestable behavior two years ago and thought the worst of him—because when he ended it, he'd *wanted* her to despise him, for it was the only way. He knew she possessed a passionate nature and would never give him up, and he couldn't very well tell her the truth—that he'd been groomed all his life to hate her, and to knock her vulgar usurping family off the throne of Petersbourg.

Yet since that time, he'd had no respite from the regret, for he never could succeed at hating her, and after seeing her tonight, he knew he still desired her as ardently as he had the first time their lips met.

Just thinking about her sweet, delicious mouth caused a stirring of need in his loins that made him wonder what the bloody hell he was doing here, waiting for her to join him for a drink. It would only intensify this wretched torture and drag him through another round of agonizing sexual resistance, and in the end he'd be forced to repeat what he'd done to her the last time, which was to push her away. Incite her hate.

Deciding that it was long past time to purge such thoughts from his brain, he rose from the chair and moved across the room in a hazy fog of frustrated desire mixed with too much wine and brandy. He stopped dead in his tracks, however, when he encountered Rose in the doorway, looking impossibly beguiling and quite thoroughly vexed.

Rose took one look at Leopold, gorgeous and godlike in the shimmering firelight, and wondered what the devil had been going through her head just now when she walked out of her room and descended the stairs.

"I wasn't going to come," she explained, feeling defensive all of a sudden as she entered the room and shut the door behind her. "In fact, I was trying very hard to go to sleep, but I couldn't stop thinking of your final words after dinner. Do you have something you wish to say to me, Leopold?"

It shouldn't matter. She shouldn't care at all—and

she certainly shouldn't be here alone with him for he looked rather menacing—but if she didn't find out what it was, it would haunt her for the rest of her days.

He gestured toward the two chairs in front of the fire. "Sit down, Rose."

With some hesitation, she moved past him. "I see that you've finished the brandy. Please do not ring for more. I do not wish to drink with you." Clearly he'd already had enough, and for that reason she needed to keep her wits about her. "Nor do I want anyone to know we are alone here."

"Understood."

He locked the door behind her, which was not what she intended to suggest, but decided it was a good thing. Heaven forbid the dowager should find out about this.

She sat down in front of the fire, her back ramrod straight, and folded her hands primly on her lap while her heart raced with trepidation. "Well, then. Let us fire a musket ball straight into the heart of the matter, shall we? What do you wish to say?"

He took a seat across from her and stared intently with those pale blue eyes that never failed to quicken her blood. She glanced down at his virile body and could not help but admire the strength of his form—the broad shoulders, muscular legs, and large, capable hands. He was a heroic cavalry officer, a true flesh-and-blood warrior, and no other man fascinated her the way this one did, not even Joseph, her fiancé, which disturbed her greatly.

She shouldn't have come.

But she needed to know.

"You're still angry with me," he said, his eyes serious.

"Yes, of course I am, but that is yesterday's news."

He relaxed back in the chair, and she wondered exactly how much brandy he'd consumed. "But I thought tonight was different," he added. "It felt like old times. You seemed cheerful and it gave me hope that you have finally forgiven me."

Rose sat back with a resigned sigh. "Why does it even matter? Two years ago you made your feelings quite clear. You did not wish any further contact with me. I accepted it, and as I told you before, I have moved on. Besides, even if I wanted to, there could be no turning back."

He regarded her with curiosity. "How do you mean?"

There was no point keeping it secret. He would know soon enough, and she *wanted* him to know. Yes, by Jove, she did. Perhaps it was wicked of her, but she wanted to jab him with it—or at the very least, damage his monstrous pride.

"It has not yet been announced," she explained, "but the truth is . . ." She paused and lifted her chin to bask for a moment in this very splendid array of satisfaction. "I am engaged to be married."

His head drew back. "Good God, I had no idea."

She scoffed. "Why? Is it so difficult to imagine? Did you believe I would pine away for *you* the rest of my life, and never give my heart to another?"

Now it was his turn to appear flustered, and she took great pleasure in it.

When he seemed unable to provide an answer, she relaxed her offensive charge and took a deep breath. "I've shocked you."

"Yes, I suppose you have."

They gazed at each other in the flickering firelight, and when he looked at her that way—with such intimate familiarity—she had to fight hard not to fall back under the spell of his captivating male beauty, mixed with all the unforgettable memories of their brief affair two years ago. Certain moments would be etched in her mind forever.

She'd once imagined their love would last a lifetime and they would never be apart. She'd believed, quite mistakenly, that he felt the same way.

How quickly dreams could be crushed. How quickly one could go from bliss and ecstasy to the throes of deathlike despair.

"Who is he?" Leopold asked.

"Archduke Joseph of Austria."

His eyebrows lifted. "Heir to the throne?"

"Yes. My father arranged for us to meet eight months ago, and we have corresponded ever since. He is a good man, Leopold. You would approve of him."

It was the truth. Joseph was decent and honest and their union would strengthen Petersbourg's political ties with Austria. It would be a successful marriage on all fronts.

Leopold sat forward and pinched the bridge of his nose. "I see. Well, then." He looked up at her with dark and broody displeasure. "Congratulations on your upcoming nuptials, Rose, but I would be lying if I said I approve."

She scoffed again. "Why? Is there no one else, besides *you,* who is good enough?"

She meant to be sarcastic, but when his penetrating

eyes narrowed, she realized with a jolt of shock that he might still entertain some measure of desire for her.

It was quite possible that tonight had not been a meaningless flirtation simply to swell his masculine pride. It was quite possible that he, too, had not forgotten the past . . . that there might still be something more simmering beneath the surface.

All at once, she felt as if she were back in that swerving, out-of-control coach and needed to grab on to something.

"It's not that," he explained. "I've always known you could have any man you wanted. You are a beautiful woman and the daughter of a king. I cannot reiterate enough how it frustrates me to think that you wanted me once, but that it simply could not be."

"Could not be? *Please,* Leopold. I would have married you in a heartbeat, and my father would have allowed it because he dotes on my every wish. You know that. Don't pretend otherwise and act as if I were the one who rejected *you.*"

He took both her hands in his, and the physical connection nearly stole her breath. His hands were large and strong, so achingly familiar . . .

Why was he doing this?

"I pretend nothing," he said with an intensity that caused every nerve in her body to quiver and burn. "At least not now, but two years ago I was not free to propose, and I need you to understand that."

She struggled to keep her breathing steady. "What do you mean . . . you were not free to propose?"

At last, the answer came.

"Since birth," he said, "I have been pledged to another."

Her stomach dropped like a stone.

There it was. The explanation she had longed for on so many nights when she was weeping into her pillow, dreaming of this man's hands upon her body, his lips upon her mouth, his vows before God at the altar.

Why hadn't he told her this before? How could he have broken her heart in the cruelest manner and led her to believe he did not care for her? That he did not desire her?

"Why didn't you tell me this before?" she asked. "Why did you treat me with such cold indifference, as if you had lost all affection for me? Do you have any idea how badly you hurt me?"

He spoke firmly. "I couldn't tell you then, and I shouldn't be telling you now because I haven't even met my betrothed yet. We are secretly engaged but have never set eyes on each other."

"You haven't?"

"No."

It sounded very clandestine. She swallowed uneasily. "Then why *are* you telling me?"

He sat back, looking all too gorgeous and dangerously seductive. "I'm not sure. Perhaps I've had too much brandy."

Rose sat back also. "I see."

A log shifted in the grate and a flurry of sparks exploded into the chimney.

Her heart was racing. The inside of her belly was on fire. She had not expected to ever have this conversation with Leopold Hunt. She didn't know what to say, what to make of it, how to manage it.

He was engaged!

"She's English, isn't she?" Rose asked. "That's why you are here and why you have been so vague about the reason for your travels."

He nodded casually to confirm her suspicions, and she reminded herself that she, too, was engaged to another.

A wonderful man who adored her.

"There are many things you don't understand, Rose," he said. "All my life, I have been duty-bound to marry this woman, and when I met you, I certainly didn't intend to fall in love. It just happened. I shouldn't have let it, but it was beyond my control."

Rose tried not to melt completely into his shocking admission of *love* and this long-awaited apology, for it was not as simple as all that.

"Nothing is beyond anyone's control," she argued. "I do not believe in such a thing. No one is a slave to their emotions. You should never have kissed me during the hunt at your father's estate, or after dinner that night. You shouldn't have shown me the secret passages that led to your rooms. I spent the night with you, Leopold, because I trusted you and thought you were going to propose."

"I never took your virtue," he reminded her.

"No, but you took my heart." She was compelled all of a sudden to rise to her feet. "You shouldn't have asked me to come here."

He stood up, too, ignoring most of what she'd just said. "You took my heart as well."

Oh God, did he have no pity? Did he not know this was torture? She was engaged to another man now, and he to another woman.

Yet despite the anger that was knotting up inside her, she relished those words upon his lips. *You took my heart . . .*

He had loved her. He truly had, but he had not been free.

Just as neither of them was free now.

"I came downstairs to put this behind me," she explained. "Now I have done so, and I really must leave."

Something wild flashed in his eyes. "But have you forgiven me?"

She hesitated. "If I say yes, will you promise never to speak of this again?"

He inclined his head, as if he were trying to work out an answer.

Why wouldn't he just let it go?

As she looked into his eyes, she couldn't seem to escape the memory of the mad love she once felt for him. She supposed it would always be a part of her, but life must go on. Eventually she would leave Petersbourg for Austria and become a married woman. When that day came, it was quite possible she would never lay eyes on Leopold Hunt again.

Which would, of course, be for the best.

"All right then," she said at last. "All is forgiven. Fate had other plans for us, that is all. I appreciate that you have explained yourself. Please know that wherever life takes you, I will wish you well."

She forced herself to hold out her hand.

He looked down at it for a long moment. There was

a visible knot of tension in his brow, and Rose feared there would be more of this unbearable torture before he said good-bye.

At long last he took hold of her hand, raised it to his lips, and kissed the back of it. Her whole body awakened with feverish sensation.

"I, too, will always wish you well." His eyes lifted to meet hers, and she steeled herself against a powerful flood of emotion. The passion she once felt for this man was kicking beneath the surface of everything. She didn't want to let go of his hand.

But she must, for it was done. He had apologized for his conduct. They were finished with each other now.

She gave a quick curtsy and turned to go. "Good evening."

"Rose . . ."

She stopped at the door, but did not turn around.

"I will examine the dowager's coach at eight o'clock tomorrow morning," he said, "to determine if it is fit for travel. Will I see you then?"

"Yes, and thank you," she said over her shoulder, while she prayed that the vehicle would be in good working order, for she wasn't sure she could manage another day in this man's presence, especially now that all was forgiven.

"It appears all is well," Leopold said to the dowager the following morning as he knocked on the outside of the coach. "She's as sturdy as a warship."

"Oh, thank heavens!" the dowager replied.

Rose stood on the stone walk in the yard and tried to ignore the way the morning sun sparkled in Leopold's eyes as he approached. "That is indeed good news," she said. "We will not need to burden you any further, Lord Cavanaugh."

"I assure you, Your Highness, it was no burden," he said with a bow. "In fact, I am exceedingly pleased we had the opportunity to dine together last evening."

He gave her that look, as if he were communicating far more than his words conveyed . . . as if they had a secret to share, which they most certainly did.

"It was a very pleasant evening," she agreed, though she had not slept well the rest of the night, despite the prescribed dose of laudanum.

"Might I inquire about your injured wrist?" he asked, looking down at her gloved hand.

She raised it to show him. "It's much better, thank you."

They stood facing each other on the stone walk while a blackbird chirped in the eaves. Rose breathed in the fresh, cool scent of the earth, damp with wetness from the heavy rains the night before, while her former lover regarded her with a rather intense look of desire.

She found herself reveling in the pleasure of his nearness and wondered if it would ever pass. Perhaps not. He was her first love, after all. She couldn't simply erase him.

"Well!" the dowager called out. "Shall we be on our way?"

Lord Cavanaugh turned. "Indeed, madam. Allow me to assist you." He moved to help her step into the coach, while Rose managed with some difficulty to put one foot in front of the other, knowing she would be next to take his hand. When she reached the vehicle, he turned to face her.

"You will be sailing back to Petersbourg soon?" she asked.

"Yes, in the next day or so, otherwise I would pay a call to your brothers at St. James's. Do give them my regards."

"I will, and I wish you a safe voyage."

"And you as well, upon your return." He never took his eyes off hers as he held out his hand.

Rose tried not to make too much of the shivery sensations she experienced when her gloved fingers slid across his palm. A few heart-pounding seconds later, she was settling into the seat and watching him in the doorway, wondering what was left to say. So much, it seemed, yet the only appropriate word was good-bye.

"It was a pleasure meeting you, Your Grace," he said to the dowager. "Perhaps one day you will visit Petersbourg. If so, I would be honored to entertain you at Cavanaugh Manor."

"Oh!" she exclaimed with a leaping thrill in her voice. "You are too kind, sir! Be warned, however, I may take you up on your offer, and then you will *never* be rid of me!"

He smiled at her with those dazzling blue eyes that had the power to seduce any woman alive, and Rose had no choice but to look away, for it was that very smile that had stirred her blood the first time they met. It was blinding, almost too painful to behold.

"Safe trip," he said.

"And the same to you, Lord Cavanaugh," the dowager replied.

It was time for him to close the door. "Good day, Your Highness," he said with a gentlemanly bow. Then he shut the door and shouted, "Onward, Samson!"

The coach jolted into motion and Rose couldn't help herself. She whirled around and stretched her body to look out the tiny back window, just for one last view of him.

Suddenly her whole being flooded with panic.

Perhaps it was a mistake to marry Joseph. Perhaps this was the only man she would ever desire and she would never truly be over him.

Leopold remained standing on the road outside the inn, watching the coach grow distant.

He must have seen her in the window, for he raised a hand to wave good-bye.

All at once, she was overcome by an uncontrollable urge to weep. Good Lord. What was wrong with her?

"What a remarkable man." The dowager sighed. "So capable and handsome. He is a dream, is he not? How is it possible that he is not yet married? Is he looking for a wife, do you know?"

The coach traveled down a hill, and Leopold disappeared from view.

Rose turned on the seat to face front. She felt slightly nauseous and was quite certain she had gone completely pale. "I beg your pardon?"

"Is he married?" the dowager asked. "Because I have a few granddaughters who would most definitely find him very appealing. I am quite sure my son would send us all to Petersbourg in a heartbeat if there was the smallest chance we could capture the marquess for one of them."

Rose carefully pulled off the glove that concealed her swollen wrist and massaged the tender flesh. "I am afraid he is already pledged to someone, Your Grace, though I do not believe they have met yet."

"What a shame," the dowager said. "I do hope this young woman will appreciate how very fortunate she is."

Rose glanced up. "I am sure she will. The very moment she lays eyes on him."

"Indeed," the dowager replied with a chuckle. "I daresay she will lay more than just her eyes on him when she discovers his many charms. I wonder who she is? What does she look like?"

Rose gazed out the window at the passing landscape and imagined what her life might be like now if that woman had never been born. "I really wish I knew."

Chapter Five

It was past dark when Leo's coach rolled up in front of the house in Lambeth where his father was plotting the long-awaited overthrow of the Sebastian monarchy. Leo knew, however, that in reality his father's presence in England had more to do with the high-priced charms of his current mistress, Georgia Stanhope—one of the less celebrated actresses on the London stage.

Her carriage was parked out front when Leo arrived (the woman had no shame) and it galled him to think that he had come all this way and sacrificed so much to do his duty in the name of the Royalist cause, when his father was constantly distracted by shinier, less permanent toys.

Leo stepped out of the coach, pulled off his leather gloves and tapped them against his thigh as he climbed the steps and met the butler at the door.

"Does he know I am here?" Leo asked as he shrugged out of his coat and removed his hat.

"Yes, my lord. I have just informed His Grace of your arrival. He has asked that you wait for him in the library."

"Fine." Leo strode purposefully across the hall to pour himself a brandy.

He waited for a quarter of an hour before his father finally appeared.

"Leopold, you're late," the duke scolded. "I was expecting you yesterday."

"The roads were treacherous," Leo explained.

There was no need to inform him about the chance meeting with Princess Rose. His father still knew nothing of their brief affair two years ago. If he had learned of it, he might have strung Leo up from the rafters.

But those days were done. He would have no more of it.

"Well, you are here at last," the duke said. "Pour me a brandy, will you?"

Leo poured his father a glass from the crystal decanter and carried it across the room. He set it down on the large mahogany desk.

His father sat down in the chair behind the desk and crossed his legs. "I am afraid there has been a change in plans," he said.

Leo sat down also and regarded his father with a dark, simmering fury he felt quite unable to control. Nothing was the same between them, and he was quite certain it was the war. He was not the same man he once was. Ever since his return from the battlefield, he was always looking for a fight, craving a forward charge. "What is it this time?"

"Don't take that tone with me, boy. You know it hasn't

been easy. We must tread carefully toward our goals or we might all end up in Briggin's Prison for high treason."

Leo's eyes narrowed. "Maybe that's where we all belong."

His father frowned. "What is wrong with you? You've been irritable of late. Have you lost your courage?"

"It was never courage that drove this cause, Father," he replied. "It has always been something else. You know it as well as I do."

The duke leaned forward and slapped a hand on the desktop. "What are you implying?"

"I imply that your desire to crush the Sebastian monarchy has nothing to do with duty or honor. On the contrary, you hunger for power, and you have been using me to attain it."

"I beg your pardon? Watch your tongue, boy!"

"Or what?" Leo replied, rising to his feet to tower over his father. "You will lock me in my room or beat me insensible? I wouldn't recommend it, Father, because I am no longer that defenseless young boy. I have been to war. I have seen far worse than the back of your hand, sir, so if you ever raise it to me again, I swear to God I will beat you back twice as hard."

Bloody hell! He had never spoken to his father in such a manner, but it had been a tumultuous year.

"Something has happened," his father said. "Why are you suddenly doubting your purpose?"

The floor shifted beneath Leo's feet. He couldn't say it. He couldn't possibly admit that since he had faced death on the battlefield, he wanted only to live and quench his *own* hungers, not his father's. And what were those hungers exactly?

He could only think of one . . .

Besides, Prince Randolph was a good man. Leo had begun to consider him a friend in recent years, and despite what the Royalists said about the New Regime, the people adored him.

"It is no longer *my* purpose," Leo replied. "It is now yours and yours alone."

"But you are pledged to Princess Alexandra Tremaine," the duke said, sounding confused. "You have been pledged to her since birth. You've always known that."

God help him, Leo had given up everything for the Royalist cause—*everything*—but he was done with that. His encounter with Rose last night had confirmed it.

"If Alexandra is so keen for me to be her champion," Leo said, "why have we not been introduced? Why is she now competing with all the other women in England for a chance at Randolph's hand in marriage? Don't look at me as if it were not true. I've read the papers, Father. I know she has been presented at court, and that she has been provided with gowns and jewels, and she is considered the current favorite to win a proposal from the future king of Petersbourg."

The duke sank back into his chair. "Dammit, Leopold. Why must you question everything?"

Leo walked to the window and spoke with bitter rancor. "Because I am not your bloody pawn."

He took a moment to make sense of all this and bring his anger under control.

"Do not lose heart," his father said with concern.

"You must continue to be patient. You know we don't have the resources to raise an army. This is the most efficient way to regain Alexandra's crown and for you to rule beside her one day, as was always meant to be."

Leo inhaled deeply, moved to a chair and sat down. "So this is the new plan? Alexandra will marry Randolph and be crowned queen all on her own without any help from us, while I simply wait in the wings for the people to realize they prefer true royal blood on the throne?"

It was a ridiculous pipe dream. It was never going to happen. And quite frankly, Leo was surprised his father was willing to accept such a passive strategy.

At the same time, Leo felt a great weight lift from his shoulders, for clearly Alexandra's marriage to another man constituted a breach of their contract.

His father stood up and circled around the desk. "Yes. Then, and only then, will we have the power to turn the tide."

Leo shook his head. "No, Father, not *we*. If she accepts a proposal of marriage from Prince Randolph, I shall consider myself released from our betrothal and no longer a part of this."

The duke hesitated. "But you cannot shun your duty. We are Hunts! We are descended from King Marcus II, while Randolph's ancestors were butchers and blacksmiths. Alexandra has no family, and the New Regime may not be kind to her when they discover she is the secret Tremaine princess. She will need your friendship and the support of the Royalists when she arrives in Petersbourg. And you are not my pawn, Leopold. Your duty is to serve the crown, not me."

It was a convincing argument, one he had heard many times before.

Duty to your true king. Honor for our family . . .

An almost violent rage filled Leo suddenly. He had sacrificed a great deal in the name of duty and honor, and perhaps if he believed Prince Randolph was a villain, he might continue to put duty above all without question. But over the past few years he had come to know Randolph and his brother Nicholas very well—and their sister Rose—and he could no longer believe that the destiny he'd always accepted as true was the proper course of action.

As a boy he was too young to understand and knew nothing but obedience to his father. As a man, however, he had come to recognize that Frederick was a great king, while his own father was a greedy dreamer and an adulterous husband.

God knows what he would do with the Petersbourg crown if he ever seized that ultimate power.

"I will have no more of this," Leo said, backing away. "If Alexandra marries Prince Randolph and one day sits upon the throne, I shall consider my duty to the Tremaines fulfilled, and I will pledge my oath to the New Regime."

"But the Sebastians are common usurpers!" his father argued. "They are not true royals. Frederick was a soldier. The throne was not his to take. It should have gone to our family. We were next in line."

"Careful, Father. You are speaking treason."

The duke's cheeks flushed red. "Do you mean to say you are no longer a Royalist? That you are forsaking your birthright?"

"What if I am?"

The duke paused. "Then you will no longer be my son."

They faced each other squarely, and Leo's heart turned stone-cold in his chest.

"If that is your decision, Father, then so be it. Goodbye."

The duke took a frantic step to follow. "Where will you go?"

"I will sail for Petersbourg in the morning," Leo replied.

"But this is not over! You will not walk away from me!"

Yes, by God, he would.

Leo gave his father one last threatening glare, then walked out and slammed the door shut behind him.

St. James's Palace, London

"How is your wrist this evening?" Prince Nicholas asked Rose as he buttoned his opera cloak inside the door. "You don't have to come with us if you are at all uncomfortable. Randolph and I can make your apologies. The regent will understand."

They had tickets to a play at Covent Garden, and Randolph was impatient to see Alexandra, the woman who had captured his heart the first moment they met. Rose had spoken to her on two separate occasions and found her to be not only beautiful, but gracious and intelligent as well. She was a good choice for a wife and future queen. Rose approved of the match.

"It is much better," she replied, "though my maid

had to help me with my gloves. It's rather awkward sometimes." She rubbed the pad of her thumb over the sore tendons along her forearm and flexed her fingers. "At least the glove hides the bandages."

"Yes. No one would ever know you were hurled about in a carriage accident twenty-four hours past and nearly met your maker."

Rose chuckled. "It wasn't quite as bad as all that. Nevertheless, I am made of stern stuff, Nicholas. It's the Sebastian in me. We are a resilient bunch."

"That we are."

They waited in the front hall for Randolph to join them. He was taking a very long time to dress. The tall case clock ticked heavily by the door. What was keeping him?

"But what about your heart?" Nicholas asked quietly. "Is it as resilient as the rest of you?"

As it happened, her heart was still aching quite stubbornly, but Rose did not seek her brother's pity. She knew he meant well, of course. He was the kindest brother in the world, but she did not wish to talk about it.

"Come now," he whispered. "You can't fool me, Rose. I was the one who wiped buckets of tears from your cheeks two years ago and offered to strangle the scoundrel with a thin rope, remember?"

She couldn't help but smile, but it was a melancholy moment. "You were very generous," she said, "but truly, I am over it. It was a long time ago and I am engaged to Joseph now."

Nicholas studied her with concern. "But are you certain that's what you really want? You don't ever have to lie to me, Rose. I know you better than anyone."

Indeed, he did, for Randolph had always been the special one destined for the throne. While he was being guarded like a priceless jewel, she and Nicholas could sometimes escape the watchful eyes of the palace guards and enjoy a little freedom together as children.

She took a deep breath and peered out the front window at the coach waiting outside. It was a clear night. There was not the slightest breath of wind.

"If you must know," she finally admitted, "I cannot purge him from my mind, though it pains me to admit it."

"I presume you are referring to Cavanaugh," Nick replied with impressive intuitiveness, "and not your betrothed?"

She turned to face him. "Your presumption is correct. I thought I was over him, but I am not sure I ever will be. Please do not tell Randolph. I don't want him to know. He was instrumental in introducing me to Joseph and encouraging our courtship. It will be a good marriage. I know it will. I do not wish to change my mind. I only wish I could stop wanting what I know is not good for me."

Nicholas nodded. "I know all about that."

They continued to wait in silence.

"Tell me this will pass," she said.

He considered it. "Of course it will, in time. I'm sorry, Rose. While I am grateful that Cavanaugh came to your rescue last night, I wish I could have come for you instead."

She couldn't meet her brother's gaze for she feared her composure might crack, and that simply would not do. Two years ago she had been to hell and back over

Leopold Hunt, but she had recovered. She had learned not to wallow in self-pity. To this day she could not bear to be pitied by others.

"Do not worry for me, Nicholas," she said. "I will forget him, just like the last time."

But would she, really? Last time, she had built a wall of anger and hate around the memory of him.

This time she had forgiven him and secretly celebrated the fact that he still cared for her. She had been overjoyed to learn that, contrary to what she believed, he had not wanted to end it two years ago. It had been difficult for him, too, but he'd had no choice in the matter, for it was a contract of betrothal which, as a gentleman of honor, he could not break.

Either way it was tragic. She still desired Leopold Hunt, but it could not be. Not then, not now. Not ever.

"Who is the woman to whom he is pledged?" Nicholas asked suddenly with a curious frown. "And why did he never speak of it before? We have been friends for years."

Rose shrugged. "I don't know the answer to that. All I know is that she is English, and that is why he is here. But he is leaving again, very soon, apparently."

Nicholas paced around the front hall. "It's odd. He hasn't met her yet, but plans to leave as soon as he does? Will he take her with him?"

"I don't know, and I don't care. Help me forget him, will you? Don't ask me about him again. I want to enjoy the play tonight."

Their brother Randolph came bounding down the stairs just then. Rose was relieved to see him. It would take her mind off things.

"Sorry I kept you waiting," he said. "I feel like a love-struck schoolboy. Someone hit me over the head, will you?"

Rose smiled. "You are referring to Alexandra, I presume?"

"Of course. My future wife, for I will have no other," he said with confidence.

"Remember, she must choose you first," Nicholas reminded him with a note of caution.

"Oh, she will. I *know* she will."

Rose took Nicholas's arm and walked out the door, hoping that for Randolph's sake, Alexandra did in fact return his affections—for it was never easy to mend all the pieces of a broken heart when such a love was not returned.

PART II
The Road Home

Chapter Six

Petersbourg, July 1814

Leaning into the wind, Leopold urged his mount into a faster, wilder gallop across the fertile green fields and relished the heady exhilaration that always came when he traveled at such speeds. It was nothing like a battle-field charge, when he was surrounded by a thundering army of soldiers overcome by one of two things: savage bloodlust or heart-wrenching terror. Nothing about this resembled that at all. The warm, humid scents of the morning filled his nostrils with clean fresh air and filled his head with an almost unrecognizable sense of peace. Holding tight to the reins, he pressed his horse into a dangerous leap over a high stone wall, then tried to put all thoughts of war behind him.

He had come home to Cavanaugh Manor with a clear purpose to embrace his title in the new realm and begin anew. He had just spent the afternoon consulting with his steward about building three new cottages down by the river and making improvements to some of the existing ones where the tenants had lately been complaining of leaky roofs and poor drainage.

There was much to be done and he was glad of the distraction. It kept his mind off certain other things and helped him to sleep better at night when he found himself reliving particular moments from the past.

The scorching sun was high in the sky when he trotted into the stable courtyard, dismounted and handed the reins to a groom, then stalked to the house for an early luncheon with his mother. The soles of his boots crunched heavily over the loose gravel as he pulled off his riding gloves and dabbed at the perspiration on his forehead.

Leopold looked up at the sky and wondered if Petersbourg had ever known such a hot summer before. He certainly couldn't remember one. It was impossibly sweltering and damned uncomfortable, and he wished the heavens would open up and dump some cold rain on his head.

After changing out of his riding boots and donning a clean shirt and light jacket, he strode into the luncheon room where his mother was already seated at the white-clothed table reading the *Petersbourg Chronicle*.

She set it down when he entered. "Leopold, I'm glad you're back. Have you seen the paper?"

He stopped in his tracks, for she had that look about her. Something had happened.

"I had an early start this morning. Why? What is it?"

He pulled a chair out to sit across from her while she folded the news sheet and handed it to him. He read the headline quickly while working to control the sudden rapid beating of his pulse.

When he finished the article, he set the paper down on the table. "Well, then," he said. "This confirms it. I am a free man."

"It appears so."

It was good news, but shocking all the same, for the woman he had been pledged to marry since birth—the secret Tremaine princess—had just wed Randolph Sebastian, future king of Petersbourg.

The article implied it was a brilliant love match, the stuff of fairy tales, for whilst in England, Prince Randolph and his brother Nicholas had switched identities to ensure Randolph found a lady willing to marry him for love, not his crown. Randolph had wooed Alexandra the old-fashioned way.

What a shocking surprise when they each discovered the truth—that he was, in actuality, first in line to the throne of Petersbourg, and she was a direct descendent of the Tremaine dynasty, a true blood princess.

Fate, surely, had intervened and brought these two together.

The story caused Leo's jaw to clench, for when it came to love, the fates had been quite uncooperative and rather obstinate in his case. All they ever did for him was keep him alive on the battlefield—a miraculous feat if there ever was one—but there were days he wondered if that had been a blessing or a curse.

The marriage of Randolph and Alexandra was a blessing for the country, the *Chronicle* reported, for it would at last unite the two opposing factions—the traditional Royalists and the progressive members of the New Regime.

"Nicholas wrote that," Leopold said, tapping his

finger on the paper. "He knows just how to present something to sway the popular opinion."

"You're probably right," his mother replied. "But how will your father feel about this? I cannot imagine he is pleased. He has coveted the throne since the day they buried Oswald. He wanted it for *you*."

Leo sat forward. "I do not care one way or another how Father feels, and neither should you."

His parents had been separated since he was ten. They parted ways not long after his two younger sisters died of typhoid.

The duke and duchess did not share the same political opinions. His father was a secret Royalist. His mother sided with the New Regime. To put it plainly, they despised each other and had not spoken in years.

"I've already told Father that I want no more part of his crusade," Leopold added.

His mother regarded him ruefully. "There was once a time you believed in it."

Indeed, there was. At one time he, too, had been estranged from his mother when he'd followed his father's banner and wanted to be king. The ambition was like a drug.

"Those days are long gone," he assured her. "I was young and wild and too easily influenced. Since then I have fought a real war. I've seen death and I've witnessed the human cost of one army conquering another."

She laid her hand upon his. "I am glad you've given that up."

He turned his eyes toward the window. "How could I not? I won't fight another war in my own country.

There are other things I want now. Besides, now that we are poised to have a Tremaine back on the throne, what is the point in fighting? The Royalist cause is now satisfied. Pray God we can all live in peace for once."

"I agree," she said. "An attempt to topple the Sebastians could not possibly end well. Your father never understood that the people of this country love King Frederick dearly, and despite the fact that there is no royal blood flowing through his veins, he has done more for this country than any other king ever has."

"I see that now." He did. He truly did.

Leopold stood up, walked to the window and looked out at the forest and lake in the distance. A hot, muggy haze obscured the horizon. Everything inside him felt heavy as well. Motionless. Anchored down. Frustratingly restless . . .

"What have you heard about the king's health?" he asked. "Has there been any improvement?"

His mother's tone was somber. "I am afraid not. They say he is dying, and that is why Randolph returned from England so quickly with his new bride. I do not believe it will be long."

Leopold continued to ponder the hot, hazy world outside the window while his thoughts traveled elsewhere, to the palace in Petersbourg where an old man lay dying in his bed.

Leopold was barely aware of the chair legs scraping across the floor behind him. He paid no mind to his mother's light footsteps circling around the table. It was not until he felt her hand on his shoulder that he recognized the magnitude of her concern.

"You are thinking of her again."

He faced his mother, who was lovely in the soft mid-day light and still looked as young as she did when he was a boy. There had always been a gentle kindness about her, while his father was quite the opposite.

Leo had always assumed he'd inherited his father's ambitious nature, as opposed to his mother's compassion and benevolence. He had certainly displayed a rather astounding talent for battle which seemed founded upon a hot-blooded desire to conquer and triumph. His ancestors were kings after all—at a time when kings wore suits of armor and commanded giant armies and took what territories they wanted by force . . .

"It cannot be an easy time for Rose," his mother said. "She loves her father very much."

At the mere mention of Rose's name, Leo felt that need to conquer rise up like a monster within him. He couldn't seem to quell it, and it was eating him up inside because he couldn't fight for what he really wanted. At least not while he was here in the quiet, peaceful countryside.

"I should go and pay my respects," he said.

His mother laid an open hand upon his cheek. "I am not sure that would be wise."

Of course it wouldn't. Rose would be vulnerable and full of grief and fear for the imminent loss of her beloved father.

Leopold would comfort her and do whatever he must to ease her pain. He would not leave her side.

"Perhaps it would be best if you just sent a note," his mother suggested.

He knew what she was thinking, and the sensible part of him agreed with her. What he really needed to do was cut all contact with Rose completely and stay away from the royal court in Petersbourg. He had to stop fighting and try to grow accustomed to a normal life.

"Please, Leopold," his mother said. "She is betrothed to the future emperor of Austria."

The mere thought of the man caused Leopold's hands to curl into fists.

"But it's not too late," he found himself saying. "I am released from my own obligations now, and they are not yet man and wife. A woman can change her mind."

His mother sighed in frustration. "There are political issues to consider. If you truly wish to be a loyal subject to your king, you will not interfere with such an important national alliance."

Leo's gut turned over. He wished life were simpler—that he was a common man, and Rose a common woman, so that he would not be forced to give her up. All he wanted to do was straddle a horse this instant and gallop into the city proper, break down the door to her private apartments, kiss her senseless until she couldn't breathe, then carry her away to his bed.

Bloody hell.

A note would not suffice. It would *never* suffice. He desired her too much. His passions were never going to burn out.

So what next? Charge headlong into battle? He didn't see any other choice. He was a soldier born to fight and he didn't like to lose.

Damn. What the devil should he do?

Rose fell asleep at her father's bedside. She was dreaming about slow waves on the ocean when a throat cleared beside her. Groggily she lifted her head from the cradle of her arms on the edge of the mattress and peered up at a footman. "Yes? What is it?"

Standing with one hand behind his back, he offered up a silver salver. "A letter for you, Your Royal Highness."

She blinked a few times to clear the sleep from her eyes, glanced at her father who was resting comfortably, then picked up the letter.

"Thank you. You may go, but could you inform Mrs. Hartford that I would like a supper tray sent up? I do not wish to leave my father's side tonight."

"Yes, madam."

She waited for him to leave the chamber before she rose from her chair and moved to the upholstered window seat to break the seal and unfold the letter. Of course, she knew who it was from. She had known the moment she saw the Hapsburg seal.

My darling Rose,

I write this to you knowing you are still abroad in England and it may be weeks before you receive it, but I decided it should not matter that you are on the other side of the sea.

I trust your visit is proceeding as planned and that Randolph is making good progress with the shipbuilding campaign.

You must write to me as soon as you are able and tell me about your journey. What is the weather like abroad? It has been a warm, dry summer here in Austria. We expect a cold winter. After that, will an early spring wedding suit you?

My sister believes we should wait until the summer when the roses are in bloom, but that is a whole year from now and I grow impatient to see you again and have you for my own.

I hope this letter finds you well.

Joseph

Rose looked up from the letter and rested her weary head upon the glass windowpane.

Clearly her fiancé did not know about her father's worsened condition when he wrote this. She found herself frustrated by the distance that separated them, for it made her feel terribly disconnected when she needed him now more than ever.

Her father was dying and a part of her was dying, too. She needed to know that there would be happiness in her future—new beginnings instead of mournful endings.

She and Joseph had been apart for too long. Though she carried a miniature portrait of him, it was not the best likeness, and it had become a challenge to remember all the details of his face. Sometimes she had to shut her eyes and work hard to summon his image in her mind when another less welcome face continued to appear tenaciously in her daydreams, always with a caring smile.

Her father stirred in the bed. Rose returned to his side as he tried to sit up.

"Lie still, Father," she whispered, laying her hands on his shoulders. "Tell me what you need, and I will get it for you."

He laid his head down on the pillows. "All I require

is right here. Ah, my dear Rose, you are such a sweet girl. You've always been the brightest light in my world. What is that you have there? A letter from Joseph?"

She managed a smile. "Yes. He writes to me of the warm weather in Vienna."

Her father took hold of her hand and squeezed it. "It pleases me to see you betrothed to such a good man. I have known Joseph since he was a boy, and he is one of the most honorable and decent men I know. I couldn't have chosen anyone better for you, and you deserve the very best. Now I can leave this world knowing that at least two of my children have found happiness. I will not worry for you, Rose. Nor will I worry for Petersbourg."

She raised his hand to her lips and kissed it. "Yes, all is well now, Father. Randolph has chosen the most perfect bride. Now all we need to do is find a wife for Nicholas."

Her father chuckled, then gave in to a fit of coughing. When he recovered, he said, "If you can convince that boy to choose a virtuous wife, I swear I will sing to you from the heavens."

Rose laughed. "I will do my best."

She held his hand and sang softly to him until he fell back to sleep.

Later that night the king suffered a series of convulsions and slipped into a deep coma. Thirty-six hours later, he was dead.

Rose had never known such grief. She was an infant when her mother died of tuberculosis, and remembered nothing about her, nor of the sorrow her father must have endured at the loss of his beloved wife and queen.

Rose had been raised at the palace by a devoted caregiver who was now retired to the country.

This was the first time Rose had ever lost a close loved one, and on the day of her father's funeral, when he was laid to rest in the royal tomb at the Abbey of St. Peter, it took every measure of strength she possessed to hold her head high beneath the black tulle veil that covered her face, and weep only silent tears.

When it was over, she walked beside Nicholas and followed Randolph and Alexandra—now king and queen of Petersbourg—down the long center aisle of the abbey while the congregation stood and the angelic voices of the choir echoed gloriously throughout the ancient cathedral. It had been a beautiful ceremony and she was grateful for the love and support of the people.

Halfway down the aisle, however, she spotted Lord Cavanaugh in attendance, standing at the rear of the church in the back pew. Their eyes locked and held as she walked the rest of the way.

As she and her brother drew closer, Leopold bowed to them. She could not bring herself to look away until they passed by.

Even then, she could still feel his intense gaze on her as she exited through the open doors and descended the steps to their coach. Nicholas helped her inside while Randolph and Alexandra rode separately ahead of them.

As soon as the vehicles pulled away from the abbey, Nicholas turned to her. "Are you all right?"

"I am perfectly fine," she replied as she lifted the black veil off her face and peeled off her gloves. "I cannot believe it's over, that he is really gone."

Nicholas squeezed her hand. "Nor I."

They gazed out the window at the crowds lining the streets. As the royal procession passed by, everyone bowed solemnly.

"Look how the people adored him," Rose said. "It pleases me to see it."

"I suppose you saw Cavanaugh in the church," Nicholas said.

"Yes." She continued to look out the window, for surely there could be nothing more to say about it.

"Did you mind that he was there?" Nicholas asked. "Or would you have preferred not to see him, today of all days?"

She took a deep breath and let it out slowly. "It may surprise you to hear it—for it certainly surprises me—but strangely enough, I was glad to see him. It made me feel . . ." She paused to reflect a moment while Nicholas waited with impatient curiosity.

"It made you feel . . . ?" he prodded.

"Valued. Did you see how he looked at me?"

"How could I not? He looked at no one else. It was as if you were the only person in the church." Nicholas paused. "What happened between the two of you in England? *Something* must have happened."

She shut her eyes and tipped her head back to rest on the soft upholstery. "I told you, we just talked. Now I don't know what to make of him. He has not yet announced any engagement, nor did he bring his betrothed home with him from London. At least not that I have heard." She opened her eyes and looked sharply at her brother. "You would tell me, wouldn't you, if you heard anything? I assure you I do not need to be protected from news of him. I am already pledged to another, and I rather wish Leopold would make haste and do the same. I believe I would find it easier to see him if he took a wife."

Nicholas listened to everything she said, and shook his head. "I haven't heard a word about any betrothal, but we've all been preoccupied lately. Would you like me to ask him while he is here in the city? I could summon him to the palace."

She gazed down at her engagement ring—a stunning emerald-cut diamond—and turned it around on her finger. "No, that won't be necessary. It shouldn't matter anyway. It's not for me to care what Leopold does." The coach rolled over a bump in the road, and she was jostled about quite uncomfortably.

Chapter Seven

The sun was just setting when Leopold's coachman pulled to a halt in front of Cavanaugh Manor. The butler hurried to meet him.

"Hello, Johnson," Leo said.

"Good evening, Lord Cavanaugh. Welcome home."

"Has Mother dined yet?" Leo walked up the steps and through the front door, where he handed over his hat and gloves.

"Not yet, my lord. Dinner will be served at eight. In the meantime, I should inform you that a package arrived for you yesterday. A rather large package."

Curious, Leopold halted and turned to face him. "Where is it?"

"In your study, my lord. There are two packages, in fact. One large and one small."

"From whom?" he asked as he started off toward the stairs.

"From your father."

He halted with one hand on the newel post as a fierce wave of displeasure coursed through him, for he did not welcome the notion of being further manipulated. His father had best not be attempting to bribe him or lure him back into his hopeless crusade—and God help the man if he intended to use threats.

"Thank you, Johnson." He wasted not a single moment before he climbed the stairs and broke the seal on the letter that had been placed on his desk. He would read it before he opened the boxes, for he was not yet sure he wanted whatever was inside of them.

> *My son,*
>
> *I have not been well since our argument in England. It is never a good thing to part ways on such terms, so I hope you will accept my most sincere apologies for all that has passed between us.*
>
> *I understand that King Frederick has also not been well and may not live to see the end of summer. I have given it a great deal of thought, and you were right about everything. It is time to stop living in the past.*
>
> *When Randolph is king, he will remember your friendship as young men, so do what you must to strengthen those ties. Alexandra will be in need of support from those who were once loyal to her family, so do your best to be a dutiful subject and a true friend to her.*
>
> *I have sent two wedding gifts for the royal couple. I leave it in your hands to deliver them.*

> *For Randolph, a Scottish claymore which I know he will enjoy. I recall a time when he expressed a desire to visit the Highlands.*
>
> *For Alexandra, I have sent a portrait of her parents—King Oswald and Queen Isabelle—which was painted before she was born. Please tell her that I have enjoyed the honor of its safekeeping since the Revolution. No one has known of its existence or whereabouts, but the time has come at last to return it to its rightful owner—the only child left of the Tremaine dynasty.*
>
> *Your father,*
> *Kaulbach*

Leopold sank into a chair and cupped his forehead in a hand. His father wrote that he had been unwell since their argument. It must be serious indeed for him to let go of his old Royalist ambitions and set his son free to live his own life as he chose—as a loyal subject of the new Sebastian king.

Nevertheless, turning his eyes to the large wooden box propped up against the bookshelf, Leo could think of only one thing: this gift provided a legitimate excuse to return to the city and visit the palace.

And see the woman he intended to make his own, by any means necessary.

Chapter Eight

After the death of King Frederick, a full fortnight passed before visitors began to arrive at the palace, one by one, to present wedding gifts to Randolph and his new bride.

Clearly the country was eager to meet the woman who had captured the king's heart, so it was decided that a banquet would be held to provide the highest-ranking peers of the realm an opportunity to meet their new queen.

The invitations were sent out and Rose was torn between her turmoil at seeing Lord Cavanaugh again—for naturally he was listed prominently on the guest list—and her shame and frustration at feeling anything other than indifference, for she did not wish to fall under his spell again. That would put her betrothal at risk and her heart as well, for it had taken so very long to get over him the last time.

When the night of the banquet was finally upon her,

she dressed in a gown of black silk with daisies embroidered on the puffed sleeves—for the daisy was her father's favorite flower—and studied her reflection in the looking glass. She wondered fleetingly if it might be better to feign a headache and avoid attending the banquet altogether.

In the end, she resolved that such absence and cowardice would only prolong the curiosity that was presently growing by leaps and bounds in her imagination.

Perhaps facing Leopold in person would douse those flames with a heavy dose of reality and remind her why she was better off with Joseph, who would never flirt with any other woman and encourage her affections when he was not free to do so. Nor would he lie to her or toy with her affections. Joseph was decent in that way. He was not flirtatious or seductive, and for that reason he was not likely to be unfaithful in the future and break her heart. She could not say the same for Lord Cavanaugh.

By the time she made her entrance with Nicholas into the reception hall, most of the guests had already arrived. The room smelled of lilacs and roses and hummed with subdued laughter and conversation.

Nicholas picked up two sparkling champagne glasses from a footman carrying a tray and handed one to Rose. Together they mingled with the guests until Randolph and Alexandra were announced and everyone fell into courtly bows and curtsies.

There was much talk of the late king during the first hour. Everyone who spoke to Rose offered kind sympathies, which she accepted gratefully, but when the dinner gong rang and it was time to move into the banquet hall, she found herself glancing more carefully around the room, searching for the one person she had not yet encountered.

She knew he was here in the city. He had come to the palace that very afternoon to present a gift to Randolph and Alexandra in the throne room. Or so she had been told.

But where was he now?

A group of gentlemen in the far corner of the room stepped apart just then, and she spotted him. He wore a dark green dinner jacket and fawn breeches, and was listening intently to the man across from him who was speaking passionately about something while waving a hand through the air in a series of gestures.

The very instant their eyes met, Rose's body began to whirr with awareness. She hid it well, however, and gave Leopold nothing more than a courteous and regal nod of her head as she passed by—as if he were any other acquaintance in the room.

Which he was not. Everything about him hit her like the zap of a lightning bolt.

More than a little shaken by her response to the mere sight of him, Rose moved into the banquet room on Nicholas's arm and sat at the head table with the rest of the royal party.

When everyone was seated, a number of toasts were made in the king and queen's honor, and there was a moment of silence for their late father.

More often than she intended, Rose found herself glancing at Lord Cavanaugh. She was intensely aware of his presence at all moments and the force of her attraction to him was greatly disturbing to her in every way—for she did not invite those feelings nor could she banish them, no matter how dutifully she tried.

After dinner, everyone moved into the ballroom where the orchestra had begun to play a cotillion.

The room was crowded. There were nearly three hundred guests, but somehow Lord Cavanaugh found her within minutes, just when she was beginning to feel a heavy sorrow in her heart over the fact that her father was not here to enjoy the music and dancing.

"Good evening, Your Highness," he said as he approached.

Rose was standing with a group of ladies from one of the more fashionable new neighborhoods, but turned when Leopold spoke.

"Good evening, Lord Cavanaugh," she replied. "What a pleasure to see you."

While they greeted each other, the other ladies seemed frightfully keen to listen in on any conversation.

"I wish to convey my deepest condolences over the loss of your father," he said. "If there is anything I can do . . ."

She swallowed over a rush of emotion that threatened to undo her carefully cultivated decorum, and found herself confessing what she truly wanted in that moment—which was something that went against her better judgment, but there it was. The words spilled past her lips before she could stop them.

"Actually, there is something," she said. "You could ask me to dance. It would do me good to focus on my feet instead of my heart."

Needing no further bidding, he offered a gloved hand.

"Will you do me the honor?" A new set began and he escorted her onto the floor. "I believe this one will be a waltz."

She suspected he was warning her that he would soon slide his hand around her waist, rest it upon her back, take hold of her other gloved hand and touch her in that manner for the entire piece.

Despite the butterflies in her belly, she kept her eyes fixed confidently on his. Under no circumstances would she permit him to know that she was the least bit unsettled. She must do everything in her power to hide it—from him and everyone else.

At last the music began and he swept her into the first few steps.

He was an excellent dancer, but she knew that already, for they had danced many times before, but never the waltz, for it was very new in Petersbourg.

"Again, Rose," he said, this time more intimately, closer to her ear, "I am sorry about your father. I know there is nothing anyone can say to make it better, but I want you to know how often you have been in my thoughts."

The wall she had constructed between them cracked slightly at his kind words, and she found she could do nothing but speak from the heart.

"Thank you, Leopold. It has been difficult, especially when I think of how far away we were when he fell ill. I will never forgive myself for not being here."

"But you came home as soon as you learned of it, and I am certain he must have been pleased by what you accomplished in England. He was proud of you.

That was obvious to everyone." He paused. "He was a great king. He will never be forgotten."

The sentiment brought her comfort, and she thanked him.

"How is your mother?" she asked as they circled around to the other side of the room. "It's been too long since I've seen her. Please tell her that she would be most welcome at court."

"I will convey your message," he replied, "but you know my mother. She hates to leave the country. She loves her gardens too much."

"She has such a gift with flowers. Thank her for the beautiful bouquet she sent. It was the loveliest of them all."

"She will be pleased to hear it."

They danced in silence for a moment or two, and Rose was relieved they were keeping to polite conversation. There was no obvious awkwardness or tension, though she had not yet conquered the butterflies in her belly.

As the dance continued they chatted about the summer heat but stopped talking as the music reached a crescendo. He held her steady in his arms and swept her lightly around the room until her cheeks were flushed and her blood was racing at a swift and exuberant pace.

She was pleased they had danced. It took away some of the fear she had felt about seeing him again.

Everything would be fine, she told herself. All would be well.

When the dance came to an end, however, she was sorry for it. She did not wish to take her hand off his shoulder.

"Thank you, Rose," he said in that appealing husky voice as he escorted to the edge of the room.

As they walked together, she glanced up at him. "It is I who must thank you for such a delightful few minutes on the dance floor. It has lifted my spirits."

They found a quiet corner to watch a number of guests gather for a quadrille.

"Look," Leopold said. "Nicholas has escorted the queen onto the floor. She seems to be adapting well to her new life here, and you have a sister now. So much about the world has changed in recent months, has it not?"

Rose watched her brother dance with Alexandra and wondered what they were saying to each other. There had been some tension between them since Nicholas learned Alexandra was a Tremaine, for she had kept that secret from Randolph during their courtship in England.

"That is very true," Rose replied. "And how are things in your world, Leopold? The last time we spoke, you told me about your engagement. Did you finally meet your intended in England?"

He kept his eyes fixed on the dancers. "I regret to say it has not worked out quite as everyone expected. As it happens, she fell in love with another fellow and is now happily married to him. It was a good match for her. I can hardly blame the woman, so there are no hard feelings." He paused and looked down at Rose. "I am now a free man, released from my obligations."

Rose swallowed hard over a sudden wave of astonishment. "I am sorry to hear it did not work out."

He spoke with a hint of bitterness. "Well. There is

nothing to be done about it now. I will begin anew and endeavor not to nurse too many regrets."

A footman came by just then. Rose picked up a glass of champagne.

"It is frustrating sometimes," she said, "how life does not unfold the way we plan. Just when we think we know which way we are headed, the path takes a turn or splits in two directions, and one must choose."

He considered that. "Yes, although sometimes one does not have a choice. Sometimes one is pushed to the left, when the right is much more desirable."

"I know the feeling, exactly."

She had become quite familiar with it when she was forced to forget the man she loved and move on with her life. She didn't even want to consider the possibility that the path was again diverging before her. She had finally come to terms with her future in Austria and had accepted her duty, and did not welcome any complications.

But Leopold was free now. He was no longer pledged to another, and clearly he still had the power to stir her blood, arouse her passions. Though she tried not to feel any of those things.

Heaven help her, what if a life in Austria was not her true fate? What if *this* was?

Rose glanced up at Leopold's handsome profile. He was watching Alexandra and Nicholas with notable concern. Perhaps he, too, could recognize an argument when he saw one.

Rose scanned the room, wondering how many others had taken notice of her brother's disinclinations toward their new queen, but everyone appeared oblivious.

Most of the guests were too busy laughing and enjoying the champagne.

"Is there something not quite right between them?" Leopold asked, as he leaned a little closer to Rose.

"You are very observant. I must confess I had my doubts about Alexandra at first. The piece Nicholas wrote for the *Chronicle* was very romantic, but there have been a few bumps and hurdles along the way, as you can well imagine. I believe Nicholas still has some doubts. You know how protective he is of Randolph."

The music came to an end, and Nicholas escorted Alexandra back to her stepmother, the dowager Duchess of St. George, then promptly walked off.

Leo turned his attention back to Rose. "Your doubts are now alleviated?"

"Yes. Alexandra and I have come to know each other very well since the crossing. I am convinced she wants to see Petersbourg united again and bring an end to the conflicts between the Royalists and New Regime. I am also certain that she loves my brother with all her heart." Rose took a sip of her champagne. "Nicholas will see that, too, soon enough. His problem is that he doesn't understand about true love. You know what he is like. He enjoys turbulent affairs that promise to be both brief and disastrous."

Leo bowed at a couple as they passed by on the way to the dance floor. "I suspect there is hope for him, yet," he said. "Remember . . . you once thought the same of *me*."

She chuckled lightly at his roguish remark, though there was nothing light about it, for she could sense the flirtation simmering beneath the surface and it excited her to no end. "I suppose I did."

Another set began, and she knew it was long past time for them to part ways. She set her empty glass down on a table and caught Nicholas's eye.

"It appears my brother is sending me signals," she said. "He wishes to remind me that I promised to dance with Lord Bramberry."

"Bramberry?" Leo smiled with teasing charm. "Is he still alive?"

Rose nudged him with her elbow. "Now, now, Leopold. He's not that old."

"Of course not. But do try not to wear him out, darling. There is a spark about you that can give a man dangerous heart palpitations—and at *his* age . . ."

She smiled at the flattery. "You are positively wicked, sir, and I am going to pretend you never said that, because if he drops dead on the floor at my feet, I will blame you completely for floating such ideas into the air."

She curtsied and made a move to leave, but Leo touched her arm. "Do you still like to ride in the mornings?"

Now it was *her* turn to experience dangerous heart palpitations. What was he getting at? "Yes, in the park, mid-morning. And you?"

His eyes glimmered with resolve. "I've been riding in the country lately, but mid-morning is my preferred hour of the day as well. It's quiet. There is less wind."

"And the dew has a chance to leave the grass."

They stared at each other for a tantalizing moment. He nodded in agreement, and as she turned to join her brother, she realized with a disturbing mixture of excitement and self-reproach that they had just arranged a secret rendezvous in the morning, without ever openly mentioning it.

Oh, he was smooth. A part of her feared it, for what if his intentions were dangerous? She knew how he liked to win. Perhaps he only wanted to prove that he still had the power to seduce her, and that he could steal her away from her fiancé in a heartbeat if he so chose.

When she reached Nicholas and turned to look back, she saw that Leopold had already crossed to the other side of the ballroom and was striking up a conversation with Alexandra. They spoke privately for a few minutes until he bowed and took his leave.

"Don't give me that look," she said to her brother as she turned to face him. "It was just a dance, nothing more."

He held up his hands as if to profess his innocence. "I said nothing about it."

"Good. Let us keep it that way. Now where is Lord Bramberry? He promised me a dance."

"Here he comes now."

Rose turned and gave the aging viscount a warm and affectionate smile, while her thoughts ventured uneasily to the temptations she might find herself confronting in the morning.

Chapter Nine

Petersbourg Palace stood at the southern edge of the city. Beyond it stretched miles of peaceful country meadows and forests. On the morning after the banquet, a warm, hazy humidity hung low over the park as Rose walked Zeus to the crest of a lush, green hill and cantered down the other side into the river valley below.

She headed for the bridle path along the river, which meandered through the woods to the top of a high ridge where she could look out over the palace and city to the north.

She had galloped out of the stables earlier that morning with her groom as an escort—a strict and necessary rule of protocol—and wished, for once, that she could enjoy the freedom of riding alone, but such was her life as a royal. She had been following rules forever, doing exactly what was expected of her. Freedom was a luxury she had rarely dreamed of, but as she slowed Zeus to a walk and entered the cool shade of the trees, she found herself resenting her lack of it more than ever before.

Perhaps it was the death of her father and a greater awareness of her mortality that caused this restlessness in her. Life was short, after all. There were no second chances.

Or perhaps it was the weight of her increased responsibilities in recent months, for it was no light matter to marry a future emperor.

Or perhaps it was something else—the lure of the forbidden . . .

As they entered the forest, Zeus's ears pricked and he tossed his head, as if he'd scented something that required a warning. A secret thrill ran through her veins.

"What is it, boy?" she asked, giving him an encouraging pat on the neck while her own instincts escalated to a heightened state of alert.

Sure enough, the sound of approaching hooves and the nicker of another horse broke the silence of the wood, and she reined Zeus in to a full stop on the path. Her groom stopped behind her.

Just as she anticipated, a handsome rider appeared from around the bend and trotted to meet her. They faced each other with mutually mischievous and knowing smiles.

"Lord Cavanaugh," she said. "What a delightful surprise to see you here."

He fingered the brim of his hat while she took in his appearance atop the impressive chestnut mare. This morning he wore a dark gray riding jacket, pale gray breeches with tassled Hessians, and a fine silk cravat tied loosely at his neck.

"Good morning, Your Highness," he gallantly replied. "Are you headed to the lookout?"

"Yes, I am. Would you care to accompany me?"

"I would be most delighted."

Without hesitation, she turned in the saddle and spoke to her groom. "Thank you, Casper. It appears I have a most capable escort. You may ride back to the palace now and wait for me there."

"But madam . . ."

"Rest assured, sir," Leo added. "I shall take every care with the princess and see her safely returned within the hour."

The groom glanced uneasily between the two of them, then bowed his head and obediently walked his mount out of the wood.

Rose waited for Casper to break into a gallop on open ground, and regarded Leo feistily in the humid air.

"He appears to be gone," she mentioned as she nudged Zeus with the heel of her boot.

"Alone at last," Leopold replied.

The suggestive intimacy in his tone provided her with an enjoyable rush of pleasure that felt very wicked and very wrong. She had no intention of turning back, however, for she needed to explore this path before she accepted another that had been laid out for her by others.

Together they fell into a leisurely walking pace along the river while the birds chirped cheerfully in the leafy treetops.

"Did you enjoy yourself last night?" Leo asked.

"Tremendously," she replied. "The mood has been

somber at the palace since my father's passing. I think we all benefited greatly from the company of others." She glanced across at Leopold, who was painfully gorgeous in the dappled shade of the morning sunshine. "Randolph mentioned you bestowed another wedding gift upon Alexandra—a portrait of her parents, King Oswald and Queen Isabelle."

"Yes, my father has been its guardian since the Revolution, but he felt its rightful place was now with our new queen."

"I believe she was very touched by the gift. She will have it mounted today in her private chamber."

They continued on in silence for a moment or two while Rose fought to resist the wanton urge to admire Leopold's powerful muscled thighs as he rode beside her. And his gloved hands, so big and strong in the chocolate brown leather gloves . . . It was impossible not to stare.

There was one other thing she could not resist either: the desire to speak openly.

"It has been a long time since we enjoyed a morning ride together," she said, recalling how they had once sneaked away during the shooting party at his estate two years ago. "So much has happened since then."

Leopold gazed at her in her dark riding habit and top hat, which she had intentionally perched forward on her head at a flirtatious angle. His eyes were as blue as the summer sky. "Yes," he replied in a low, husky voice that stroked her like velvet. "You became engaged, while I became . . . *un*engaged."

"That is true," she said, "but it is minor in comparison to your accomplishments in the war."

She glanced across at him, but he looked away in the other direction.

"When we met in England," she continued, "I told you I had thought of you very little since our parting, but I feel I must confess the truth." That seemed to garner his full attention. "The fact is," she said, "I *did* think of you often when you were abroad. I prayed for your safe return, and I was happy for you when your heroics were recognized."

He regarded her doubtfully. "You were happy for me? Truly, Rose? I find that difficult to believe."

"Why?"

He chuckled. "I know you too well. You probably tossed the newspaper into the fire when you read it. Didn't you?"

He was referring, of course, to the announcement of Napoleon's downfall the previous October. Leopold had distinguished himself in battle and received the Petersbourg Medal of Honor for his bravery. It was also noted that he had never been defeated in battle, not once. He had come home to a mad crowd of cheering admirers who tossed flowers at him in the street, and a nation of women who openly adored and desired him.

Rose swallowed uneasily at his probing question, for he had hit too close to the mark. For a moment she considered how best to respond and convince him that she had been pleased about his triumphs, but she could not tell a lie. It was no use anyway. He would see straight through her, for it was exactly as he described. He knew her too well.

She rolled her eyes good-naturedly. "Fine. I admit it.

I crumpled the paper and threw it into the fire. There. Are you happy now?"

He regarded her steadily. "I am happy that you told me the truth, but sorry that you remained angry with me for so long."

The humor of the moment vanished as she looked into his striking eyes. "Yes, I was angry," she finally confessed. "But I was angry at myself for caring. I *did* think of you and I worried for your safety. I hated the fact that I knew nothing of what you were enduring. I wished you could have written to me. I didn't like being kept in the dark and reading about the battles in the newspapers. There were so few details."

He nodded with understanding. "It was better that way."

"Why?"

"Because you wouldn't have enjoyed hearing about what it was really like. It's not for a lady's ears."

"Now, see here," she argued. "You know as well as anyone that I am not like most women."

She had watched her father strangle a man dead when she was not yet old enough to tie her own shoes. It was an image she would never forget. It had both hardened her heart and fueled her passion for life.

Leopold was one of the few people who knew about that incident. She had confessed it to him when she sneaked through the secret passages at his father's country house and stayed up all night with him . . . *talking.*

"I apologize," Leopold said. "You are indeed unlike other women. I've never thought otherwise."

She steered Zeus around a large exposed root on the

path and felt very daring all of a sudden. "Do you remember when we spent that night together?"

"Of course," Leopold replied.

"We promised each other we would never hide anything, that we would always be completely open."

"I remember."

She turned to him. "Then tell me about the war."

He paused and gave her a look of warning. "As I already said, Rose, it's not something a man talks about."

"But surely you can talk about it with *me*."

Her emphasis on the last word did not go unnoticed, and his eyes warmed to the acknowledgment of the bond that existed between them. "You may ask one question," he said. "What would you like to know?"

She did not hesitate. "Were you ever wounded?"

A shadow fell over his eyes. "There were scratches and bruises almost every day."

"That is not what I mean, Leopold. Were you ever seriously hurt?"

There was no change in his expression as he leaned forward and patted his horse. "Twice. I took a musket ball in the arm during a skirmish in Spain and required some time to recover. Another time, my horse was shot out from under me during a full charge, and I went flying forward out of the saddle. Before I could get my bearings, I was slashed by a rather murderous steel bayonet. It was lucky I was fast on my feet, for it was just a surface wound. That foot soldier could have cut me in half, the way he was swinging his weapon."

"What happened to him?" she asked.

Leopold did not respond to the question, but she saw the answer in his eyes.

"I see," she replied. "That was going to be my next question . . . if you ever killed anyone."

"We agreed there would be just one."

She nodded and retreated into silence, but found it impossible to suppress her curiosity about so many things.

"They wrote in the paper that you were fearless."

He shook his head. "I don't believe there is such a thing as a fearless soldier."

"But some are braver than others, surely."

"I suppose. Somehow I always managed to keep my head when all hell was breaking loose around me. When I was shot in Spain, I felt no pain in my arm until the skirmish was over. Afterward they delivered me unconscious back to the hospital tent. Evidently I collapsed on top of a dead British artillery officer after taking charge of his regiment and firing enough cannons to take out half of the French cavalry."

He spoke of it as if it were nothing at all to take a bullet in the arm and continue fighting for his life.

"How long did it take you to recover?" she asked.

"A few weeks. Luckily the musket ball went straight through and completely missed the bone."

He stopped talking suddenly and shook his head. "I do beg your pardon, Rose. Surely you did not wish to hear such gruesome details."

"To the contrary," she replied. "I wish to hear anything you are willing to share. I do not need to be protected from the truth, no matter how grisly or unsettling."

They rode in silence for a few minutes up the gradual incline that would take them to the top of the ridge. A gentle breeze blew through the treetops and Rose looked up. "I am glad Napoleon is captured and that King Louis is back on the throne. I hope we never go to war again."

He closed his eyes. "It's strange. . . . There were times I thought I might go deaf or mad from all the cannons exploding around me, and the chaos of a thousand men riding hell-for-leather straight into enemy lines. At the time, I didn't think I would survive long enough to experience a peace like this ever again, and believe me, I dreamed of it. But since I have come home, I've felt restless. It's almost too quiet." He gazed at her in the hazy morning sunshine. "Except when I am with you. Then everything comes alive again."

She should have taken exception to such a comment, or perhaps brushed it off as a shameless flirtation meant only to flatter her, but instead she steered Zeus closer to the center of the path and reached out a gloved hand to him. He took hold and squeezed it.

They regarded each other intimately in the cool shade of the wood, then let go and moved apart.

"Now I must change the subject and ask *you* a question," he said.

"Fire when ready."

"Does your brother know you agreed to meet me this morning?"

Rose chuckled. "First of all, my lord, I did not 'agree' to meet you. This is pure coincidence, and I will not have you suggest otherwise."

His eyes glimmered with amusement. "As you wish."

"And yes, both my brothers are well aware that I am out riding. It is my usual routine to ride before breakfast."

"Ah, but would they be displeased if they knew you sent your groom back to the stables on his own?"

She considered it. "Randolph would be, for he was instrumental in the arrangement of my betrothal to the archduke. I don't doubt he would be displeased if any untoward gossip found its way to Austria before the wedding day. Nicholas, on the other hand, has always been a rule breaker. He's very protective, but understands my heart. He lets me be adventurous when I wish to be."

"Is that what this is?" Leo asked. "An adventure?"

His eyes touched her like a caress, and she wondered again about his intentions. Was this a well-planned seduction, simply because he enjoyed a challenge? He had already confessed that this peaceful existence seemed somewhat dull to him, for he was a man who thrived on dangerous battles and lived for the breathtaking quest for victory.

"I don't know the answer to that question," she replied. "I knew it was wrong to send my groom away, but I couldn't help myself, and I am not sure why."

"I can think of a few reasons."

"Is that a fact?" Her tone was intentionally haughty, while deep down, despite all her doubts, she relished the possibility that he desired her and wanted her for himself and would say what he must to bring their attraction out into the light.

To force her to admit to it.

For a long moment he watched her thoughtfully, then took a deep breath and let it out on a sigh. "Shall we race to the top?"

"Better that than continue *this* conversation," she replied.

With a quiet laugh, he gestured with a gloved hand. "After you, Your Royal Highness."

She took full advantage of his chivalrous offer and shouted *"Yah!"* as she tapped Zeus's rear flank with her riding crop. He was a masterful runner, and she thrust forward up the hill like a shot. It wasn't long, however, before she heard the thunder of hooves closing in on her from behind.

"Faster, Zeus! Faster!"

Her impressive steed pushed forward with renewed vigor, and she flew up the hill to the clearing at the top, where the grass was tall and a warm wind was blowing mightily.

Leo emerged from the wooded path a few seconds later. "I am no match for that incredible beast of yours. What did you feed him for breakfast? Gunpowder?"

Rose laughed. "You let me win, and do not try to deny it. Next time, give it your best and we shall see what we are truly made of."

Feeling decidedly out of breath, she said, "Help me down, if you please. I am overwhelmed and the horses need to rest."

Leopold dismounted at once, reached up to her and lifted her to the ground. She ran a gloved hand over the skirt of her habit and loosened her cravat, for she was exceedingly warm after the exertion of the race. "Upon my word, that was thrilling."

Leo patted his horse and tethered both of them to a tree.

Seduced by the spectacular view of the palace and cityscape below, Rose wandered to the edge of the clearing and sat down on the grass.

Leo joined her there a moment later. "I am glad you came," he said, as he removed his gloves and stuffed them into his breast pocket. "If you must know, I've been up and down that bloody path a dozen times since dawn."

Secretly aroused by the flattery, Rose leaned back on one elbow and smiled provocatively. "I am not sorry to hear it. You deserve to suffer for what you did to me two years ago."

His eyes were full of daring. "I thought you said all was forgiven."

With a hint of mischief, she puckered her lips. "I did say that, didn't I? Oh, blast it. I suppose the truth is out. I am still bitter and will probably make you pay an ungodly sum for the rest of your God-given days."

He, too, leaned back on an elbow and crossed his booted legs at the ankles. Rose was instantly lost in the splendor of his impossible male beauty and the divine perfection of every word that passed his lips, yet nothing could have prepared her for what he said next. *Nothing*.

"For a lifetime with you . . . I would pay any price you desire, Rose. For as long as you wish."

The morning breezes whispered through the tall grasses while she struggled to contain the intoxicating fire in her blood, and fight this dangerously tempting emotional involvement with a man she had never been able to forget.

He was rugged and virile beyond any imagining, and she could not fully comprehend the power he possessed over her. Despite everything that happened in the past and her recent engagement to a future emperor, all he had to do was enter a room and she melted.

"What are we doing?" she asked breathlessly in one last attempt to gain control over her desires. "We both know this cannot be."

He drew back slightly. "I know nothing of the sort, for there is something between us that cannot be denied, Rose. Did you not feel it come alive again when we met in England?"

She sat up and looked out over the spectacular panorama below. "Yes, but I am engaged now."

His voice was like a thunderbolt that shuddered through her body and shook her deeply.

"Do you love him?" he asked.

Her emotions were in a tumultuous state. She did not like the question.

"I do genuinely care for him," she replied. "And I respect him. He is decent and kind and he loves me. I think."

"But do you love *him*?"

Rose swallowed hard. She was concerned about where this was heading. "What I feel for him is not the same as what I feel for you."

He leaned back on his elbow again. "Vague, but it's a start." He plucked a long piece of grass and absently wrapped it around his thumb. "What, exactly, do you feel for me?"

"That is a very bold question, Leopold, and I do not wish to answer it because I honestly do not know what I feel. My head is telling me one thing, but my emotions are pulled in two different directions."

He regarded her with those penetrating blue eyes that never failed to beguile her. "So there is hope, then."

She scoffed. "Hope for what? That I will have one last fling with you before I leave for Austria? Or do you imagine I will break off my engagement and pledge my heart to you instead?"

"Would you, if I asked you to?"

She stared at him in shock. "Good God, what a cowardly question."

"Me? Cowardly. How so?"

"It is completely hypothetical and requires me to divulge the secrets of my heart, while you have committed nothing at all beyond a simple 'what if.'"

Feeling angry all of a sudden, she rose to her feet and brushed the grass from her skirt. "I am not your plaything. Do not presume I am available to you the moment you have a change of heart and beckon me with your famous trigger finger."

He stood up as well. "I presume no such thing, Rose, and I apologize if I have offended you. That was not my intention."

She frowned. "Then what *was* your intention?"

His chest rose and fell quickly as if he had just sprinted a great distance. "To convey that I have not known a single day in recent years that was not interrupted by thoughts of you. I cannot purge you from my heart, so if it is a commitment from me that you desire, it is yours for the taking."

She hadn't known what to expect when she rode out to meet Leopold this morning, but she had certainly not expected *this*.

"Do you have any idea what you are saying?" she demanded to know. "I am pledged to another man. Archduke Joseph of Austria! It is a political marriage to unite our two countries, and it was arranged by my father before he died. You cannot make me an offer. You have no right."

He took hold of her arm. "But do you love him, Rose?"

All her haughty mettle sailed out of her body in a wild rush of recklessness. She was confused suddenly by the grief she felt over her father's death and the undecided condition of her heart. Leopold was standing before her, pledging his love. Joseph was a thousand miles away.

Heaven help her. She had been so sure of her decision to marry Joseph, for not only was he a kind and courteous gentleman, it was also a great boon for her country. It had pleased her father on his deathbed and had patched up all the holes in her wounded pride after Leopold's terrible rejection.

But here she stood on this gorgeous summer morning with the sun reflecting in the luminous blue of his eyes while he held tight to her arm, not allowing her to escape him.

Not that she wanted to. Her traitorous body was on fire with need, and she wanted him with a ravenous hunger that knew no bounds.

Joseph was polite and thoughtful. He did not tempt her this way. He did not set her passions on fire.

"I don't know what I feel," she said at last. "I just lost my father. Nothing is easy or clear. Everything feels upside down."

Leopold's grip on her arm loosened, and he lowered his hand to his side. "Forgive me, Rose."

They faced each other in the hazy summer heat. She felt almost dizzy with confusion.

"Again you ask me to forgive you," she said. "I should say no. I should tell you that I am offended beyond repair and I never wish to see you again."

"But you won't tell me that," he insisted, "because it is not true. And you don't love the archduke."

"How do you know what I feel for Joseph? You know nothing about me. All you know is how to fight for what you want, and how to win it at any cost. I don't think you even know how to lose. It is beyond your comprehension."

Turning quickly, she gathered her skirts in her fists and waded through the tall grass to fetch Zeus. She took hold of the reins and patted his neck.

"Don't leave yet," Leopold said as he followed.

"I will do as I wish, and what I wish to do is to return to the palace. I require your assistance to mount, if you would be so kind."

She faced him expectantly.

"Rose . . ." His voice was seductive and soothing. His hands cupped her face.

A wood pigeon cooed from somewhere in the brush, and for a moment Rose felt completely conquered. What was the point in fighting this? Despite all her fears and doubts, her attraction to this man was a fierce and potent thing. The mere touch of his hands on her cheeks made her forget who she was and the importance of her duty as a royal.

"Do not give up on me," he said. "Perhaps Randolph would understand. Perhaps there is a chance he would let you choose for yourself."

Some sort of madness overcame her. She covered his hand with her own, turned her lips into his palm and kissed it. All sensible thoughts escaped her, and before she could weigh any decisions about her future, Leopold's mouth covered hers in a deep kiss that made her tremble all over with shock and ecstasy.

He let out a husky groan of need as he tilted her head to the side, looped an arm around her waist, and pulled her close to the incredible searing heat of his body.

Inflamed by memories of past kisses and intimacies, Rose reached up to lay her hands on his broad shoulders and squeeze the heavy fabric of his riding jacket. She couldn't seem to get enough of the delicious sensations and sighed with pleasure as he thrust his body closer, pulling her tight against him.

His mouth was soft and damp. The warm pressure of his tongue caused a throbbing ache between her legs, and all she wanted to do was surrender to whatever he proposed. She wanted to sink down to her knees and lie back on the grass, invite him to cover her body with his own, and wrap herself around him like a glove.

As he blazed a trail of sweet kisses across her cheek and down the side of her neck, she tried to wake herself from this dream, but alas, she could not.

After the sorrow and darkness of the past few weeks, this surging physical connection was like some kind of drug. Warmth and sunshine rained down upon her, and she felt alive again. She was overwhelmingly happy to be back in Leopold's arms after the terrible loss of him so very long ago. How many nights had she dreamed of this and prayed for one more chance to be with him? Even when she had accepted Joseph, she had nursed a sad regret for the final death toll of that wish.

"Ah, Rose," Leopold whispered in her ear. "I beg of

you . . ." He took her face in both hands and looked into her eyes. "Consider my suit as well. I am heir to a dukedom and a great fortune. My ancestors were kings of this country. Surely Randolph would consider the possibility of a union between our families."

She heard what he said but couldn't seem to form words or reason out an answer. All she could do was press her lips to his again and kiss him with all the pent-up passion that was buried so deeply in her soul.

Her aggression ignited a matched response in him, and he clung to her with unstoppable desire. One large warm hand cupped the nape of her neck while he ran the other hand down over her hip and around to her backside.

He carried her to the shade of an ancient oak at the edge of the clearing. Slowly, gently, he knelt on one knee and set her down on the grass, removed her hat and set it aside, then gazed at her with those determined dark-lashed eyes.

Quite naturally she parted her legs to welcome him into her open arms, and he kissed her with tantalizing lust and loving affection.

"Why can't I resist you?" Rose sighed.

"You're not meant to resist this because we are destined to be together. Do not marry Joseph. You are mine. You've always been mine."

How easily she was swept back into the obsession that had once nearly destroyed her. She did love Leopold, still. She had never stopped. She had only convinced herself that she hated him in order to survive.

"It would cause a terrible scandal," she said, as she arched her back beneath him and nearly fainted at the pleasure of his lips on her throat. "I don't know what Randolph would say."

"Tell him you love me. Tell him you will be miserable if you are forced to marry a man you do not love."

It was a sobering thought to imagine such a conversation. And what of Joseph? How would she ever explain it to him? He thought the world of her. He believed her to be virtuous and dutiful and pure of heart. What would he say if he could see her now, thrusting her body wantonly in the throes of passion with an ex-lover in the grass?

Oh God, what was she doing?

"Please stop." She placed her open palms on Leopold's chest. "This is wrong. Let me up."

Scrambling to her feet, she smoothed out her skirt and picked up her hat. Pressing it firmly back onto her head and tucking in a few loose tendrils of hair, she strode toward Zeus.

"Rose, wait," Leopold said. "Do not do this."

She whirled around to face him. "Do what? Come to my senses? Remember my betrothal? I don't know what just happened, but I'm not that sort of woman. I lost my head."

She took hold of Zeus's lead rope and walked him to a fallen tree, where she stepped up onto the trunk and mounted into the sidesaddle without assistance.

Her father would be so disappointed in her. Was he watching her from heaven above? Did he know what she had done this morning?

She wheeled Zeus around to steer him to the path that would take her home, but Leopold grabbed hold of the bridle. Zeus tossed his head and trotted backward, but Leo would not set them free.

"I must escort you back," he said.

"That is not necessary. I know my way."

"I gave my word to your groom, and we cannot part like this."

Her heart was racing. She took a few deep breaths and fought to calm herself. "Very well, then. We must return together and behave as if nothing improper has occurred. Please do not betray me, Leopold. I need time to consider all of this."

"I am your servant in all ways," he replied. "I will wait forever if I must."

Zeus stomped restlessly and reared up, forcing Leopold to release them and step aside.

"You may catch up to me in the meadow beyond the wood," she said. "But I must leave you now. Without any promises."

Responding to the firm kick of her heel, Zeus carried her across the clearing into the cool shelter of the forest. Only then did she slow him to a walk and shut her eyes.

Leopold would soon follow and be upon her. She must strive to regain her sanity and think rationally. She was a royal princess and had agreed to a political marriage that would benefit her brother's realm.

She loved Randolph. He was the best brother in the world.

Her father had sanctioned the marriage. He was not alive to advise her now, which was a tragic circumstance, for he had always put her happiness and well-being above all.

But happiness and well-being were sometimes two very different things.

She was not entirely certain that Leopold was good for her. He had caused her terrible pain in the past.

Her father had never known of it, for their affair was kept secret from everyone except Nicholas. Though she suspected Randolph knew. She could never confess it to her father, for it was wicked and wanton. She had desired Leopold so desperately that she had sneaked through the secret passages of his father's manor house to visit him in his bedchamber and spend the night with him.

Not unlike what she had done this morning by agreeing to a secret rendezvous in the woods.

What was it about Lord Cavanaugh that brought out the worst in her? She was not a fast or wild woman. She was a dutiful princess and a virgin.

She did not behave like one, however, when she was alone with Leopold Hunt.

Chapter Ten

"Upon my word, Rose. You are much better at this than I am." Alexandra lowered the archery bow to her side and grimaced at the fact that her arrows had landed deadly strikes in two tree trunks and an elderberry bush beyond the target. Meanwhile Rose had hit the target every time and had come very close to the bull's-eye.

"I've been practicing since I was twelve," Rose explained as she waved a servant closer to bring her another arrow. "It was one of Father's favorite summer pastimes."

She raised her bow, took aim, and let another arrow fly. That one hit the bull's-eye, dead center.

"Marvelous!" Alexandra said, tucking her bow under her arm to applaud Rose's skill. "You are a true master."

While a servant hurried to collect all the arrows, Rose and her sister-in-law strolled to the refreshment tent to enjoy some cool lemonade.

It was stiflingly hot on the lawn. Rose was perspiring despite the fact that she was dressed in a gown of the very lightest muslin. Her maid handed her a sunshade. She twirled it around as she sipped the cool drink and looked out over the flat expanse of green lawn where the targets had been set up.

There were very few people about, except for the servants. No one was fool enough to brave the heat and humidity, she supposed, but it provided a welcome opportunity to speak to Alexandra about her current quandary.

"May I ask you something?" she said as they strolled along the hedgerow with their lacy sunshades.

"Of course, unless it concerns archery, in which case I shall be of very little assistance."

Rose linked her arm through Alexendra's. "How do you know when you love someone? How do you know if it's real?"

Alexandra gave her a curious sidelong glance. "I presume you are referring to your betrothed?"

"Yes, of course," Rose replied, for she did not wish to confess her transgression on the ridge with Lord Cavanaugh three days prior. She hadn't told anyone about it, and until she determined what was best for her and the country, she would continue to keep it secret.

"Are you unsure of your feelings for him?" Alex asked with both understanding and concern.

"Not entirely. I like him well enough. He possesses a pleasant demeanor and is quite handsome. You haven't met him, but you will. He promised to visit Petersbourg again in the spring before I depart for Austria."

"Are you worried that you haven't had enough time to become better acquainted with each other?"

"Yes, there is that, but we have our whole lives ahead of us, so that will come in time. What concerns me is that I do not . . ." She paused. "I do not long for him in the way I feel I should. Nor did I ever feel particularly . . ." She paused again. "I don't quite know how to say it, so I shall be as blunt as possible. He has never made my heart go boom. You know, like a cannon."

Alexandra did not chuckle or seek to appease her. To the contrary, she stopped on the gravel path and lowered her sunshade. "Does this concern you?"

Rose fanned her cheeks with her hand. "I don't know. How was it with you and Randolph? You were prepared to throw away your chances at becoming queen when you did not know he was heir to the throne. Now you have everything you wanted—a passionate romance with your husband, while doing your duty at the same time. You are very fortunate."

"Yes, I am, but I would have married Randolph even if he was not the heir. It was a love I could not deny."

"When you say 'love,' do you mean passion? Or was it something else that told you he was the one?"

Alexandra lifted her sunshade and they resumed their pace on the gravel path. "It was most definitely passion, and to be honest, I didn't know what I was doing at the time. It was as if the whole world had spun out of control. I tried very hard to be sensible and listen to my head, but in the end, my heart won the war. Thankfully it all worked out, but now I know there is not a single chance I could have been happy marrying anyone else but him. My whole life would have been a lie. The nights would have been torture."

"The nights . . ."

"If I had to give myself to one man, while I was in love with another," she explained. "But that is not your problem, or is it? Do you love someone else? Because if you do, you must speak to Randolph. Surely he would not force you to be miserable for the rest of your life in the name of duty."

Rose swallowed uncomfortably. "No, I do not wish to speak to Randolph about it. At least not yet. Not when I am so unsure of my feelings. I admit there is someone who excites me, but I do not trust my heart. It could simply be that Joseph is very far away and I have been melancholy since Father's death. Perhaps when we see each other again, I will be more certain of my affection for him."

Alex was quiet for a moment. "This man who excites you . . . is he here at court?"

Rose spoke carefully. "He is a citizen of this country, yes, but I would prefer not to reveal his identity, for this infatuation may simply pass, and I would not wish to incriminate him as a person of danger."

"I see." She paused. "Well, please know that you can come to me, Rose. I only want to help. I cannot speak for Randolph, but I would not wish to see you marry a man you do not love."

"Thank you, Alex. You've been very kind."

Rose glanced toward the targets and the servants standing in the sun, perspiring heavily while waiting for them to return.

"What do you say?" Rose asked. "Shall we go shoot some more arrows?"

As they turned toward the archery range, they noticed a footman walking briskly toward them.

"He seems in a hurry," Alex said.

"He is carrying a letter," Rose replied.

"I wonder who it is for—you or me."

"Your Royal Highness," the footman said with a bow as he held out a gold-plated salver to Rose.

Her heart pounded fiercely in her chest as she picked it up and examined the seal.

"It is from Joseph," she said with a pang of disappointment.

"Ah, there, you see? He may be far away, but he thinks of you. Perhaps this letter will remind you of the affection you share."

"Yes . . . I am sure that will be the case."

She waited for the footman to leave before she broke the seal and unfolded the letter.

"Take your time," Alex said. "I shall go and hone my archery skills."

She walked off, leaving Rose alone in the sun to read the letter.

My dearest Rose,

Please accept my condolences over the passing of your father—a great man and a great king. I wish I could be at your side during this difficult time, but alas I am very far from your borders.

Please know that I hold his memory close to

my heart and have no doubt that his soul is now resting peacefully with the angels. I will be returning soon to Vienna for the Congress in October. I wholeheartedly anticipate a prosperous summit, and I look forward to meeting with your brother, King Randolph.

As always, I think of you fondly and look forward to our wedding day.

Yours truly,
J.

Rose lowered the letter to her side and watched Alexandra exclaim her astonishment when one of her arrows penetrated the target. All the servants applauded. Alex laughed and gestured for one of them to hand her another arrow.

I think of you fondly.

Rose raised the letter and reread Joseph's plain, dispassionate words. Then she looked at the beautiful diamond engagement ring he had given her, which sparkled blindingly in the sunlight.

He was fond of her, to be sure, but did he love her? Did he desire her with all his heart and all the passion in his body? Did he even know what passion was? And if there were some impediment to their marriage, would he promise to wait for her forever? Would he fight for her if she ended their betrothal, or would he recover quickly and seek another wife before the year was out?

She thought of all the moments they had shared when he'd visited her country. He had been a perfect gentleman and had kissed her only once, briefly on the cheek, before he said farewell on the day he departed.

The kiss was polite. There had been no weakened knees, no racing hearts, no tears upon his departure—and certainly no hot-blooded sexual madness that left her judgment impaired.

She sighed heavily. Perhaps a quieter, calmer sort of love was the better choice. Perhaps there would be less chance of heartache in the future.

She folded the letter and handed it to her maid for safekeeping, then lowered her sunshade and handed that over as well before returning to the archery range to pick up her bow.

An hour later, after an invigorating competition with Alexandra—whose aim was improving at an impressive rate—Rose returned to her private apartments to rest before dinner. When she entered her room, however, she was surprised to discover another letter under her door.

With a blazing rush of exhilaration, she bent to pick it up, tore at the seal, and hurried to the window to read it.

> *Dear Rose,*
>
> *I write to inform you that I must return to the country today to attend important estate matters, and I do not expect to be back in town until the coronation.*
>
> *I fully intended to leave the city without any communication to you for you were clear on that matter, and I do not wish to cause you any further distress.*
>
> *I could not yield to those noble intentions, however, for my heart still burns for you, more*

ardently than ever before. I ache to hold you in my arms, and I pray that one day I will know such bliss.

Please think of me while I am gone. I will think of you with all my heart and a love so profound, no words can possibly convey it. Such intimacies can only be expressed through body and soul. By God, if you were my wife today, I would take you home with me to Cavanaugh Manor, carry you to my bed, and spend an eternity proving to you the power of my undying love—my sweet darling.

I have not given up. I will never give up. You should have been mine two years ago, and I will fight for you until I draw my last breath.

Your devoted and most passionate servant,
Leopold

Without thinking, Rose immediately pressed her lips to the letter and hugged it to her breast.

She wished she could be indifferent toward Leopold, but any chances of that were suddenly dashed. She loved him and desired him with a passion equally as ardent and profound as he described in his letter. No words could possibly convey it to anyone.

What was she to do, then? Speak to Randolph and discuss the possibility of ending her engagement? But what if this was not real? What if, like before, Leopold could not be trusted to remain true? She knew from experience that his passions could turn cold in an instant. He had seemed devoted to her once before, but he had broken her heart in the end.

Had he truly changed, or was he simply too charming for his own good? And for hers?

Though she wanted to run away with him this very instant and pledge her whole heart before sunset, she forced herself to see reason and be patient. She must continue to be careful. She was a Sebastian, and could not afford to do anything rash.

Chapter Eleven

Leopold pounded hard upon the inside door of the coach and shouted to the driver, "Stop here!"

The heavy vehicle rumbled to a halt in the forest, less than two miles from Cavanaugh Manor. Leopold knew this property like the back of his hand and couldn't pass by the old swimming hole without cooling off in it before his arrival at the house, for it was damnably hot inside the coach and he was drenched in sweat and close to suffocating.

Quickly shrugging out of his jacket, he left it on the seat and flung the door wide open. "Good God, it's stifling." He spilled out of the vehicle and wiped a sleeve across his forehead. "I am going to take a dip in the river just beyond that knoll," he said to his coach-man. He untied his cravat and tossed it back into the coach, then unbuttoned his waistcoat and removed it as well. "Wait for me here. I will be back in a quarter of an hour."

He tugged his shirt out of his breeches and tramped into the woods, quickening his pace to a light jog over the soft ground, which was covered in a blanket of golden pine needles. As he breathed in the fresh scents of the evergreens, he realized that if he didn't soon cool off, he might lose his bloody mind—and it wasn't just the humid summer heat that plagued him. It was this damned relentless obsession with the princess.

He hadn't wanted to leave town, but had little choice in the matter for one of the tenant cottages had suffered a collapsed roof. Fortunately no one had been inside when the disaster occurred, and he was grateful for that, but now he had to assess the damage and decide what was to be done. Repair it or knock the whole place down and start over.

After skidding sideways on the edge of his boots down the steep bank of the river, he reached the water and pulled his shirt off over his head, removed his breeches, boots, and undergarments, and dove naked into the slow, swirling waters.

The chill of the river was a welcome shock to his senses. It woke him from the fog of erotic dreams that had been filling his head since he left town. What else was there to do, after all, during a long and tedious drive into the country but daydream about Rose?

For that reason, he was as horny as a bull and something had to be done. Otherwise he'd arrive at the manor house in a quite improper state . . . frustrated as he was by Rose's engagement to another man.

Uttering a bitter oath, he slapped a hand across the surface of the water to send a silvery spray of fury into the air.

He wished Archduke Joseph of Austria had never been born.

All at once, a flash of hellish memories surged into his brain—*explosions, terror, the violent all-consuming compulsion to kill, or be killed* . . .

Taking a deep breath, he sank quickly into the river's depths, dunking his head and remaining there for quite some time while the water filled his ears and nostrils and drowned out those vivid images of battle.

He thought of Rose and the soft touch of her lips. The sound of her voice. The warmth of her smile.

Slowly, the out-of-control pounding sensation in his chest began to subside.

A short while later, feeling somewhat cooler but no less frustrated by the reality of Rose's engagement, he dressed himself and tramped back up the hill.

He was driving up the tree-lined drive to the manor house and pulling to a halt out front when he spotted his mother. She was quick to meet him at the door as he alighted from the vehicle. "Leopold, I am so pleased to see you! Your hair is wet. Did you go for a swim?"

"Yes. I couldn't take the heat." He gave her a quick kiss on the cheek.

"I share your woes. We have all just been saying how uncomfortable it has been lately, and how delightful it would be to cool off at the river."

He regarded her with some displeasure. "*We?* Do we have guests, Mother?"

He had been looking forward to some peace and quiet. Time to reason out his feelings and calm the inescapable urge to lash out at everything that seemed to threaten him. Namely Archduke Joseph of Austria.

He felt he needed Rose for that. Everything would be fine if he could just get her back.

Or would it? He worried suddenly that something was wrong with him. He felt so damned restless and agitated lately.

With a mischievous smile, his mother linked her arm through his and led him to the drawing room. "As a matter of fact, we do. You remember my dear friend Lady Palmeter? She has come to visit with her charming and beautiful daughter, Elise. You may recall that you once played together as children."

Ah. He could spot a matchmaking scheme from a hundred paces and could usually dodge those bullets, but it was too late to do anything about it now, for he'd already walked straight into the fray.

"I do remember her," he said, "but I trust you haven't given the young lady false hopes, Mother. I am not presently seeking a wife."

"No?" Her disappointment was obvious.

"No," he firmly answered.

She let out a tiny *hmpf*.

"There is no point even trying," he told her. "Not at the present time."

She inclined her head a fraction. "Why? Did something happen while you were in town? Were you given reason to hope?"

His mother knew what he wanted. She also understood the delicacy of the situation.

And yes, he *had* been given reason to hope—the moment Rose turned her face into his palm and kissed it with tender affection and desire. The whole world had turned golden before his eyes; the touch of her lips was like magic. He had felt transported back to the way things used to be. Just thinking about it now sent a hot rush of yearning down the hard length of his body.

"I would rather not explain all the particulars," he said, "but the princess's marriage is not yet set in stone, nor will it be until she speaks her vows before God."

His mother stopped in the hall and faced him. "Please be careful, Leopold. This is not a game. She is not like other women."

"Believe me, I know it."

"Does the king know of your intentions? Has Rose gone so far as to make promises to you?"

He took a deep breath and let it out. "Not officially, but do not concern yourself. I will not do anything foolish."

She dropped her gaze to the floor. "I was so relieved when your father set you free from that secret betrothal to Alexandra. I knew it would be dangerous to plot an overthrow, and that you would gain many enemies in the process. I always made it clear to him that I am a loyal subject of the New Regime, which is why your father and I now live apart." She looked up. "But I do not wish for you to step out of that frying pan straight into another fire, Leo. Why can't you simply fall in love with a less complicated girl?"

He couldn't help but recognize his mother's own version of plotting an overthrow—one of a more romantic nature.

"Like Elise?" he asked.

The color returned to her cheeks. "Precisely. She is very beautiful and remarkably intelligent. You have a great deal in common with each other, and I am certain you will like her, if you will just give someone else a chance."

He took hold of his mother's hand and kissed the back of it. "I will meet her if it will make you happy."

But there was no chance that his passions would be led astray. When he was with Rose, he felt like the man he was supposed to be. The man he had not yet become. She was the one he wanted for his future.

They started up the stairs to the drawing room where a light lunch was already being served.

Lady Elise was indeed an enchanting creature. She was, in fact, one of the most classically beautiful women Leopold had ever encountered, with shiny ebony hair, full cherry lips, and a flawless, creamy complexion. When she smiled, her blue eyes sparkled with warm sensuality and deep dimples formed on both her cheeks.

His mother had not exaggerated about her intelligence, either, for he soon learned that Lady Elise had been educated in France, spoke three languages fluently—English, French, and Spanish—and had a strong natural talent for music. She played the piano like no one he had ever heard. She could read complex sheets of music, and it was quite a spectacle to watch her slender fingers fly across the keys at an impossible tempo.

If that was not enough, she was a gifted artist, as well (her mother was painfully eager to show him one of her watercolors), and she also enjoyed chess.

"How lovely your gardens look," Lady Palmeter said to him that evening in the drawing room after dinner. "The flowers are holding up very well in this wretched heat."

"That is my mother's doing," he replied. "She is the gifted one in the family."

"Gifted with gardens, you mean?" Lady Elise said. "But surely you have gifts of your own, my lord. One cannot defeat a terrible villain like Napoleon and return home a decorated war hero without certain rare and indispensable qualities."

She watched him intently over the rim of her china cup as she sipped her tea.

"I suppose that is so," he replied, hoping she would not press him to talk about it. He was weary of reciting the same stories over and over to strangers, always finishing to a round of cheers and applause, while most of the truth about the battlefield was left unsaid.

"Forgive me," Lady Elise said, seeming to recognize his unease. "Now is hardly the time to talk of war." She sat forward to place her teacup and saucer on the table. "Napoleon has had far more attention than anyone deserves. I daresay we ignore him altogether, at least for this evening."

"Here, here!" her mother agreed.

"What say you, Lord Cavanaugh? Perhaps a game of chess would appeal to you? I promise to be a worthy opponent." Lady Elise sat up primly with her hands folded on her lap, staring at him with keen eyes.

Though he would have preferred to go straight to bed, for he'd had an exhausting afternoon helping to clear away the rubble from the collapsed roof, he did the gentlemanly thing and accepted her challenge.

As he escorted her to the chess table on the far side of the room, he heard the quiet murmurs of approval from their mothers and realized he was going to have to be exceedingly careful in his behavior with this woman, for he did not wish to do anything that might trigger a misunderstanding.

They set out the chess pieces and began to play while chatting casually about the weather, his recent trip abroad to meet his father in England, and of course the marriage of King Randolph and Queen Alexandra.

"What a shock it was," Elise said, "when we read the newspaper that morning and learned that the woman he chose for a bride was none other than the fabled Tremaine princess. Are they absolutely certain she is who she claims? I thought King Oswald died without heirs."

Leopold moved a knight on the chessboard. "Yes, they are certain. She was smuggled out of Switzerland at birth and was raised in England under a false name."

"Smuggled out by whom?" she asked. "The paper did not disclose that information."

He watched her forehead crinkle while she considered how to make her next move. "A man by the name of Nigel Carmichael. He was one of Oswald's chief advisers and has been her protector all these years. He resides in Petersbourg now and has been welcomed back at court."

"You don't say. Well. I am sure the queen will be an outstanding monarch. She seems charming and lovely."

They continued to talk of light matters until they finished the game, at which time Leopold politely thanked Lady Elise, made the usual excuses, and retired for the night.

"Is he everything you thought he would be?" Lady Palmeter asked as she sat down across from Elise in front of the unlit fireplace in her guest chamber.

Elise was slouched down so low in the facing chair, it was a wonder her neck didn't snap.

Dressed in a pale pink silk nightgown with a low neckline and nothing on her feet, she fanned herself grumpily.

"He'll do well enough, I suppose," she replied, "but I am still angry with you about Randolph. It is your fault he married Alexandra."

"*My* fault? How can it be my fault? I didn't tell him to go to England to find a bride."

"You should have let me debut last year!" Elise shouted. "I asked you a hundred times over! I begged and pleaded, but you wouldn't allow it. You insisted I wait. Now look what has happened!"

"You were barely seventeen, and he had just ended his engagement to Lady Elspeth. It would have been pointless last year."

Elise growled in displeasure and flew out of her chair. "You told me I could marry the future king!"

"I said it was *possible* that you could. Not that you *would*. That sort of thing never comes with guarantees."

Elise shot her mother a seething look of pure venom. "I wanted to be queen."

Lady Palmeter shifted uneasily in the chair. "Chin up, darling. You can still be a duchess. Lord Cavanaugh is heir to his father's title, and do not forget, he is descended from true kings, while the Sebastians are commoners by blood. There are still some who believe they are lowly usurpers who should be executed for what they did during the Revolution."

Letting out a huff, Elise slapped at the bed curtain and sauntered back to her chair. "Oh, do shut up, Mother. The bright side reeks of second-best."

"But Lord Cavanaugh is a shiny golden prize!" she argued. "He is without a doubt the very best there is available at the moment. He is a famous war hero and I daresay the most handsome bachelor at court. You cannot deny that. And if you want to catch him, you had best keep your eye on that target, Elise, or he will be snatched up by some other ambitious young lady who recognizes an opportunity when she sees one. As soon as word gets out that he was recently jilted by a secret fiancée that no one knew existed, he will be more sought after than ever before."

Elise lounged back in the chair again. "Stop trying to frighten me. I am not intimidated by other women. It is they who should be intimidated by *me*. I am not the least bit concerned." She snapped her fingers. "I can have him just like *that* if I want him. I am only angry that I did not have a chance with Randolph. If he had met *me* first, he wouldn't have bothered to travel all the way to England to find a bride, and he wouldn't have married that stupid Tremaine cow."

"Hush, Elise! She is your queen!"

The reprimand was met with a careless scoff, then Elise stood up to admire herself in the cheval glass. She ran her fingers through her long dark wavy tresses and turned her cheek left, then right, to admire the soft lines of her jaw and the fullness of her lips. "Since I cannot have the king," she said cantankerously, "I suppose I shall have Lord Cavanaugh instead."

Lady Palmeter let out a heavy sigh of relief. "That is wonderful, darling."

Elise's blue eyes narrowed with malice as she regarded her mother in the glass. "Unless I change my mind again, of course," she warned. "I may decide I want Prince Nicholas instead. He is second in line to the throne after all, and if Alexandra cannot give Randolph a son, he would be king."

Her mother blinked at her. "But Nicholas is a terrible rake. He leaves a trail of broken hearts and ruined reputations wherever he goes."

Elise climbed onto the bed. "Oh, for pity's sake, sometimes I wish you would stuff a stocking into your trap, Mother. I haven't made up my mind yet, and I will most likely keep both of them on the hook until I do. Now tell me where those cottages are, for I intend to get in Lord Cavanaugh's way tomorrow."

Apprehension flashed across her mother's face. "What will you do?"

Elise rolled her eyes. "What do you *think* I'll do?"

"Elise . . . ?"

"Don't worry, Mother. I'll be sweet and virtuous." She flopped back onto the pillows and twirled a long tendril of hair around her finger. "I don't believe it will take much effort. Watch and see. Lord Cavanaugh will be hopelessly infatuated with me before the noonday meal. Then all I'll have to do is say yes to his proposal."

"You will be charming, I am sure."

"Of course I will. Now get out. I'm tired."

Her mother rose from the chair and quietly crept from the room.

Chapter Twelve

Cantering at an easy pace toward the east cottages to ensure the repairs were under way, Leopold continued to ponder his mother's concerns and wishes. She'd made no secret of the fact that she wanted him to move on with his life and let go of his desire to have Rose as his future duchess. She wanted him to consider Lady Elise instead, which was not such a very bad idea, for he was in hell at the present moment, wanting a woman who was already pledged to another man.

Slowing his horse to a walk, he let his mind wander back to their encounter on the ridge overlooking the palace and recalled the sweet intoxicating flavor of her open mouth when he kissed her.

Erotic images flooded into his brain, and he couldn't help but envision the irresistible pleasures that would be his on their wedding night—if only he could have her for his own.

He grew uncomfortable in the saddle as he fought

an inconvenient surge of arousal, then heard the sound of someone calling his name.

"Lord Cavanaugh!"

Glancing across the fields toward the south river, he spotted a splash of pink and blue against the rolling green landscape. It was Lady Elise with a basket on her arm and a pretty straw bonnet on her head, ribbons flapping everywhere as she came barrelling down the steep hill.

He pulled his mount to a halt and was just swinging a leg over the saddle—for he felt obliged to stop and say hello—when Lady Elise stumbled and fell forward onto the grass in a great heap of flying fruit and fluttering fabrics.

Seconds later, he was dropping to his knees at her side before she even had an opportunity to realize what had occurred. "Are you hurt, Lady Elise?"

"Oh my!" she exclaimed, sitting up and clutching at her ankle. "I do apologize!"

"No apologies are necessary," he replied. "It is I who should apologize to you for the unpredictable slope of my property. You took quite a spill. Are you certain you are not hurt?"

"Oh," she sighed. "I fear I may have sprained my ankle." Without the smallest show of modesty, she flung her skirts up over her knee and reached down to massage the lower part of her shapely leg.

Leopold immediately lifted his gaze to scan the surrounding countryside and ensure there were no witnesses about—for a scandal involving a young lady lifting her skirts for him was not what he needed right now. Ascertaining that there was no one in the vicinity, he gave her his full attention.

"You are in no condition to walk," he said. "Please allow me to take you home."

"Oh, you are too kind, my lord, but I cannot possibly inconvenience you. I shall limp back to the manor house on my own. It will be no problem at all. I will only require some assistance collecting the cherries I just picked in the orchard. I had hoped to have your cook bake a pie for the poor family that suffered a collapsed roof. Yes, your mother told me about it and I could not bear to imagine what they must be enduring. 'Surely a cherry pie would lift the spirits of the children!' I thought to myself last night as I was drifting off to sleep."

He stared at her intently. "That was very gracious of you, Lady Elise. I am sure they will be most grateful to receive such a gift. Now let me help you to your feet."

"Thank you, my lord. You are the most heroic of men."

As he slid one arm under the curve of her lower back and hooked the other under her knees, she wrapped her arms around his neck and smiled alluringly at him in the early morning light.

He could not help but wish he was carrying quite another young woman to his horse this morning, holding her in his arms in this way and promising to see her safely home. To *his* home, where she belonged.

Bloody hell. Perhaps his mother was right. Perhaps it was time to consider a woman who was not beyond his grasp—a woman who did not require him to fight another battle.

He had to marry one day. It was his duty as a future duke. Lady Elise was too young, however, and clearly very impatient and impetuous to have broken into a run down a steep slope.

But she had only recently had her debut, he reminded himself, and was still a child in many ways. In time, she would mature.

He felt her soft warm breath on his cheek and the brush of her lips across his jawline.

"You are a very handsome man, my lord," she said. "How is it possible you have not yet taken a wife? Surely you have many admirers."

"If I do, I should be very flattered."

"Well, of course you do!" she exclaimed. "I feel fortunate to be in your arms this morning, even though I am injured."

He carried her to a low stone wall and set her down on the ground. Keeping one hand on his shoulder, she hopped on one foot.

"Bear with me," he said. "I shall summon my horse and deliver you to the house in no time at all, and we will do what we must to hasten your full recovery." He whistled to Goliath, who came trotting over. "We shall use this wall as a mounting block. Can you put your good foot in the stirrup?"

"With your assistance, my lord, I believe I can accomplish anything."

"Very well, then. Up you go." He took hold of her under the arms and hoisted her onto the wall, then grasped the bridle to hold Goliath steady while providing support to Lady Elise with his other arm.

Within seconds, she was sitting in the saddle, wiggling her bottom to find a comfortable position. "I wish I had the courage to ride like a gentleman," she said, "but I am quite certain Mother would brain me."

Leopold chuckled. "No need to risk it. I shall lead you back slowly."

He went to collect the cherries that had spilled from her basket and brought them back to her. She slipped one gloved hand under the wicker handle and held on to the pommel.

"Ready?" he asked, squinting to look up at her against the radiant morning sun.

"Undeniably," she cheerfully replied.

They made their way along the wall and back onto the lane, where they walked for a short while without conversing. Then Lady Elise cleared her throat. "I understand your father has been abroad in England for many months. Will he come home in time for the coronation?"

"I believe that is his intention."

"How wonderful. You will be pleased to be reunited with him, I am sure."

"Yes." Though the last time they spoke, they had argued heatedly, and Leo wasn't entirely sure his father was sincere in his newfound loyalty to the Sebastian dynasty. To be honest, he wasn't looking forward to their reunion.

"What has he been doing in England all this time?" Elise asked. "I thought most of our diplomats would return after Bonaparte's defeat, yet he lingers there. I suppose he is enjoying the celebrations."

Warm under the scorching heat of the sun, Leopold considered how best to reply. He couldn't very well explain that his father had been striving for months to orchestrate Leo's marriage to Queen Alexandra. Nor could he reveal that the duke's London mistress provided enough entertainment to keep him there indefinitely. So he simply lied about it.

"He continues to act as an ambassador, and as you can imagine, there are many details to work out now that the war has ended. It's more important than ever to secure positive relations with all our allies."

"How right you are, my lord. We are fortunate to have your father acting on our behalf. Someone from the old guard, so to speak."

Growing suddenly uneasy, Leopold kept up a steady pace on the lane. "What do you mean?"

"He is a Royalist at heart, is he not?"

Leopold cleared his throat. "He was once a friend to King Oswald, to be sure, but has declared himself King Randolph's loyal subject. Now, with Alexandra as queen, I believe any quarrels that once existed between the Royalists and the New Regime are resolved. The old Tremaine dynasty is effectively restored."

"Yes, yes, of course," she quickly replied. "You are quite correct. It is a wonderful thing, and I believe the Coronation Ball will be the most spectacular social event of the decade. You will be there, I presume?"

"Of course."

"It is a pity you were in England when I had my debut, Lord Cavanaugh. It, too, was a spectacular event. I hope you will make up for it by dancing with me at the Coronation Ball."

"Naturally, I will be honored," he replied, as he quickened his pace to reach the manor house, for he had much work to do and did not wish to give the young lady any further encouragement.

Chapter Thirteen

Love was both a blessing and a curse. Rose knew this for a fact, as she'd had much time to contemplate the matter while helping her brother and sister-in-law prepare for their coronations.

Leopold had left town for the country and stayed away for weeks without writing a single letter. Though it felt more like months.

She couldn't be angry with him, for she had asked him to allow her time to consider her feelings. He was respecting her wishes and for that she was grateful, but it left her no further ahead in terms of a decision. She had thought her passions might cool under the forced separation, but instead her traitorous emotions had taken root and dug in very deep.

Now, on the night of the coronation after weeks spent alone—and not a single letter from either Leopold or her fiancé—she found herself longing for the one man she had never truly swept from her heart the first time.

Leopold Hunt, Marquess of Cavanaugh. Decorated war hero. Future Duke of Kaulbach.

As she stood in the crowded reception hall and looked around at all the guests who were arriving for the ball, she weighed the fact that he would be present this evening, unlike her fiancé who could not attend. Joseph was occupied with the arrangements for the Vienna Congress, which was set to begin in less than a month.

She considered that fact in terms of her future marriage.

Wasn't it better that Leopold was a citizen of her own country, not a foreigner? If she married *him,* she would not have to leave Petersbourg and reside in Austria.

Oh, but listen to her. Perhaps she was dreaming. Perhaps Leopold would walk into this room, pick up a glass of champagne, and there would be a horrible repeat performance of the last time he'd jilted her.

Feeling all at once terribly agitated by that memory, she entered the banquet hall on her brother's arm and took her seat at the head table.

It was the first time she truly and bitterly resented her rank as a princess, for it dictated who she must marry. Perhaps she was not as dutiful as she'd always imagined herself to be. Perhaps instead she was a rebel at heart and it was time to start behaving like one.

Randolph and Alexandra were first to dance at the ball. They waltzed around the parquet floor in a swirl of color from Rand's striking scarlet regalia and Alexandra's shimmering gold silk gown. She wore a string of pearls around her neck with earrings to match, and long white gloves.

When the music came to an end, they stepped apart and bowed and curtsied to each other, then did so again to acknowledge their appreciation of the applause and cheering.

As the orchestra began a new set, Randolph and Alexandra gestured for the other guests to join them.

Rose was led onto the floor by the prime minister, Mr. Carlton, a handsome older gentleman with a sharp wit and a brilliant ability to win most any argument in the House. He'd been a good friend to Rose's late father and had known her since she was a young girl.

They were just beginning to dance a minuet when she spotted Leopold not far away, leading another young lady onto the floor. The woman—who was exceptionally fresh faced and appeared quite young—was unfamiliar to Rose. Slender as a twig, she was blessed with shiny dark hair and high cheekbones, full lips and delicately arched eyebrows. She wore a sea-green gown with pearls sewn into the puffed sleeves and peacock feather designs embroidered on the hem of the skirt.

Leopold was attentive as he danced with her, and Rose felt as if she had just been flung back in time to the night he jilted her at a ball not unlike this one. He had danced with every woman in the room but her, and when she confronted him at the end of the night, he had treated her with frosty indifference.

"What is wrong?" she had asked, after taking hold of his arm and forcing him to stop and explain himself before he left. There had been a beautiful Spanish-looking woman on his arm. "Why did we not dance together?"

"I wasn't aware we had made such an arrangement,

Your Royal Highness. Perhaps next time . . ." With a courteous bow, he escorted the lady out.

Rose had never been more angered or humiliated in her life, and would not under any circumstance repeat such behavior tonight.

The dance ended and Mr. Carlton led her off the floor. She barely had a chance to catch her breath before Leopold's soft, husky voice spoke softly in her ear. "You look beautiful tonight."

Turning quickly to face him, she steeled herself against the urge to smile too brightly. "Thank you, my lord. Are you enjoying yourself?"

"I am now." He settled in beside her to watch the dancers. "Will you be my partner at least once tonight? Twice if you are feeling generous?"

She lifted her chin. "I suppose."

He regarded her with a curious frown. "Are you angry with me?"

"Not at all."

"Yes you are. I see it in your eyes. I hear it in your voice. Is it because I was dancing with that silly chit who has an ego the size of Portugal and a mother who is desperate to marry her off, just to be rid of her?"

Now it was Rose's turn to shoot him a surprised look. "I beg your pardon?"

"She is the youngest daughter of the Earl of Palmeter," he explained, "and spoiled rotten. Her mother brought her to Cavanaugh Manor recently, and they camped out for a bloody fortnight. I nearly went mad, I tell you. It was all I could do to keep from riding back to town to see you and assure myself that not all women were such selfish creatures. I wanted to write to you, Rose, and tell you every silly word she said."

In that moment, all of Rose's insecurities from the past faded away as she regarded Leopold in the golden light from the chandeliers and let herself fall into the magic of the music. "I really wish you had."

His eyes met hers, and time stood still. Her heart pounded like a drum. She couldn't escape the pull of whatever it was about him that would not let go of her heart, not even when he was miles away in the country.

He gazed at her with heated desire. A muscle flicked at his jaw. "Is there somewhere we can go?" he asked in a dangerously persuasive voice.

She understood his meaning. He wanted to be alone with her. She understood because she wanted the same thing. She could not possibly deny it.

Glancing over her shoulder, she swallowed over the fear that someone would take one look at them and recognize their secret passion. Surely someone would know that she was not thinking of her fiancé. She was thinking only of how wonderful it would feel to fall into Lord Cavanaugh's arms and know the sultry caress of his hands on her body and the tantalizing allure of his kiss.

"Meet me in the library in the Van Eden wing at midnight," she said without looking at him. "Do you know how to find it? You must exit into the center courtyard and reenter the palace through the double doors behind the white rose arbor. I will make sure they are not locked, and you must ensure that no one follows. Can I trust you with this?"

"Of course," he replied, also without meeting her gaze.

Chapter Fourteen

Rose stood in the dark with only the bluish glow of the moonlight shining in through the window when the library door began to open.

She had been waiting nearly ten minutes. She'd tried three times to sit down and relax on the upholstered settee in front of the bookcase, but could not sit still. After only a few seconds, she stood and paced back and forth in front of the window.

Now, as the door finally creaked open, she felt almost dizzy with fear and excitement.

Fear that her secret rendezvous with her ex-lover had been discovered . . .

Excitement that he had come at last and would take her into his arms and again whisper sweet promises in her ear. Passionate promises that he would love her forever and never stop fighting for her.

She realized in that blazing moment of anticipation that she could not exist any other way. She could not marry a man she did not love. Her passion for Leopold was undeniable, and he had declared his wish to marry her. To choose another man and another future would force her to live a lie, and she could not do that, not even for the good of her country. Perhaps it was selfish of her, but if it was, so be it.

With bated breath, she stood motionless while Leopold entered the room and closed the door. She stared at him in the moonlight and quivered with desire.

He felt it, too. There was no doubt in her mind that they were utterly together in this madness.

"You're here," he softly said as he slid his hands behind his back and turned the key in the lock. *Click* . . .

They were truly alone now. No one else could enter.

Her senses ignited with heat and her body melted like butter at the sight of him pushing away from the door, crossing over the plush Persian carpet, and circling around the desk to reach her at the window.

As they stood face-to-face, she felt as if she were sitting on a cloud, floating in a thick haze of rapture.

"We must move away from the window," he said. His fingers weaved through hers, and she wished they were not wearing gloves, for she wanted to feel the heat of his skin.

Slowly, with a deliciously erotic note of command, he led her to the settee and whispered, "Sit down."

She sank onto the soft cushions and reclined back against the head rest while he shrugged out of his jacket. He turned to lay it on a nearby chair, then removed his gloves and set them down as well.

He sat on the edge of the settee and laid one hand on the curve of her hip, while the other cupped her chin.

The soft pad of his thumb feathered lightly across her lips.

With careful movements, as if he feared she might spook and bolt if he moved too quickly, he leaned down and touched his lips to hers. The tips of his fingers feathered down the side of her neck, sending a ray of gooseflesh across her body. His tongue mingled with hers, and the pleasure ached between her legs where a deliciously sweltering heat began to fill her senses. All this, from just a kiss . . .

As he came away and let his gaze roam over all the details of her face, she tugged at the fingertips of each glove and slowly pulled them off. The delicate fabric slid across her skin, arousing her to a heightened state of desire that knew no bounds.

Nothing seemed to exist beyond this private encounter. The rest of the world, past, present, and future, simply disappeared.

"Tell me there is hope that you will be my wife," he said. "Tell me you will speak to your brother and explain to him that you cannot marry the archduke—that by doing so you will be sacrificing your happiness forever."

"Yes." She took his face in both her hands. "I will speak to him and I will beg to be released from my obligations. I want to marry you, Leopold, for I have never stopped loving you. Even when I hated you, I loved you."

His eyes filled with emotion, and he touched his forehead to hers. "You have made me very happy."

His lips found hers again and this time the kiss was deep and ravenous. The ache to feel him with her hands and devour him with her mouth was overwhelming in its intensity. She nearly fainted with rapture when he inched closer on the settee and slid his hand under her back to pull her closer. Soon he was lowering his heavy body to hers, kissing her neck and stroking everywhere with his strong, passionate hands.

She wrapped her legs around his hips and felt the firm evidence of his arousal which he pushed against her pelvic bone.

Her mind was telling her to stop, that this was wicked and wanton, but her soul did not agree. Again, it was as if she were floating on a cloud, rising up to heaven, and she knew this was not wrong. It was what she was meant for—to share her life, her heart, and her soul with this man who somehow understood her more than any other person ever could. When she was with him, she was her true self.

Leopold blazed a trail of hot kisses down the side of her neck, and she arched her back beneath him while clutching at his shoulders. His mouth moved to the tops of her breasts, just above her satin-trimmed décolletage, and she quivered with tingling ecstasy when he darted his tongue into the crevice between her breasts.

"Your gown is lovely," he said, "and you are beautiful in it, Rose, but I would dearly love to slide it off you."

She laughed softly. "I believe I would enjoy that as well, but it might raise some suspicion when I return to the ballroom."

"*If* you return," he said with a devilish grin, "because I may decide to kidnap you."

Her hands stroked through his wavy, chestnut hair,

which gleamed in the moonlight shining through the window, and she smiled at him in return.

"It's not kidnapping when your captive runs off with you willingly."

He slid a hand across the top of her thigh and slowly tugged her skirt upward, one glorious inch at a time, while he continued to kiss and tongue the tops of her breasts. "If only it could be so."

A quiet melancholy settled over her while she ran her fingers through his hair and squirmed with delight at all the erotic sensations he aroused within her. For he was right. It could not be so.

If Rose—a princess pledged to marry the son of the Austrian emperor—ran off with her secret lover, the Sebastian dynasty might never recover from the scandal. The people of Petersbourg—the Royalists and Revolutionaries alike—valued virtuous beliefs and moral conduct, and would not react well to another member of the royal family displaying a lack of self-restraint. Her brother Nicholas had pushed those limits by stirring up his share of scandals, which was one of the reasons Randolph had brought Alexandra home from England to sit on the throne at his side. No one could dispute the fact that she had royal blood flowing through her veins, while the Sebastians were constantly judged by their behavior, for they were born of butchers and soldiers.

"You are lost in thought," Leopold said, shifting his body to lie beside her on the settee and resting a hand on her belly. "Talk to me."

Rose met his gaze. "I am thinking of the future and how I will tell Randolph that I cannot satisfy his wishes for a political marriage."

"He will understand," Leo said.

"Perhaps, but it is an important alliance that I will be breaking."

Leopold, who was leaning up on one elbow, ran a finger across the pearls that were stitched into her neckline. "Are you having second thoughts?"

There was an unmistakable menace in his voice. She could not see it in his eyes, for he'd lowered his gaze to look down at her body. Her leg was exposed above the knee and she was still half dazed from the fever of her arousal.

She cupped his face in both hands and urged him to look at her. "No, I am not having second thoughts."

"Then why are you still wearing that ring?"

She paused and looked at the engagement ring Joseph had given to her. Many times she had watched it sparkle in the light, and always felt torn between what was expected of her and what she truly wanted.

"I have no choice," she replied. "I haven't spoken to Randolph yet and I must consider appearances. People would notice if I took it off. We must be patient."

"For how long, Rose?" he said irritably. "I want you *now*."

"I want you, too, but it won't be easy. Randolph will not be pleased, especially with the Congress approaching. He leaves for Vienna in a week and will be staying at Hofburg Palace with the emperor. I do not see how I can bring this up at such a time when all the great nations of Europe will be negotiating for new borders and renewed alliances."

Leopold was quiet for a moment. "You do realize I am attending the Congress as well."

She sat up. "I beg your pardon? You did not tell me this before."

"It was only decided tonight at the reception before the banquet," he explained. "As you know, my father has returned from England and Randolph has personally requested his presence at the Congress. Naturally my father asked me to accompany him, as I will inherit his title one day and he wishes for me to meet our neighboring monarchs. It is quite an opportunity. The Congress will be a historic event that will shape the future of all Europe."

Everything he said made perfect sense, but all she could think of was the fact that he would travel to Vienna and possibly . . .

No, not possibly. He would most *assuredly* meet Joseph.

"Where will you be staying?" she asked. "Not at the Hofburg, surely." It was the palace that belonged to Joseph's family. His home. It would be *her* home as well if she went ahead with the marriage.

Leopold exhaled deeply. "You're upset."

"Yes! I most certainly am. How can you be telling me this *now*?"

"You needn't worry," he argued. "I will be very discreet. We are in this together, Rose."

"Do you *promise* to be discreet? With Joseph especially?"

"Of course."

Though she trusted Leopold, she couldn't help but worry, for she recognized the depth of his passion for her. It was fierce and dogged—which is what she loved about him—but pray God he would show restraint when he met her fiancé.

Her initial shock began to subside as he stroked a finger along her arm and managed to calm her nerves with the magic of his touch.

"What are we going to do?" she asked. "Should I tell Randolph about us before he leaves? I feel that I must, but I don't want to weaken his position once he reaches the conference. Now is not the time for Randolph to be insulting the son of the Austrian emperor by telling him that his fiancée no longer wishes to marry him because she has taken up with an ex-lover."

"Randolph may be our king," Leo said, "but he is your brother first. I do not believe he would force you to do anything you do not wish to do."

"Perhaps you are right."

Leopold covered her hand with his, pulled it to his lips and kissed it tenderly. "Whatever hardships you must endure, know that I will be at your side. Do not despair. I lost you once before. I will not lose you again. I do not care what it takes, even if I have to wait a lifetime, I will. If you would prefer to wait until after the Congress to tell Randolph, I will honor your wishes and I will reveal nothing to anyone about what exists between us—as long as you are mine in the end."

Her heart warmed at this clear proof of his devotion, but she could not relax just yet. There was still so much uncertainty. "We will have to tread very carefully," she said.

"I always do."

She couldn't bear it any longer. She had to touch him, feel closer to him. Sitting forward, she took his face in her hands. "Please kiss me. We don't have much time before I must return."

At the mere mention of returning to the crowded ballroom, he pressed his lips firmly to hers.

His hand slid down her leg and found its way under her skirts. She shivered at the pleasure of his caress as he rolled onto her and continued to kiss her passionately on the mouth, his tongue softly probing, teasing her with its sweet, sensual eroticism.

"Oh, Leo," she whispered on a breathless sigh of delight. She tipped her head back to offer him full access to her neck and shoulders. "I want you so badly."

"I want you, too." He slid his hand to the damp center of her womanhood.

She gasped at the shock of the intrusion, but immediately took pleasure in it as he stroked her tender folds, exploring all her secrets, sliding his finger everywhere.

"My sweet virgin," he whispered in her ear. "Tell me you'll be mine."

"I will be," she replied. "I am."

He shut his eyes, losing himself in the rapture of her words while he pleasured her gently with his hand and kissed her deeply on the mouth.

Soon her body began to quiver and pulse with a current of sexually charged heat. She thrust her hips forward, pushing against his hand and pulling him closer.

"It feels good," she sighed, as a tremulous orgasm came upon her suddenly and unexpectedly. She had no power to keep it at bay and shuddered beneath him in a series of tiny spasms and moans.

Their mouths collided as she cried out. She realized he was doing what he must to smother her cries of pleasure, in case anyone was lurking in the corridor.

When the wave of ecstasy receded, she laid her head

down and smiled. "I dreamed of a moment like this. Many of them, actually."

He withdrew his hand and lowered her skirts over her knees. "As have I, and I will continue to dream— now more than ever."

"Does this mean I am no longer a virgin?"

He kissed her lightly on the nose. "I was very careful," he explained. "I only touched you on the outside."

"Why? I told you I was yours. I want to give myself to you completely, and no one else. Not ever."

"That pleases me, Rose, but your maidenhead is not mine to take. Not until we are man and wife. I will not dishonor you that way, and certainly not like this, on a sofa in a back room at a ball. When I make love to you, it will be special. We will take our time. It will not be rushed."

She wrapped her arms around his neck. "That only makes me want you more. How will I ever survive until then?"

"There are other things we can do," he whispered suggestively in her ear, teasing her with his seductive appeal and ensuring her that he was committed.

After what he'd just shown her, the probability of her marrying another man was reduced to nothing.

"Other things . . . Such as?"

With a sexually charged smile that sent her reeling, he kissed her trembling lips. "I will teach you everything, darling, but for now, we must deliver you back to the ballroom."

He stood and helped her to her feet, then bent to pick up her gloves. While she pulled them on and ran her hands over her hair to ensure all was in order, he pulled on his jacket and gloves.

"How shall we proceed?" she asked. "Will you go first, or shall I?"

"You," he replied. "I will watch from the window as you cross the courtyard to satisfy myself that you have reached your destination safely. Then I will follow a few minutes later."

She kissed him fiercely. "How long will it be until we are alone again? I must see you before you leave for Vienna."

He took hold of her hands. "Let's meet again when you go riding."

"That wouldn't be wise. If my groom revealed that I met you a second time, it would arouse suspicion. I must be very careful. Nicholas has done enough damage to this family with his rakish ways, and if I become the root of another scandal, Randolph will be far less sympathetic toward my feelings and more likely to ship me off to Austria."

"You are meant to belong to me, Rose. No one else."

Her heart beat wildly with distress. What if none of this was possible? What if this wonderful happiness would soon come crashing down all around her?

No, she wouldn't let it. She would do whatever it took.

"I will tell him as soon as possible," she said, "but we should still be discreet until I am free."

She waited for Leopold to make a suggestion.

His eyes glimmered with renewed purpose. "Can you slip out of the palace after dark? Borrow a dress from your maid and a hooded cloak. If you could reach the outer gates, I will meet you there and pick you up in my curricle. We can spend the night together at my town house. I would have you back before dawn."

"What about your servants?"

He paused. "A hotel, then."

She shook her head. "No, that is too risky. Can we not sit out under the stars somewhere?"

His determined expression remained unchanged. "When? I leave for Vienna the day after Randolph."

"Then we could meet that final night, after he is gone. One o'clock in the morning. I will exit through the south door and take the path along the tall cedar hedge. It's dark there. No one will see me. Now I must go."

With that, she hurried back to the ballroom feeling certain that her life was at last on the right path to happiness, for she was in love. She was in wonderful, magical love, and nothing—*nothing*—was going to keep her from the man who was surely destined to be her husband.

Chapter Fifteen

The following evening after dinner, Rose sat with Alexandra in the drawing room while Randolph and Nicholas enjoyed brandies in the library.

"Do you remember that sweltering afternoon on the archery range," Rose said, "when we talked about my marriage?"

Alexandra set her glass of sherry down on the table. "Of course."

"I have been thinking about it a great deal, and I feel I must speak to Randolph about it."

The lamp beside Rose sputtered and hissed as if expressing its disapproval.

Alexandra, however, inclined her head with understanding. "You do not wish to marry Joseph?"

There was such finality in the honest answer to that question. Rose was not entirely comfortable with it, but could see no way around it. It was time to bring her feelings out into the open and make her decision.

"No, I do not."

"You do not love him?"

Rose shook her head.

"Is there any chance you might grow to love him in time?" Alexandra asked.

Rose took a deep breath. Oh, how she hated this. "I do not believe so, for I have never felt anything but friendship toward him, and lately the idea of becoming his wife has caused me a most regrettable distress. In addition to that, I do not wish to leave Petersbourg. This is my home."

Alexandra laid a hand on her knee. "Then you must speak to Randolph. I am certain he would not wish you to be unhappy."

"That is what I believe as well, but I fear it is dreadfully ill-timed with the Vienna Congress only a week away. I do not wish to be the cause of poor international relations. I cannot imagine a worse time to jilt a fiancé—when we are about to negotiate a historic peace treaty with all the great allied powers."

Alexandra considered it. "Yes, the timing is most unfortunate. That is why you must speak to Randolph right away. You must give him time to consider the options."

Rose's heart began to pound. "Do you think he would be willing to hear me out this evening?"

"I don't see why not."

At that moment, both her brothers entered the room, and Alexandra gave Rose an encouraging nod.

"What is it?" Randolph asked. "You look white as a sheet."

Rose followed him across the library to the settee where she had lain with Leopold the night before. Her brother handed her a small glass of brandy and urged her to sit down.

Perhaps this was a poor choice of locations in which to have this conversation, but it was too late now. She must complete what she had begun.

"I apologize in advance for what I am about to say to you," she said, "for I know it will not be welcome news, especially now when you are preparing to leave for Vienna."

Her hands were trembling when she raised the glass to her lips, but she welcomed the strong flavor of the brandy as it slid down her throat.

Her brother—her king—sat down at the foot of the settee. "What is wrong? You must tell me."

With a deep breath to summon courage, she raised her chin and spoke frankly. "I am not in love with Archduke Joseph. I don't love him. I never did."

Randolph stared at her for a long time, unblinking, then frowned in the suddenly hellish-looking firelight.

"Please speak to me," Rose said. "I cannot bear to think I am a disappointment to you. I do not wish to be, but we have always been honest with each other, so I must confess my true feelings."

"What are they exactly?" he asked. "You tell me you do not love the man you agreed to marry. Is there more to it than that? Do you not wish to marry him?"

She set the crystal glass down on a bookshelf behind her and steeled her nerves for what was to come, for she could not back down now.

"No, I do not wish to be his wife. I have only feelings

of friendship toward him, and I am hoping with all my heart that you of all people will understand, for not so long ago you left Petersbourg and masqueraded as Nicholas in order to find a bride who would love you for yourself. You went to great lengths to avoid a political marriage. Yet now you ask me to carry that burden, when all I really want is to have a husband who loves me passionately, as you love Alexandra. I do not believe Joseph is that man."

"But he is an honorable gentleman and would never treat you unkindly. I would not have encouraged the match otherwise. Do you not find him handsome enough? Is that the problem?"

"No, he is very good-looking, and I agree that he is a decent and kindhearted man. I know it in my head, but it is my heart that desires a different sort of love." She stood up. "I want what *you* have. I want passion and devotion. I want to marry a man who would lay down his life for me."

"Perhaps Joseph would, if you gave him a chance."

She moved to the window and looked out at the moon, which was bright and full in the incredible star-speckled night sky. All she wanted to do was dash out of the palace this very instant and find Leopold waiting for her in his curricle beyond the cedar hedge, but it was not to be. At least not tonight.

She heard Randolph rise and pour himself a drink from the crystal decanter on the drinks tray. "You haven't seen your fiancé in months," he said. "How could you possibly know how you feel about him?"

Rose whirled around to face her brother. "I know

my heart," she told him. "I am not a child any longer. I am a woman. I know what I feel, and I do not appreciate your condescending tone."

Randolph regarded her with astonishment and set down his glass.

"Do you realize what you are asking me to do? You want me to break off your engagement to the eldest son of the Austrian emperor? Francis is hosting the Congress, for pity's sake! Austria is one of the greatest nations in Europe. Have you no care for the future of your country?"

"You are a fine one to talk," she argued. "When you married Alexandra, you had no idea how the people would respond to her. You even did so without Father's permission or blessing because you were mad for her. You would have eloped to Scotland if you had to, so I beg of you, Randolph, to understand that I cannot sacrifice my happiness by marrying out of duty. I want more than that. I want to choose for myself."

He returned to the settee, sank down onto it, leaned forward and rested his elbows on his knees. He bowed his head and raked a hand through his hair.

"Christ, what a mess this is going to be." He looked up suddenly and frowned. "Is there someone else, Rose? By God, if any man has dared to encourage your affections while you were engaged to another, I will strangle him with my bare hands."

More than a little taken aback, Rose swallowed uneasily. "No, of course there is no one." The lie slid over her lips before she had a chance to fully comprehend the fact that she had lied not only to her brother, but to her king. But she could not reveal the truth to him when he was in such a mood. God knows what he would do to Leopold. All hope would be lost.

No, she must be released from her engagement first. Then, and only then, could she present Leopold as a possible husband.

Moving closer to sit down beside her brother, she cautiously asked, "What are you going to do? Will you tell Joseph when you arrive in Vienna? Or should I come with you and speak to him myself?"

Randolph laid his hand on hers. "No, it would be best if you wrote him a letter, which I will deliver to him personally."

"But I would prefer to come."

"No, Rose. I need you to stay here with Alexandra. She is still so new to the country. She needs the company of those who care about her. I don't know how long I will be gone. The Congress could last weeks, even months, if there is conflict between the nations."

"Really? That long?" Her thoughts flew instantly—as they always did—to Leopold. It seemed as if she had been waiting forever to be with him, and now it could drag on even longer.

"Are you sure about this?" Randolph asked. "Because if it is what you truly want, I will respect your wishes, but perhaps if you give it some time, you might grow to love Joseph."

"No," she firmly said. "There is someone else out there for me. Someone who will love me the way you and Alexandra love each other. That is what I want, and I won't change my mind."

She pulled the engagement ring from her finger, took

one last look at how it sparkled in the candlelight, and handed to her brother.

He slipped it into his pocket, then put his arm around her, pulled her close and kissed the top of her head. "What do you think Father would say if he were here? Would he have talked you into staying the course?"

She almost laughed out loud. "No. He always let me get away with murder. He spoiled me rotten, and if he were here now, he would have said exactly what you just did. He would be holding me in his arms, and he would tell me that everything is going to be all right."

Randolph squeezed her shoulders. "Then I will say that as well. Everything will be fine, Rose. I promise . . . because we Sebastians know how to look out for each other."

"Indeed," she replied, "for there are always enemies lurking about, aren't there? Skulking about in the shadows . . . plotting to dethrone us . . ."

She spoke in jest of course, but felt a cold shiver of unease run down her spine as the words passed her lips. She wasn't sure why, and felt compelled to sweep the sensation away as quickly as she could.

Chapter Sixteen

It was a cloudy day, uncomfortably muggy and damp, when the Petersbourg Palace coach, followed by an envoy of vehicles carrying servants, secretaries, and a number of court ministers to advise on the negotiations, drove through the cobblestone streets of the city on its way to the peace conference in Vienna.

Crowds of onlookers gathered along the city walls to bid farewell to the procession as it passed by in all its glorious pomp and ceremony.

When at last they crossed the bridge and rolled onto the old coach road that would take them through endless meadows and forests, Randolph removed his hat and tipped his head back on the upholstered seat.

"This is going to be a difficult conference," he said. "When do you suggest I deliver the letter to Joseph? As soon as we arrive, I suppose. It wouldn't do to put it off. I cannot very well behave as if all is well. Heaven forbid he should wish to discuss wedding plans."

"That would be awkward indeed," Nicholas agreed. "But are you certain about this? You don't think it is simply a case of cold feet on Rose's part?"

Rand shook his head. "You know our sister. She's always known what she wants and will settle for nothing less. I cannot bring myself to force her into matrimony. I wouldn't want to, and to be completely honest, a part of me is relieved. I was dreading the day when we'd have to pack her off to another country. It's so bloody far away, and besides that, I was having some trouble with the notion of her marrying into the same family that offered one of their own daughters as a wife to Napoleon. Could you ever imagine Father doing such a thing to Rose?"

"No, but those days are over," Nicholas reminded him. "Austria is no longer at the mercy of that tyrant. Francis regained his honor at Leipzig."

The coach rumbled noisily for a while along the rutted dirt road.

"You don't suppose this has something to do with Cavanaugh again, do you?" Nicholas asked, sitting forward on the seat. "Because it seems odd to me. She liked Joseph well enough when he came to visit last spring, but ever since that carriage mishap in England . . ."

"I asked her if she was in love with anyone else," Randolph replied, "but she denied it. Why do you bring it up? Do you truly think she's hiding something?"

Nick gazed out the window at the passing haystacks in the fields. "Who knows? At any rate, maybe it doesn't matter. She wants to choose for herself. I just hope she doesn't get hurt again."

"Like she was hurt last time when she fell for Cavanaugh?"

Both men fell quiet. "Exactly," Nick replied. "I've seen the way she looks at him, and though she once claimed to hate him, she seems to have forgiven him since we returned from England."

"He came to her rescue that night," Randolph said, "and for that I am grateful."

"As am I, but I wonder if he has given her some encouragement, and that is why she has lost interest in her Austrian fiancé. Would you object if she wanted to marry Cavanaugh?"

Randolph gazed out the window as well, and listened to the sound of the horses' hooves clopping along the packed ground. "I suppose not, as long as she waits a respectable amount of time after her break with the archduke. We wouldn't want to stir up another scandal."

Nicholas agreed. "At least Cavanaugh comes from a long line of illustrious Petersbourg aristocrats and kings. He's not a bad choice, actually, and the people adore him since his return from the war."

Randolph sighed. "Yes, but let us not forget how he broke her heart once before. I swear, Nicholas, if he treats her shabbily again, I won't care a fig about the royal blood in his veins. I'll string him up and hang him out to dry."

Nicholas regarded his brother intently in the swaying coach. "If we're bringing up his shortcomings, we shouldn't neglect to mention that his father has always been a secret Royalist. To tell you the truth, I've never trusted Kaulbach, and never understood why Father made him president of the Privy Council."

"Father always believed in the old adage: keep your friends close—"

"And your enemies closer," Nick finished for him. "Perhaps he thought he could win his loyalty in time."

"He did think that, and by all accounts, he succeeded. The duke served him well and played an important role at Leipzig."

"As did Leopold."

Randolph nodded. "Yes, he was brilliant on the battlefield. I cannot imagine we could have distinguished ourselves nearly so well without him."

"Which is why you invited him and his father to Vienna," Nick reminded him.

Randolph sighed. "Yes, but perhaps that was a mistake. I don't know. Let us keep an eye on both of them, just the same. The duke especially."

Nicholas sat back, looking satisfied and very much at ease. "It shouldn't be difficult. I suspect they'll be attending all the balls and soirees. The duke has always enjoyed meeting new women."

"Which was a pity for his wife," Randolph mentioned. "I always thought the duchess was a lovely woman. I never understood why Kaulbach insisted on straying from her bed."

"She's well rid of him, I say," Nicholas agreed.

Rand chuckled. "Is that not the pot calling the kettle black? You've never refused an opportunity to meet new women."

"Unlike you," Nick replied, "because you are hopelessly bewitched by your new, expectant wife."

Rand gazed out the window again. "Bewitched . . .

Yes. Good God, I miss her already. Let us hope this conference is over in a snap."

Heaven help me if I am discovered, Rose thought as she hurried along the hedgerow in the dark. *For it would cause a scandal like no other . . .*

She scurried to the outer gates at the servants' entrance and said, "Good evening," to the guard who was posted there.

"A bit late to be sneaking out, ain't it, miss?" he said.

"It most certainly is," she casually replied, "but I trust you will keep my secret."

She spotted the curricle approaching and waved a hand to signal to it.

Leopold, dressed in a plain gray overcoat with a black hat pressed low on his head, pulled to a halt and waited for her to dash across and leap into the vehicle without assistance. "Take hold of your hood," he said, snapping the lines to urge the horse into a canter. "The wind may knock it away from your face once we get moving, and we must be cautious."

She leaned into him and made a great show of sliding her hand into his coat and stroking his chest, while the guard whistled in amusement, watching them as they sped by.

"Clearly he did not recognize you," Leopold said, turning his head to kiss her on the mouth after steering the curricle down a quiet lane.

She couldn't keep her hands to herself. All she wanted to do was climb onto his lap and tear brazenly at the buttons of his jacket and waistcoat.

"Where are we going?" she asked as he dragged her

hungry lips across his cheek and down the side of his neck. "Not far, I hope. I don't want to waste a single moment driving. All I want to do is devour you. You must think me shameless."

He chuckled when she threw a leg over his lap and straddled him. Gentleman that he was, he voiced no objection, despite the fact that she was obstructing his view. He kissed her hotly in return and waited for her to bring the sizzling kiss to a graceful finish before he leaned to the side to peer around her in order to avoid driving straight into a tree.

He turned up the lane that circled around the back of the palace toward the park where she went riding in the mornings, and found a narrow cart road that took them into the apple orchard.

The October night air was crisp and cool and the scent of the fresh apples filled it with a sweet, natural perfume.

Leopold pulled the horse to a halt just over a gentle rise and set the brake. Wasting no more precious time, he leaped out of the vehicle. His boots hit the ground with a thud. He spread a blanket out on the grass, and held his arms out to Rose.

A flashing second later, they were entwined in each other's arms on the blanket, kissing passionately. She sat up and quickly ripped off her cloak while he tossed his hat aside.

"I thought this night would never come," she told him breathlessly. "I nearly went mad in my impatience."

"I suffered the same agony," he replied, settling himself snugly between her parted thighs. "Every moment away from you is a moment I never wish to repeat."

Their lips met in a fierce and violent kiss that set Rose's heart on fire. The world spun circles all around her. She had never felt more alive, never more sure of any decision in her life.

"I want tonight to be the night," she said, arching her back in rapture while he blazed a trail of hot, succulent kisses down the side of her neck to her collarbone. "I want you to make love to me."

Breathing hard and fast, he rose up on both arms above her. A gentle breeze blew a part in his hair. The full moon over his head glowed brilliantly. "If I make love to you, there will be no turning back. You will be mine, Rose. My wife in God's eyes. Forever. No man—not even your brother the king—will keep you from me."

She nodded. "I give you my word—I am yours."

He sat back on his haunches, tugged at his cravat to untie the knot, and reached around the back of his neck to unclasp a chain.

"I cannot yet give you a ring, but take this." He held out a gold medallion that swung like a pendulum before her eyes. "Keep it with you always and know that it holds my promise of forever."

She sat up, leaned on one arm while she reached out with the other hand to rub the pad of her thumb over the gleaming gold treasure. "What is it?"

"A family heirloom. It belonged to my ancestor King Edmond the Fourth. I will entrust it to your care until we are together again, and one day we will pass it to our eldest son."

He clasped the chain at the back of her neck. She looked down at it and fingered the shiny surface embossed with the Kaulbach coat of arms. "I am honored to wear it."

He came down upon her again, and she welcomed him with open arms. "I wish we could get married now. In secret."

His hand journeyed down the side of her body and over the soft curve of her hip. While he laid hot kisses on her neck, Rose opened her eyes to look up at the beautiful night sky, framed by the rows of apple trees on either side of them. Crickets chirped all around, and a breeze whispered gently over the grass.

With sweet, feathery caresses, Leopold stroked her body and aroused her to an almost delirious fever. His lips were everywhere, moving gracefully over her eyelids, her cheeks, her neck, the tops of her breasts. He hooked his fingers under the neckline of her dress, tugged it down over her shoulder, then kissed the sensitive flesh there and tasted her with his tongue. He sucked at her tender skin, and the sensation caused a fresh flurry of arousal in her core. She gasped at the shocking intensity of it.

Leopold regarded her with hooded, seductive eyes while she ran her hands down the muscular surface of his shoulders and arms.

"We will take it slow tonight," he whispered. "I want to make this perfect. I want to give you everything."

Sliding her hands slowly across all the slopes and hollows of his strong, fit body, she gave a dreamy reply. "Then let me explore every inch of you."

Carefully she found her way to the front of his breeches. He let out a soft groan and rolled onto his side to face her.

She, too, rolled to her side and slid her hand over the tops of his breeches to firmly stroke the length of his arousal.

All her desires culminated in that magical moment of discovery. Cautiously, but with clear determination, she fixed her eyes upon his, unbuttoned his waistcoat, ran her open palms over the fine linen fabric of his shirt to stroke his chest, then tugged it out of his breeches.

Without uttering a sound, she slid her hand inside and felt the shocking size and overwhelming virility of his manhood.

Instinct told her to be gentle, but she saw by the flicker of arousal in his eyes that he took pleasure in a firm stroke of her hand.

"What do you like?" she asked. "I've never done anything like this before. I don't know what a man wants."

"Do what you want, darling. There are no rules. Just enjoy yourself."

She stroked him for a long time, learning what pleasured him by watching his expressions and listening to the sounds he made. She paid close attention to the pace of his breathing.

After a while, he rolled onto his back and she inched closer to continue exploring all the treasures inside his breeches. His lips parted and every so often his body jerked in a tiny spasm of excitement. He was breathing hard and turned his head to look at her. "I cannot take this much longer," he said.

She nodded while he slid a hand down to lift her skirts and caress her as he had done on the soft settee in the palace library. As before, his fingers slid over her with great ease. With a soft moan of rapture, she thrust her hips upward, needing to push herself against his palm.

He stared at her for an intense moment of deliberation, then inched his body lower and disappeared under her skirts.

The shock of his kiss upon the sensitive flesh of her inner thigh caused a fresh flood of desire to crash thunderously into her belly. When he plunged his open mouth into the damp center of her womanhood, she was done for.

Rose gasped in shock and sank her fingers into the thick wool of his jacket at his shoulders, clutching at it. Thrusting her hips in response, she relaxed back on the blanket and gazed up at the stars, twinkling like thousands of tiny diamonds. She felt as if she were rising up into the cosmos and floating around like a celestial being.

Another gentle breeze hissed through the orchard, and she closed her eyes, hearing only the sound of Leopold's mouth pleasuring her.

The orgasm came upon her suddenly, like an explosion of sparks in a hot fire. All the muscles in her body tensed as the pleasure flowed through every limb, from the top of her head to her fingers and toes. She arched her back and cried out into the darkness, completely unable to control the quivering, pulsing contractions between her legs. The climax ended in a frenzy of pleasure, and all the while Leopold continued until she was completely weak and boneless.

When he climbed up over her on all fours and looked down at her with a smile, she could barely speak. She felt drunk with passion.

"You look quite satisfied with yourself," she said, letting out a deep, husky chuckle.

"It's *you* I'm satisfied with. I love how you respond to every touch and stroke. I feel as if we were born to be lovers."

"I believe we were," she replied, feeling weak, but still wanting more.

As if reading her mind, he lowered his body to hers and embraced her tightly on the grass. She wrapped her legs around his hips and stroked his hair, shoulders, and arms. "I love you," she whispered.

"And I love *you*."

He entered her then, shockingly with a slow, natural ease that minimized the pain of her ruptured maidenhead, for she was completely open and ready for him and wanted him desperately in every corner of her soul.

He moved in and out of her with tender, loving care while kissing her mouth and nuzzling her cheeks. She had never in her life felt more cherished, and knew this was the right choice. Leopold was the man of her dreams, and this was her ultimate commitment to that dream. There would be no going back now, and she was glad of it.

Soon he reached a tumultuous climax that equaled her own earlier orgasm in its intensity, but he withdrew in time to prevent a child and spilled his seed onto the blanket. As he collapsed beside her, he fought to catch his breath while he clasped her hand tightly and held it.

"Are you all right?" he asked.

She nodded.

"I'm not sure if *I* am," he replied. "I feel transported—as if everything is finally as it is meant to be, yet I don't recognize myself."

She rolled to her side to face him and frowned with some concern. "What do you mean?"

"I've never known peace before," he said, bewildered. "I've always been fighting for something—even you."

"Do you feel peace now?"

He looked at her directly. "I'm not sure. I still feel like I need to fight. I think it's because you are still engaged to *him*. I cannot bear it, Rose. I cannot even speak his name. I need to know he is truly out of your life."

She could not deny that his jealousy pleased her. It was part of his passion, which was what she loved most about him.

"He will be out of my life soon enough," she assured him as she relaxed and rested her head on his shoulder.

While they took time to recover from their lovemaking, they talked about the future and the Congress in Vienna. They spoke of borders and politics and what Napoleon must be thinking and feeling in his exile.

"Surely," Rose said, "such an ambitious conqueror must be going half mad on such a small island with nothing to do but regret his strategic mistakes."

Leopold expressed his frustration at how generous and hasty Tsar Alexander had been in negotiating for Bonaparte's abdication. "We should have stripped him of his titles and shipped him off to St. Helena," Leo said. "He should have been treated like a prisoner, not a deposed monarch. Two million francs a year! That is what King Louis must pay to him to keep him content. But mark my words, a man like that will grow restless on Elba, and we will all be thrust right back into another war."

Rose leaned up on her arm. "Do you really think so?"

"Elba is only seven miles off the coast of northern Italy. It's an easy trip to France if he chooses that direction, which I suspect he would. Let us not forget, Rose, he took a thousand members of his Imperial Guard with him." Leopold glanced up at her for a moment, then invited her to lie down again. "I am sorry, darling. Perhaps I am wrong. I hope I am."

Another breeze blew across the tops of the apple trees. Dawn was not far off. They held each other tightly, knowing the dreaded moment of separation would soon be upon them.

When the sky began to brighten on the horizon, they forced themselves to rise and fold the blanket. Leopold tossed it into the coach and held out his hand to her. "Let us not go just yet. Are you hungry? Would you like an apple?"

He was stalling and she knew it, for the idea of saying a hurried good-bye at the palace gate was too horrible to bear. Her heart was beating out of control, and her stomach was in knots. But she kept that to herself, for she did not want to spoil the magic of their last moments together.

Never letting go of her hand, Leopold led her to the nearest tree and told her to select the apple of her choice.

"That one," she said, pointing to the one that was the brightest red in color, yet low enough so that he would not need to climb.

He jumped to grab hold of the branch, pulled it low so she could reach it. "It is yours for the plucking."

She smiled at him as she picked it, then held it out to him.

He took a big bite, crunching into the crisp flesh. "Sweet and juicy. Your turn now."

She turned it over in her hand to inspect the surface, and selected a spot next to the place where he had taken the first bite. As she crunched into it, the flavor stimulated her senses.

Arms wrapped around each other, they took turns finishing the apple, then he tossed the core deep into the orchard.

Her heart sank. "I suppose this means we must go."

He nodded. "Before the sun comes up."

He helped her into the curricle and went to pick another apple, which he fed to the horse before climbing up beside her. Soon he was snapping the lines and they were under way.

Rose linked her arm through Leopold's, and rested her head on his shoulder as he steered the curricle around a tree and began heading out in the opposite direction.

"I will never forget this night," she said. "Not as long as I live."

They spoke very little on the return, but words hardly seemed necessary. Everything that mattered was contained in the bond she felt with Leopold while her head rested on his shoulder and he held her close, keeping her warm against the early morning chill.

As they drew closer to the palace, however, the dread

moved in like a dark cloud, and she knew it would soon be time to let him go.

"We should say our good-byes now," he said, "for if we linger too long at the gate, we may be recognized."

He pulled the vehicle to a halt and took her into his arms. "Wait for me," he whispered. "When I return, things will be different. I will win Randolph's support in Vienna and seek his permission to marry you."

"I am not worried," she replied. "I know this is meant to be. But you must be careful in Vienna. Keep our plans secret from Randolph. He did not respond well to the idea of another man wooing me away from Joseph. Wait until he returns from the Congress. Only then can we begin a respectable courtship."

He kissed her passionately. Rose threw her arms around his neck. She could hardly bear it. She didn't want to say good-bye, but knew she must. "It feels as if my life will stop and pause in silence while you are gone. Only when you return, will the music begin to play again."

He kissed her cheek. "I will be back as soon as I am able."

He drove closer to the gate.

"Good-bye," she quickly said as she shielded her face with her cloak and hopped out of the carriage. Hurrying across the lane, she ran past the guard.

"Did you enjoy yourself, miss?" he teasingly asked.

She did not respond, for she could see no humor in the moment as the horse began to trot away and Leopold was again pulled from her world.

Chapter Seventeen

In his pocket, Randolph carried with him at all times the private, intimate letter from his sister, Rose, to Archduke Joseph, heir to the Austrian throne and eldest son of their generous host, Emperor Francis.

Randolph had hoped to deliver the letter the day he arrived, but was informed that Joseph had not yet returned from his diplomatic visit to Naples, though he was expected to arrive home at any time.

As a result, Randolph went about the business of the Congress, meeting with the other European monarchs while establishing a strong rapport with Prince Metternich, the Austrian foreign minister and influential president of the peace conference.

He also attended an important dinner with Talleyrand, the French foreign minister, and the following evening he and Nicholas were invited to the Duchess of Sagan's salon at the Palm Palace, where he spent most of the evening wishing he were at home in Petersbourg with Alexandra, spending the hours alone with her, naked in bed. All he wanted to do presently was return to his apartments at the Hofburg and write to her about the events of the day and all that he had seen and experienced thus far.

He regretted not bringing her. She was his queen, after all, and they were newlyweds, but she was in a delicate condition with her pregnancy and the palace physician had advised against it.

Just then, the butler announced a late arrival to the Duchess of Sagan's intimate soiree. "His Imperial Highness, Joseph Francis."

The duchess went quickly to greet him while Randolph put a hand to his breast pocket. Was he carrying Rose's letter this evening?

Nicholas appeared at his side just then. "Well, this is a surprise. Will you tell him tonight? Seems a shame. He only just arrived."

"I believe these things are best dealt with head-on," Randolph replied.

"At least let him have a drink first."

The archduke—who was an exceedingly dignified gentleman, richly dressed, with light blond hair and a freckled complexion—kissed the duchess's hand, then lifted his gaze and spotted Randolph across the room. His expression brightened, and he excused himself from the duchess's company.

Randolph and Nicholas each greeted him. "Welcome back, Your Highness."

"Your Majesty," he cheerfully replied. "What an unexpected pleasure. My father and I were pleased you could both attend the Congress. But first, please accept my sincere condolences over your own father's passing."

"Thank you," Randolph said. Nicholas nodded in agreement.

"And Rose?" the archduke asked. "How is she? What a shame she couldn't join you."

Randolph set his empty glass down on a table. "Yes, indeed. In that regard, I have a letter for you. If you will excuse me for one moment?"

He left Joseph with Nicholas while he sought out their hostess to request the use of a more private location— her dining room perhaps. All the while, his heart was filling with dread, for he genuinely liked the archduke. He was not going to enjoy disappointing him in this manner.

Ten minutes later, the archduke lowered the letter to his side and sank into a chair at the table.

Randolph, who was already seated, said nothing for a moment. He wanted to give Joseph an opportunity to absorb the contents of the letter.

Joseph pinched the bridge of his nose and let out a heavy sigh. "Well, I suppose it's good to learn these things at the outset, rather than let it drag on and on. Did she tell you why exactly? Was it something I did, or did not do?"

"Of course not," Randolph assured him. "She holds you in the highest regard, but I believe she was finding it difficult to imagine leaving Petersbourg."

Joseph nodded. "I see. Well . . . it would no doubt be difficult to leave one's home country." He paused. "I wonder if I should have done something more when I learned of your father's passing. I fear I should have traveled to Petersbourg to be at her side. It was wrong of me to have placed so much importance upon the distance and the time it would take to make such a journey. I felt uncertain about it at the time. I should have spared nothing." He met Randolph's gaze. "I *did* think of her, and I was very sorry for your loss. Please apologize to her for me, will you? Tell her I bear no ill will toward her for this change of heart. That I understand and accept her decision. And thank her for the letter. It was very kindly worded. Did you read it?"

Randolph shook his head. "No, I believe it was meant to be private."

Joseph looked down at it. "She says she hopes I will forgive her. Tell her I do, and that I hope she will always consider me a friend."

They both stood up. Randolph reached into his pocket and withdrew the ring, which he had been carrying in a small velvet bag. He handed it to the archduke.

An awkward silence ensued.

"Well," Joseph said. "I should probably make my excuses to the duchess and bow out early. I don't think I will be cheerful company this evening."

"I am sorry, Joseph."

He waved a hand. "No, no. Please do not apologize. I appreciate her honesty, and it is best that we discover these things early on. Thank you for delivering the news personally, Your Majesty. It couldn't have been easy."

With that, he bid Randolph farewell and left the duchess's salon.

Rand returned to the party and picked up a glass of claret from a footman's tray.

Nicholas approached him. "It couldn't be helped," he said. "At least it's done. You have fulfilled your duty."

Rand nodded. "He took it well. He's a good man. It's a shame, really, that Rose couldn't feel some affection for him. Perhaps I should have done more to encourage the match."

"Don't punish yourself. Love is funny that way. Most of the time, someone gets hurt. You did the right thing. It would have been wrong to force her into matrimony, and it is best that the archduke found out sooner rather than later."

Rand finished the drink, then also made his excuses to the duchess and left the salon early, for after witnessing a good man's heart being broken, he found himself missing his own wife more than words could say.

PART III

Disappointments

Chapter Eighteen

Petersbourg
December 3, 1814

It hardly seemed possible, but here she stood at last, strolling with a feigned appearance of boredom around the potted palms in the palace conservatory, waiting for Leopold to meet her.

Finally, he had returned to Petersbourg. He had come home early from Vienna for he could not bear to be away from her another day. He also claimed he had good news.

What was it? Rose wondered impatiently as she paced back and forth upon the gray flagstones. He had not elaborated in the brief note he'd sent the night before. Other than that, they had not written to each other for fear of being discovered.

But none of that mattered now. He was home at last, and in a few short minutes he would be holding her in his arms.

The sound of footsteps at the entrance to the conservatory reached her from a distance, and a sizzling thrill of anticipation coursed through her.

She stood motionless, watching and waiting . . . Was it him? Was it Leopold, her great love?

At long last, he appeared from around a flowering rhododendron and stopped in his tracks when he spotted her.

The rest of the world vanished while she took in the breathtaking sight of his tall, muscled form beneath an elegant dove gray jacket and pristine white cravat. He was so handsome in the bright wintry light shining in through the conservatory windows, she felt almost dizzy with awe.

"My love," he said, taking a few swift strides toward her. "I thought this day would never come."

All at once, the world came alive again as he pulled her into his arms and kissed her. His lips were soft and moist, yet fiercely demanding. Her heart couldn't keep still. Her flesh tingled with excitement.

"I thought you would never get here," she said, trying to keep her voice low when she wanted to shout out loud from the highest mountain.

"How I missed you," he replied, "but I am here now, at last." He kissed her passionately until the chirp of a bird caused them to step apart and look up. "I thought we were alone," he said good-naturedly.

Rose watched the tiny sparrow dart around, up and over the treetops, just below the glass ceiling.

"Sometimes I wonder if she wants to escape this place, or if she truly enjoys being here." She met Leopold's gaze. "There were days I felt trapped here just like that little bird. I wanted to break through a window and fly off to Vienna to be with you."

He held both her hands in his. "There shall be no

need for broken windows, darling, for I am here now, returned to you."

They heard voices just beyond the entrance, so they began to stroll casually along the path.

"Did you visit Alexandra?" Rose asked, for he had mentioned that he would do so first before coming to the conservatory. It had been his excuse to pay a visit to the palace.

"Yes, I just came from the queen's chambers. I had a stack of letters to deliver from Randolph, and she asked me about the conference. That is why I am so late. There was much to tell. She was curious about the peace talks and wanted to know all about the whirl of the social calendar. I believe she is missing her husband terribly."

"There can be no question about that," Rose agreed. "She waits very impatiently for his letters. There haven't been any for a while, so I am pleased you were able to deliver some. That will keep her occupied, no doubt. But you said you had good news. What is it, Leopold? Please, I beg of you, put an end to the suspense."

He glanced over his shoulder as if to check for prying eyes and ears, then stopped at a bench and invited her to sit down.

"First, before I say anything, have you heard from the archduke? Has he accepted that your engagement is officially ended?"

She clasped both his hands. "Yes. Randolph gave him my letter and returned the ring, and Joseph has since written to me to say that he accepts my decision and bears no ill will toward me. He hopes that we will be friends and wishes me happiness in the future."

Leopold regarded her quietly. "I must tell you, Rose, that I met him while I was in Vienna. On more than one occasion, in fact. There were many dinners and balls. It was impossible not to mix with all the conference attendees, not to mention our Austrian hosts."

Rose felt a terrible pang of guilt in her heart. "You didn't mention me, I hope."

He shook his head. "No, I promised I wouldn't. I spoke to him about the peace treaty issues. . . . Honestly, if I had not made love to you before I left and felt certain that you were mine, I might have challenged him to a duel or taken some other drastic measures to triumph over him. I'm not proud of it, but my jealousy knows no bounds."

"I don't mind that you are jealous," she said with a smile. "I quite like it, actually."

He pulled her close and kissed her forehead. "There is so much I want to tell you about the peace talks, but we must save that for later, for we don't have much time."

She glanced over her shoulder. "No, I must return to my apartments soon, before anyone misses me. It wouldn't do for me to be caught unchaperoned with a handsome gentleman in the conservatory."

He smiled. "Of course not. Allow me to get straight to the point, then. Last week there was an organized hunt at Schönbrunn Palace. I spent some time with Randolph, and he told me of your broken engagement. I acted surprised of course, then he asked me quite bluntly if I still had feelings for you."

Rose drew back in surprise. "You are joking. I didn't

think he knew. I've said nothing to him about you since our meeting in England, but perhaps Nicholas did. They both remember how I suffered two years ago when everyone thought we were sweethearts, and then we weren't. Whatever did you say?"

"I told him I held you in the highest regard and regretted what happened between us. I even confessed that I was at that time secretly engaged to someone I had never met, and that is why I was forced to discourage your affections. I explained that it was over now and I was free. I did imply that I would like to court you again, if he had no objection."

"What did he say?" she asked, sitting forward slightly, powerless to curb her impatience.

Leopold smiled. "He did not object, but asked that I wait until he returned from the Congress to ensure that any new courtship does not overlap with your broken engagement. He simply asks that we be patient. That is all."

Overcome with joy, Rose raised his hands to her lips and kissed them. "Oh, Leopold, I am so happy! But will the waiting never end? It has been so difficult. Sometimes it feels as if I've been waiting forever to be with you."

He glanced over his shoulder again, listening for intruders, then pressed his lips to hers, but only for a moment, for they heard voices again, echoing in the corridor just outside the conservatory.

Rose forced herself to pull away from him when all she wanted to do was hold him forever.

"I must go now," she said. "When will I see you next?"

"I will contrive a reason to visit the palace again soon. Continue to be patient. I will send word to you."

She kissed his hand quickly, and hurried out.

With Christmas approaching, Rose was kept busy with numerous charitable endeavors, which she helped Alexandra to organize and carry out. They paid visits to the poorhouses to serve soup and bread to the less fortunate, and they also embarked upon an ambitious project to engage the help of many aristocratic ladies to knit mittens for a gift-giving on Christmas Day.

The event was widely publicized in the *Chronicle,* and the news provided an excuse for Leopold to visit the palace again to deliver a pamphlet about knitting to the queen, which he hoped would be of some use to her. He managed to get word to Rose the day before. Again, they met in secret in the conservatory.

"When will Randolph come home from Vienna?" he asked as they moved behind a thick, fragrant rose-bush. "I want to court you properly."

"I want that, too," she replied, "but I cannot afford to behave improperly. My family's reputation is hanging by a thread as it is. Did you read what was printed in the *Chronicle* last week? They said Randolph was consorting with his former fiancée, the Countess of Ainsley, in Vienna, and it implied that he was unfaithful to Alexandra. I swear, will it ever end? I am certain it is yet another plot to damage Randolph's reputation, headed by the Royalists, no doubt. They are always trying to remind the people that we were not born into royalty and are therefore unworthy of the crown."

"I read it," he confessed, keeping his gaze lowered. "But you mustn't worry about that. They are only trying to sell newspapers. Nothing accomplishes that as well as a good scandal. It will blow over. They always do." He lifted his gaze again.

She jumped at the sound of the bird chirping from somewhere above. "I am so afraid we are going to get caught. They will say I was unfaithful to my fiancé, and single-handedly destroyed Petersbourg's influence at the peace conference."

"Do not fret," Leopold said.

How could she help it? Everything seemed so uncertain with Randolph and Nicholas out of the country, while the public was throwing roses at their new Tremaine queen. The Sebastian dynasty seemed somehow less secure.

"Alexandra was terribly vexed by what they printed about Randolph and his former fiancée," she said. "I fear she half believes it. You were there in Vienna. Did you witness anything? Did you see Randolph flirting with the countess?"

Leopold inclined his head. "Are *you* worried there is truth to it?"

"No, of course not. Randolph is in love with Alexandra, but sometimes appearances can create a whole new reality. Alexandra is trying to ignore it, but she cannot help but feel very alone. She has left her country behind, and must wait for the spring for her sisters to arrive. I do my best to assure her that everything is well, but the press can be so very cruel."

"There is no need to worry," he said. "And the press

is hardly being cruel to Alexandra. The people adore their new queen. All her charitable work has not gone unnoticed. She is incredibly popular. Does she not realize that?"

Rose let out a sigh. "She was pleased about the headlines, but nothing could take the sting off the news about Randolph and the Countess of Ainsley."

Leopold kissed both her hands. "Let us not talk any more about sensational newspaper headlines and fallacious infidelities," he said. "I've missed you, Rose, and I look forward to Randolph's return. Everything will be different then, I promise."

She took his face in her hands and touched her forehead to his, working very hard to believe it would be so.

Chapter Nineteen

December 19, 1814

Leopold was on his way out the door to meet Rose in secret for a third time at the palace, when the sound of a coach clattered to a halt in front of the Kaulbach town house.

He strode to the window in the front parlor, pulled the curtain aside, looked out and recognized his father's shiny blue-painted vehicle.

"Bloody hell," he whispered.

So much for arriving at the palace on time. He wondered how long Rose would be able to wait, for they had arranged to meet by chance at the mews when he trotted in for a visit with the queen. Rose would be—coincidentally, of course—returning from an afternoon ride in the park at that time.

He watched his father alight from the vehicle while the servants scurried about in a panic, which was quickly subdued when the duke walked up the front steps. By that time, the butler had already opened the door to greet him.

"Good day," the duke said as he removed his hat and handed it to Jameson. "You are surprised to see me, no doubt."

"Indeed, Your Grace," Jameson replied. "We did not expect you until Tuesday."

Leopold stepped into the front hall as well. "Hello, Father. How was your journey?"

They had not spoken since Leopold left Vienna with Randolph's letters to deliver to the queen.

Be a comfort to her, his father had suggested. *She is bound to be lonely with the king so far away and occupied by the peace treaty negotiations . . .*

"It was as fine a journey as one can expect in the deep chill of winter, but I'm home now. That is the main thing. Where are you off to, boy? I see they brought your horse around front."

"I need some air," Leopold replied, not wanting to reveal his intention to meet Rose. That must wait until he had Randolph's formal permission.

"I see," his father replied. "Well, off with you then. We will catch up at dinner. In the meantime . . ." He turned to Jameson. "Do you have the newspapers from the past fortnight? I wish to see what I've been missing here at home. I hear the queen has been winning the love of the people."

"Indeed she has, sir. She is a true royal, in every way. Shall I bring the papers to the library?"

"Please do, Jameson." The duke climbed the stairs. "Thank God the people are finally realizing what they have been missing for the past twenty years."

He disappeared at the top of the stairs, leaving Leopold to speculate uneasily about his father's loyalty to the New Regime and his stubborn Royalist beliefs.

At least Leopold was released from his own obligation to marry the Tremaine princess. It didn't matter what his father thought. If he did not wish to be a loyal subject, that was his own grave to dig.

Leopold had other plans—plans that involved a pretty golden-haired princess, who was waiting for him at the palace stables.

"What a coincidence," Rose said as she trotted into the stable courtyard and found Leopold dismounting from his horse.

He bowed to her. "Your Royal Highness . . ."

"Have you come to see the queen about the Christmas concert?" Rose asked.

She had informed the gatehouse guard that Leopold was expected that afternoon, which gained him an entrance to the palace, even though no such meeting was scheduled to take place.

"Yes," he replied. "Shall we walk together?"

"That would be delightful."

They each handed over their horses to the grooms and strode out of the stable and across the gravel courtyard to the side door of the palace.

As soon as they entered, Rose took hold of Leopold's hand and pulled him fast into an alcove behind a potted tree fern.

"We have only a few minutes," she whispered, "so I want to make the most of it." She reached into the pocket of her riding habit and withdrew a small leather case which she handed to him.

"What is it?" he asked, lifting his striking blue eyes to regard her with flirtatious curiosity.

"Open it and find out."

She watched his hands as he turned the case over and freed the clasp. Inside he found a lock of her hair.

He looked at her again with meaningful affection. "I will treasure this, Rose. I have something for you as well." He reached into his coat pocket.

"But you have already given me something—the medallion, which I keep with me always."

"This is something else." He handed her a small gold box tied in a red ribbon. "You must wait until Christmas to open it."

That was going to prove very difficult. "Shouldn't I open it now while we are together?"

"No, you must wait, but we are very good at that, are we not?"

"We've certainly had plenty of practice."

Slipping the box into a pocket in the folds of her habit, she wrapped her arms around his neck. "When will you leave for the country?"

He briefly glanced away. "In a few days. My father has just returned from Vienna and will wish to talk to me about what went on since I left. I expect he will be spending Christmas at Kaulbach Castle with his mistress, so I will spend Yuletide with my mother at Cavanaugh Manor."

Rose ran a finger over his soft lips. "Lady Elise won't be there, will she?"

He narrowed his gaze. "Are you still worried about her?"

Rose shrugged. "I cannot help myself. I feel certain that every woman in the country wants to throw herself at you, while I remain unavailable."

He kissed her on the nose. "I don't expect she will be there, but it wouldn't matter either way. All women are invisible to me, Rose. All women but one."

He touched his lips to hers, and his kiss was the greatest gift of all.

Though there was much to be happy about, Rose could not forget that it was her first Christmas since the death of her father.

His passing still lingered like a dark shadow in her heart, and when she attended mass on Christmas Eve with her brothers and Alexandra, she recalled the many times her father had held her hand in church when she was a child to prevent her from fidgeting. What a kind and loving father he had been. The world was a lesser place without him, and she continued to mourn the loss of him each and every day.

She consoled herself, however, with thoughts of Leopold and their future together. She was quite certain her father would have approved of the match, for Leopold might not be the son of an Austrian emperor, but he was a decorated war hero whose skill on the battlefield helped defeat Napoleon.

On Christmas morning she woke to bright winter sunlight beaming in through the windows. Outside, the city was cloaked in a thin sheen of glistening ice, and the church bells were ringing triumphantly.

Her maid brought her a cup of tea. Rose sat up in bed to sip it, but set it aside as soon as Mary left the room.

Rose slipped her hand under her pillow and found the gold box from Leopold, which she had placed there the night before. *You must wait until Christmas to open it.* Well, today was Christmas, and even if it wasn't, she doubted she could have waited another day, for the suspense was a torture all on its own.

Pulling the ribbon free, she lifted the lid and found a blue velvet bag inside. She slid her fingers into it and withdrew a stunning diamond and ruby brooch in the shape of a rose.

With great fascination, she beheld the beautiful piece, but there was a note attached to it, and the sight of Leopold's penmanship was just as thrilling as the blinding sparkle of the jewels.

> *My darling Rose, I had this made for you in Vienna by an unknown artist of unparalleled talent, who I suspect will be quite famous one day. He spent countless hours crafting it, but it was worth the wait—as are you, my love.*
>
> > *Happy Christmas,*
> >
> > *L*

She hugged the letter to her chest, closed her eyes and took a deep breath. Reaching for the brooch again, she examined the fine workmanship and longed for the moment she and Leopold could finally be together.

Chapter Twenty

January 7, 1815

"I am afraid it does not look good for King Randolph," the palace physician said as he stepped away from the bed and moved to explain the prognosis to Alexandra and Nicholas. "I believe it is a hereditary affliction, identical to what ailed his father. It is a cancer that spreads quickly through the humors."

For days Randolph had been complaining of fatigue and headaches and had finally collapsed. His symptoms were the same as her father's, and Rose couldn't bear to think of what the future might hold should anything happen to him.

Please, Lord, do not take my brother, too.

And what about the crown? she wondered frantically. If Alexandra did not bear a son, would it pass to Nicholas who was next in line to the throne, or would the people demand that Alexandra be queen in her own right? For she was a Tremaine, after all.

While Rose held Randolph's hand and bowed her

head to pray, Alexandra and Nicholas left the room to pray in the chapel.

If only Leopold were here. How she needed and wanted him here at her side when she felt so alone.

For a long time, Rose sat with her brother, but he did not regain consciousness. He was as pale as a sheet and so very still on the bed. He looked half dead already.

Her stomach churned with misery, and she shook him roughly. "Wake up, Randolph. Please! You're young and strong. Whatever this is, you can fight it."

To her surprise, his eyes fluttered open and he frowned at her. "What is wrong with you?"

Rose gasped at the sight of his anger. "Nothing! Oh, thank heavens you're awake!" Leaning over him, she dropped a kiss onto his forehead. "How are you feeling? Do you remember anything?"

He shook his head on the pillow. "No."

Rose tried to explain. "Alexandra found you in your bedchamber last night. You collapsed on the floor and she couldn't wake you. The doctor says you are ill, but I am convinced you will recover in no time at all."

He shut his eyes. "My head is pounding."

"You will be all right now." She fluffed his pillow and tucked the blanket all around him. "Can I get you anything? Are you hungry or thirsty?"

"Thirsty, yes. Hot broth?"

She tugged on the bell rope to call for a maid. One quickly arrived and Rose asked for a tray of broth and tea to be brought up.

As soon as it arrived, she stood. "I will go and fetch the doctor and send for Alexandra as well. Lie still for a moment."

Rose left him with the maid. She ventured into the corridor to see if the doctor was waiting outside. There was no one about, so she headed quickly to the library where the doctor preferred to sit and read while attending the king. That had been his habit, at least, when her father was ill.

Sure enough, he was seated before the fire with an open book on his lap. He stood when she entered.

"The king is awake," she told him. "I believe he is better, but it would be best if you could come and examine him."

The doctor set the book on the table and followed her to Randolph's chamber.

They had not yet reached the door when Rose heard the terrorized sound of Alexandra's scream.

"Help us! Please help us!"

Randolph suffered a seizure that morning. Unfortunately, the doctor feared the worst, for the symptoms had been the same with their father—though King Frederick had not been afflicted with such violent seizures quite so early on.

The illness appeared to be more aggressive with Randolph, and the doctor had no explanation, nor could he offer a cure. The best he could do was prescribe laudanum as a sedative to keep Randolph comfortable.

Alexandra immediately demanded a second opinion and sent for a team of young doctors from the university who might have more modern knowledge of such mysterious diseases.

The medical men arrived early that afternoon, examined Randolph thoroughly, consulted with each other, and referred to a number of books before arriving at a diagnosis that shocked everyone present and set the palace into an uproar.

The king—and most likely his father before him—had been poisoned with arsenic.

Nicholas immediately ordered a search of the palace kitchens where a supply of arsenic was indeed detected in the food stores. All members of the staff were questioned, which led the High Constable to suspect a young kitchen maid who had been hired last spring but had disappeared early that morning.

The poison was uncovered in her room within minutes and a search began throughout the city. But who had hired her? Surely she was not working alone.

That evening, Rose helped Randolph out of bed so he could sit by the fire, where Alex and Nicholas were setting up a game of chess.

"How long before you will begin to feel more like your old self?" Rose asked her brother. "The doctors said the poison will eventually leave your system, and you will be fine as long as you do not ingest any more of it, but they did not say how long it would take."

"I am not sure they know," he replied. "One of them suggested at least a week, but it was only a guess. They said it was a near lethal dose to have caused me such a rapid decline. I am lucky to be alive."

"We are all lucky," Rose added as she helped him into the chair. "But what if the High Constable does not find the maid? How will we know who was behind this?"

"There will be a very thorough investigation," Nicholas assured her. "We will leave no stone unturned."

"Good." She sank into a chair beside them and let out a heavy sigh.

Alexandra laid a hand on her knee. "You should go and get some rest, Rose. "You've been up all night tending to your brother, but all is well now."

"What about you? Are you not exhausted, too?"

"Of course, and I will retire soon enough, once I have beaten Nicholas at this game he claims to know so well. Go, Rose. Thank you for all you've done today."

Reluctantly, she stood up and left them to their chess game.

A short while later she slipped into bed. For a long time, she lay staring at the silk canopy above.

She wanted desperately to tell Leopold about the attempt on Randolph's life before he read about it in the newspaper. She also wanted to talk to him about her father, for months ago she had accepted his death as a natural passing, but now—to learn that he was poisoned while she and her brothers were abroad in England—it was like opening an old wound and filling it with salt.

Perhaps if they had not been out of the country, they could have discovered the plot and saved his life. How she wished her father could have been here to celebrate Christmas with them and enjoy the prospect of becoming a grandfather.

Rolling to her side, she rubbed the pad of her thumb over the surface of the medallion Leopold had given her in the apple orchard. Not once had she been without it. She raised it to her lips and kissed it, and forced herself to be strong for a few more days until they could be together again—this time out in the open, with her brother's permission and blessing.

Thank God Randolph was all right. Thank God they had stopped the wretched culprit in time.

The following morning, Rose slept very late and woke to another clear but cold winter day. A light snow had fallen through the night and the palace grounds were cloaked in a silvery blanket of white.

Rose's maid entered with a cup of tea. Later, while Mary helped dress Rose for the day, she assured her that His Majesty was feeling much better. In fact, Mary had just seen him heading out to the courtyard to meet someone.

"Really?" Rose asked, as she sat before the looking glass, watching Mary slide a decorative mother-of-pearl comb into her upswept hair. "Who would he meet outdoors on such a cold day? Should he not be resting?"

"I believe it is the Marquess of Cavanaugh, madam. At least it looked like him from a distance. He's very handsome, that one."

In her mad haste to rise to her feet, Rose nearly knocked over the stool. "Cavanaugh, you say? Are you certain?"

"Yes, madam. He was waiting by the cedars."

Rose was momentarily stunned; then she dashed for the door to ascertain that this meeting was indeed taking place and to learn what it was about.

Perhaps Leopold had not been able to wait any longer. Perhaps, not knowing of Randolph's illness, he had requested an audience today.

But why would they meet outside? Why not in the library or Randolph's private apartments?

Without taking the time to fetch a cloak or shawl, she

hurried through the palace corridors, descended the stairs, and reached the back hall window just in time to see her brother draw his sword and knock Leopold to the ground by the frozen reflecting pool.

No . . . !

Her brother must have learned of their clandestine meetings before Leopold left for Vienna, of that night in the orchard when Leo had claimed her, body and soul, before he had the right . . .

But who had told him? How in the world did he discover it? She hadn't shared any of that with a single soul.

Rose watched in horror as Nicholas and five palace guards appeared from behind the row of cedars. Two guards pulled Leopold to his feet. He shouted something at Randolph as they dragged him away.

Rose's blood went cold in her veins. What in God's name was happening?

Randolph resheathed his sword, staggered slightly, and collapsed to his knees. Rose watched Nicholas rush to his side, and the next thing she knew she was pushing through the palace doors and darting outside onto the terrace.

The cold air shocked her with its stinging intensity, but nothing could slow her pace as she ran toward her brother, who was rising weakly to his feet.

"What is happening?" she demanded to know.

"The marquess has been arrested for high treason and attempted murder," he explained.

Rose drew in a quick breath that chilled her lungs. "No, that cannot be . . ."

It was some kind of mistake. Leopold had done none

of those things. He was guilty only of improper intimacies with her. That had been wrong—yes, she knew it was—but there was no need for such extreme punitive measures.

Did he say attempted murder?

What?

Rose felt dizzy all of a sudden. Her vision clouded over with a strange and sickening white haze. Randolph had already left her side. He had returned to the palace.

Nicholas appeared suddenly in front of her and took hold of her arm. "You shouldn't be out here," he said. "It's freezing. You're not wearing a coat."

She realized she was shivering uncontrollably. "I don't understand. Where are they taking Lord Cavanaugh? Surely there has been some mistake."

He glanced uneasily in the direction of the palace prison. "There is no mistake, I'm afraid. Cavanaugh is a devout Royalist and has been secretly engaged to Alexandra since the day he was born. He and his father plotted for years to put her on the throne. The duke financed her debut in London so she could meet Randolph. He paid for all her gowns and jewels. It was all a deep and complex conspiracy."

Rose frowned in bewilderment. "You mean to say that *Alexandra* was Leopold's fiancée? That she was involved in the poisoning?"

Good God! It couldn't be true! This was madness!

"No," Nicholas firmly replied. "As far as we can tell, she was a pawn and knew nothing of the plot and has never even met the duke. Their plan was for her to return to Petersbourg, secure the throne, and win the love of the people, and then, when Randolph was out of the way, Leopold would step into his shoes, marry her, and sire the next king."

Rose felt sick to her stomach and feared she might faint. None of this was making sense. Leopold never mentioned anything about this. He told her his engagement was over and done with.

But all his secret visits to the palace . . . Had she unknowingly helped in the plot?

"Has he confessed?" she asked as they crossed the terrace and approached the door.

"Not yet," Nicholas replied, "but I will interrogate him personally and get to the bottom of it."

Rose swallowed uneasily. She would have to confess her relationship with Leopold. She could not allow anything to be missed.

"How did you discover all of this?" she asked.

"The Countess of Ainsley, Randolph's former fiancée, came forward this morning to confess her involvement. Evidently she was paid a handsome sum to seduce Randolph in Vienna, make him look like an adulterer, and create a scandal that would ruin the Sebastian name once and for all. I've been a victim of it myself as you well know. The press is always dragging me into the gutter. You're lucky they haven't tried to turn *you* into damaged goods."

She remembered the night at the orchard. The seduction in the library. Was that all part of this terrible plot to bring shame to her family?

No, she refused to believe it! Leopold loved her. He wanted to marry her.

"Nicholas," she said, still shivering as they entered the palace. "There is something I must tell you. It is important that you know everything before you question the marquess." A lump rose up in her throat. "Oh God, I don't even know where to begin."

He is accused of murder. The murder of my father and the attempted murder of my brother.

After telling Nicholas everything about her secret love affair with Leopold, Rose entered her bedchamber and shut the door behind her. All normal sounds seemed to fade into a garbled hum of chaos in her ears. Her head was spinning.

She still did not believe it could be true. Despite everything that Nicholas had just told her about Alexandra's benefactor in England and the Duke of Kaulbach's arrest that very morning, none of it seemed possible. Her heart didn't believe a word of it. Leopold was her one true love. He had promised to be faithful to her forever, and she had never doubted his passion.

Was it all part of a traitorous Royalist plot?

No, she could not accept it. Yet she was so bloody angry! Why had he never told her the name of his former fiancée? Why had he not mentioned the depth of his father's involvement in such treasonous schemes? Was Leo still a part of it, or did he only wish to protect his father?

Rose wanted to believe that he was innocent, but all the evidence suggested otherwise. She wished she could interrogate him herself and look into his eyes when he explained everything. Surely she would know the truth when she saw it.

A knock sounded at her door just then, and she nearly jumped out of her skin. Was there news already?

Had something more been discovered? Perhaps it was a mistake after all and this was nothing but a bad dream.

She opened the door to find a footman standing in the corridor holding a gold-plated salver.

"A letter has come for you, Your Royal Highness."

She stared at it uncertainly, then picked it up and dismissed him before shutting the door.

At first she thought it was something from Leopold—an explanation, perhaps, which he might have written that morning, knowing he was about to be arrested. But the letter did not bear the Cavanaugh seal.

This letter had come from Austria.

Chapter Twenty-one

Dear Rose,

I promised myself I would not do this. I promised your brother I would set you free, but I cannot keep my word. Since the day I read your letter that ended our engagement, I have been crushed by a despair I never imagined possible. For months I was happy in the dream of having you as my wife, but all joy has vanished from my life since the day I learned you did not feel the same passion as I.

I blame myself for the loss of your affections and am quite certain I deserve this suffering. I should have come to you when I learned your father was ill. How I long to turn back all the clocks in the world and choose a different path. If I could, I would return to Petersbourg on the night we first met and never leave the country without *you. I should have married you when I had the chance last spring, when you still believed we could be a success as husband and wife.*

Do you not remember how we danced at the spring ball? Do you forget how I looked at you when we were introduced at the reception?

Perhaps you did not feel what I felt. Perhaps you did not know that every moment I spent with you was the greatest happiness of my life. I was overcome by an all-consuming passion that has not left me since that first day.

I cannot think, I cannot function knowing that I have not done all I could to convince you of my undying love. I must therefore beg you to reconsider your decision.

I will not try to convince you of the importance of a political alliance between our two countries. I am writing to you not as the son of an emperor, but as a man who is brokenhearted and desperately in love.

I still want you as my wife. If you will change your mind, I promise to spend an eternity giving you everything in my power to give and making you as happy as any woman can be.

Please write to me, Rose. Or better yet, come to Austria, be my future empress, and make me the happiest man alive.

> *Yours forever and truly,*
> *Joseph*

Rose covered her mouth with a hand to smother a terrible, gut-wrenching sob.

She had never meant to hurt Joseph. In fact, she had not believed her change of heart would cause him any pain at all, for he had not expressed his affections in the past, and she had not recognized the intensity of his feelings.

Or perhaps she had recognized it, but the months apart had caused the memory to grow dim. His letters had conveyed no passion whatsoever, and she had therefore assumed he was not in love with her. She had been so sure that it was a political marriage and nothing more than that.

She was absolutely shocked by this letter.

Clearly she had misjudged Joseph. A terrible regret racked her body, for she had unknowingly broken his heart.

Perhaps if she had known of this sooner, she might not have been so easily wooed away by Leopold.

And what about Leopold? He was the one she loved. Even now, knowing that he had lied to her about so many things, she could not turn her back on him. Not until she knew the whole truth.

With an aching heart and a flood of anxieties coming at her from all directions, Rose sat down and waited for Nicholas to return from the interrogation.

It took hours, and Rose could do nothing but pace in her room, waiting fretfully and wondering what was transpiring in the prison.

Please, God, let it all be a terrible misunderstanding. Leopold could not have poisoned Randolph or her father. He had kept secrets from her, certainly, but had not committed murder. Surely not that.

At last a knock rapped at her door, and Nicholas entered the room. He looked exhausted and weary, as if he had not slept for many days.

"Well?" she asked. "What happened? Did you uncover the truth?"

He dropped his gaze to the floor as if he were filled suddenly with despair. "This is not going to be easy for you to hear, Rose. You had best sit down."

Her stomach careened with sickening apprehension, but she was determined to keep a steady mind. She would hear the truth, whatever it was, and she would weather it.

Taking a seat in the dark leather armchair in front of the fire, she invited Nicholas to sit down as well. They faced each other in the late-afternoon sunshine beaming in through the windows while the fire crackled and snapped in the hearth.

Nicholas inhaled deeply, then exhaled before he began. "I will come straight to the point. Lord Cavanaugh has confessed his secret engagement to Alexandra. He says he knew of her existence and was pledged to marry her since he was a young boy, and had always believed it was his destiny and duty to remove our family from the throne and restore the true monarchs."

"The Tremaines."

"Yes. He also believed it was his duty to restore his own family dynasty to the throne, for as you know he has a distant claim to it by blood. His ancestors were once kings of this country, while ours were blacksmiths and butchers."

She worked hard to keep her breathing steady and swallowed over a jagged lump of unease. "Continue."

"He also denied any sort of relationship with you. He said he never came to the palace to see you, nor did he arrange to meet you secretly the night before he left for Vienna. When I explained that you had already told me everything, he reluctantly admitted to it, so we are now obliged to doubt his truthfulness about anything."

"He was only trying to protect my reputation," she explained in his defense. "We cannot use that against him."

Nicholas paused. "If I believed that were true, I would spare nothing to ensure the court's leniency toward him."

"But you have reason to believe otherwise?"

He stared at her for a long moment, then leaned back in the chair and glanced anxiously around the room. "Is that wine in the decanter?" he asked, motioning toward the tray by her bed.

"Yes. I had it brought up an hour ago. Would you like some?"

"Please."

She rose to go and pour him a glass, then returned to the hearth, sat down and handed it to him.

"It must be serious," she said. "You don't look well at all."

He took a sip. "It's bad, Rose. There is so much more. You have no idea."

Clasping her hands together on her lap, she said, "Do not try to protect me, Nicholas. I am a grown woman. I will survive whatever you say."

He took another sip of wine, then set the glass on the small table next to his chair. "All right, then. First off, we have located the maid who brought the poison into the palace. She is still being questioned in the prison, along with Leopold's father and his father's valet."

"How is the valet involved?"

"He is the maid's brother. They are loyal servants at Kaulbach Castle and dedicated Royalists. It was the valet who approached the Countess of Ainsley and paid her to try to seduce Randolph in Vienna. He was also responsible for the scandal that was reported to the papers last spring—the one about me seducing and ruining the Duke of Tantallon's daughter at the Hanover Hotel."

Rose frowned. "But you *did* seduce that young woman if I remember correctly," she reminded him.

"Did I?" he replied. "Or did she seduce me? She was ridiculously willing as I recall, and she was ruined long before I ever touched her. As it turns out, her family is flat broke. We are looking into it now to find out if she was offered money as well."

"My word," Rose said. "How deep does this go?"

"Deeper, I'm afraid. Here is the worst part, Rose. I was grateful before that you had been spared from the scandals, but it seems now that you are next to be skewered."

"How so?"

He shut his eyes for a moment as if he could not bear to deliver the news, then he spoke frankly. "Your letters to Leopold have been shared with the *Chronicle*. Your reputation is—" He stopped. "I'm sorry. I cannot go on."

She struggled to understand what Nicholas was saying, while her stomach clenched with anger at this unthinkable betrayal. "Can we stop the editor from printing them? What else do they intend to reveal?"

"Everything," he replied, "and it's too late to stop it. The papers are already distributed as a special edition along with news of Randolph's near death at the hands of a murderer."

She frowned. "Are you trying to tell me that Leopold did all of this to ruin me? That he seduced me in order to make the people demand that we be declared unfit to rule and should be deposed?"

"Yes. It is more than clear to both Randolph and me that this has been the plan all along. The maid admitted to it as soon as they closed the prison cell door behind her. She spilled everything in a matter of minutes."

Rose was having trouble breathing. "I still do not believe that Leopold lied to me like that. I believe he cared for me. It couldn't have been a trick."

Nicholas shrugged. "I don't know what is in his heart. Perhaps he does love you. I think it's quite possible he does. How could he not? You are a lovely woman, but the fact remains . . . He is a Royalist, and all his life he has been groomed to seize the throne. He traveled to England last spring to make sure his future with Alexandra would be secured."

Rose fought hard against the bolt of anger rising up in her throat. "But they never even met each other. Why did they not present Leopold to her sooner? Why did they let her marry Randolph?"

"Because the duke knew he would never have enough supporters to overthrow us, even if Alexandra was revealed as the lost Tremaine princess. He wanted her to secure the throne quietly, without incident, then get rid of us in a more underhanded way. That is why Leopold came home early from Vienna. To win her friendship while Randolph was allegedly straying to another woman's bed."

Rose pressed a hand to her chest. "No, that cannot be true. To hear it spoken like that, to imagine that Leopold was involved in such a dark plot, years in the making, and took advantage of me in that way . . . It makes me sick."

"I'm sorry, Rose."

She collected herself and met her brother's gaze. "Has he admitted to any of this?"

"He has confessed to treason and the plot to marry Alexandra but denies knowledge of the arsenic. At this time, we don't know what to believe. That will be up to the court to determine. In the meantime, you must brace yourself for the scandal that is about to hit all of us."

She bowed her head and closed her eyes. "I don't care about the scandal. Thank God the plot was discovered in time. Randolph is alive and Alexandra is safe from the villains who would have used her to gain back their position on the throne."

They were quiet for a long time. Nicholas looked toward the window. "It's snowing again."

Rose turned in her chair. She felt strangely numb all over, but there was no chance of tears. Her heart seemed to be freezing over with ice. "It's quite pretty, isn't it? It makes the world seem almost normal."

"But it's not," he replied.

"No, far from it." Her eyes darted to Joseph's letter on her bed. She had read it a number of times while she waited for Nicholas to return with news of the interrogation and wasn't sure what to feel about it now.

"There is something I should show you." She stood to retrieve it.

"What is that?"

"A letter from Archduke Joseph." She did not wish to hand it over, for it was personal and private, so she attempted to explain in her own words. "He still wants to marry me. I didn't realize it, but he was deeply hurt by my change of heart."

Nicholas stood and approached her. "Joseph did seem very low the entire time we were in Vienna."

She turned the letter over in her hands. "I never meant to hurt him. Now it feels as if I am being punished for that. I should have been faithful. I should not have let myself be seduced away. Joseph was always such a gentleman. Now I fear I was very foolish, and if I am to be ruined, he will be glad to have escaped such a reckless wife."

Nicholas regarded her with great care and sensitivity. "I beg your pardon, Rose, but I must ask the question. Are you truly ruined?"

She knew what he was asking. This was all so dreadfully unpleasant.

"If you wish to know if I am still a virgin . . ." She paused. "No, I am not."

A muscle flicked at Nicholas's jaw and his hand curled into a fist. "How do you feel about the archduke now?" he asked, not putting her through the agony of explaining the sordid details. "Do you think you might be able to care for him if he still wanted to marry you? Because I believe he would be very willing to come to your rescue. He was devastated over the loss of you. I am sure he would do whatever it took to save your reputation, for clearly you were deceived in the worst possible way."

Rose looked down at the letter again. "I couldn't use Joseph like that."

"But would you be using him? You were willing to marry him before. Now, after all of this, do you not think you could genuinely care for him?"

She sat down again and cupped her forehead in a hand. "I don't know, Nicholas. What about Leopold? I did love him, and I think, despite everything, I still do. How very foolish I am."

Nicholas knelt down before her and clasped both her hands in his. "His entire family is headed for disaster. The duke will likely be stripped of his title and property, and may very well hang for his crimes. It's difficult to say what will happen to Leopold. It depends on what the court decides. He denies knowledge of the arsenic, but even so the rest of it makes him guilty of treason and conspiracy to overthrow us."

"It all seems very bleak."

"Yes, but we must be thankful that we discovered the plot in time."

She thought about everything for a long moment. "What should I do?"

He sat back on his heels. "I think you should go with Randolph to Vienna when he returns to the Congress. Talk to the archduke. Be honest and tell him what happened. If he will still have you, then be happy, Rose, for I know Joseph. There is no doubt in my mind that he is worthy of you."

She could no longer hold back her emotions. She wept into her hands while Nicholas kissed the top of her head and promised that everything was going to be all right.

When she had managed to wipe away the tears and recover her composure, another knock sounded at the door.

Nicholas went to answer it. "What is it?" he said to the footman.

"The *Chronicle* has arrived, sir. You said to deliver it immediately."

Nicholas shot a rueful glance at Rose. "I did not mean for it to be brought *here*."

"Please do not apologize," she said. "There is no point hiding it from me. I will see it eventually."

She reached for it before either of them could stop her and read the headline:

PRINCESS IN LOVE
OR LUST?
NEW SEBASTIAN MONARCHY
DISGRACED AGAIN

Frantically, she read the full story and nearly exploded in a fit of rage when she saw her private letter to Leopold printed in black-and-white for all the world to see.

Meet me at noon at the stables . . . Do not be late. I long for your touch . . .

Crumpling the newspaper in her hands, she clenched her jaw in anger and pitched it into the fire.

She had never in her life felt more betrayed by anyone.

Why hadn't Leopold told her about his engagement to Alexandra? He'd already broken her trust once before, but he'd led her to believe he deserved a second chance.

Clearly she had been very wrong to give him one.

The prison door slammed shut behind her, and she jumped at the sound of it—like a judge's gavel—while her gaze fell upon the man she had come here to confront.

He was already standing in the center of the cell, as if he had known it was she outside the door. She, who had once adored him. Trusted him. Desired him.

He wore the same fashionable clothing from a few short hours ago when he was arrested in the palace courtyard and dragged away for high treason and attempted murder.

For he had tried to kill her beloved brother.

Her heart squeezed like a wrathful fist in her chest, and for a moment she couldn't breathe.

"You seem surprised to see me," Rose said, lifting her chin and resisting any urge to rush forward into his arms and beg to hear that he was safe and unharmed, for his welfare did not matter. She should not care about that. He deserved to rot down here with the rest of the rats, and she hoped he would.

"Yes," he replied. "And no, because all I've done since they dragged me here was pray you would come to me. I could think of nothing else."

Rose scoffed. "There it is again. The flattery and seduction. Did you imagine I would learn of your peril and try to rescue you? Did you think I would drop to my brother's feet and beg him to set you free, because I had fallen in love with you? Even after what you did to my family and how you used me?"

He stepped forward, but she held up a hand. "Stay where you are, sir. I know everything. My brother told me of your plot to replace him on the throne. I know how you came to the palace to win the queen's affections. I know that your father has been planning your marriage to her since the day you were born so that you would one day rule this country at her side. You have been deceiving us all, and for that reason I came here to tell you that anything I felt for you in the past is annihilated. Nothing I said remains true any longer for I was misled, and I certainly have no intention of helping you escape your sentence, whatever it may be."

Her heart broke into a thousand pieces as she spoke the words. She nearly doubled over in agony.

He shook his head in disbelief. "You're lying. If you felt nothing for me, why did you come here? If I did not matter to you, you would simply watch my head roll."

Her fury erupted again, for he was not wrong. She was not indifferent, but damn him for recognizing it. Damn him for pointing it out.

The chill of the prison cell seeped into her bones, and she rubbed at her arms. "I will never forgive you," she said.

He stared at her. "Yes you will, Rose, because you know I am innocent."

She felt nauseous suddenly. A part of her wanted to weep at the loss of him. Another part of her wanted to strike him and shake him senseless until he confessed that he had treated her wrongly and that he was sorry. That he regretted all the lies and betrayals, and that this was all just a bad dream.

"I know no such thing," she replied nevertheless. "My brother was poisoned with arsenic just like my father, who is now dead. You of all people know how much I loved my father. Yet you, as a devout Royalist, were behind the plot to kill him."

He made a fist at his side. "No, I knew nothing of that, just as I knew nothing of the attempt on Randolph's life. I love you, Rose. You know that. You know I would never do anything to hurt you."

He tried to move closer again, and what was left of her heart split in two. He was still the most beautiful man she had ever known, and despite all her cool, contemptuous bravado, she could never forget the passion they shared, how his touch had ignited her whole world into a boundless, shining realm of happiness.

But she must push those memories aside, for she was devastated by his betrayal and by the total destruction of her first love.

How could she have been so foolish? How could she not have seen the truth? He fooled her once before. How would she ever recover from this?

"Please," he said, spreading his arms wide in open surrender. "Tell Randolph I had nothing to do with the arsenic. I confess I was raised as a Royalist, and yes . . . my father wanted to remove your family from the throne and I knew it. But since the day we met on that muddy road in England, Rose, I have cared less and less for politics and thrones. I fell in love with you. You know it in your heart." He inhaled deeply. "Speak to Randolph on my behalf. Tell him I am sincere. I knew nothing of the attempt on his life or your father's murder. Treason, yes . . . I am guilty of that. I was part of the plot to take back the throne, at least in the beginning, but I am no killer."

Her heart was beating so fast she feared she might faint, but it was not like before, when her heart raced simply because Leopold Hunt, Marquess of Cavanaugh, entered a room. This was different. Everything had changed. She was not the same naive girl she was six months ago, and her infatuation was now crushed.

"It will fall on the court to determine whether or not you are a killer," she told him. "I cannot help you in that regard, for clearly I am incapable of sensible judgments where you are concerned."

"That is not true."

A part of her wanted to believe him, but she clung to the dark shadow of contempt that had taken over her soul.

"Yes it is," she replied, "for you were the worst mistake of my life."

All the color drained from his face—as if she had thrust a knife into his belly.

"I pray you will not feel that way forever," he said.

She laughed bitterly. "Why? So that there might be a chance for us? Or perhaps you hope my feelings might change in time to reduce your sentence."

"It has nothing to do with that."

For a flashing instant, her thoughts flew back to that muddy road in England when the world was a different place and she still believed in heroes and fairy tales. She quickly pounded the life out of that memory and shoved it into a deep grave.

"If I must repeat myself, I will," she replied. "I want nothing more to do with you. I want to forget what happened between us and move on with my life. I wish you luck in the trial, but I will not be here to witness it, for I will be leaving Petersbourg as soon as possible. I intend to marry the Archduke of Austria as planned."

"Rose, wait—"

Again, he took a step closer but she swung around, fearful that he might touch her, hold her, weaken her resolve. She rushed to the door and rapped hard against it with a tight fist. "Guard!"

The bar lifted and the door opened. Rose rushed out.

"Is everything all right, Your Highness?" the guard asked, looking more than a little concerned.

"I am fine," she lied.

While she struggled to resist the treacherous urge to change her mind and return to Leopold's side, the door slammed shut behind her.

Suddenly, to her utter shame and chagrin, she wondered what would happen if she spoke to Randolph on Leopold's behalf. Would he show mercy? Life in prison perhaps, instead of death?

No. No! She would do nothing of the sort! She was a Sebastian and had a duty to fulfill. Her brother's new monarchy had only just begun. She must remain strong, serve her beloved country, and marry Joseph.

She would forget about Leopold Hunt, and she would be more sensible from this day forward. She would not spend another moment wondering how this unthinkable heartache had come to pass, nor would she wonder what she could have done differently to avoid it.

What was done was done. He was dead to her now. It was time to leave Petersbourg.

Chapter Twenty-two

January 14, 1815

"Are you sure you have everything?" Alexandra asked as she dropped to her knees to help Rose lower the lid of the last trunk and fasten the buckles.

"I believe so."

Rose stood and looked around her bedchamber—the place where she had grown from a young child without a mother into a woman of the world, who had seen far too much of it lately, and learned many painful lessons.

She was sorry to be leaving. She would miss her family, the palace, the people of Petersbourg, who had rallied to support her after the scandalous story in the *Chronicle*. Shortly thereafter, blame had fallen squarely on the Duke of Kaulbach and his son, Cavanaugh. Rose's innocence in the plot had been recognized.

"Are you sure about this?" Alexandra asked. "Because it is not too late to change your mind. If you arrive at the Hofburg and Joseph is unforgiving, or if you discover you could not be happy there, you can always come home again. Randolph and I have discussed it. We would support you in any decision."

Rose picked up her reticule and opened it to check the contents. It contained something very important, which she must deliver to Nicholas before she left.

Two footmen entered the room to collect the trunk. Randolph followed them into the room.

"Do you have everything?" he asked.

"Yes. This is the last of it."

They waited for the footmen to carry the trunk into the corridor before Alexandra moved forward to hug Rose. "I will miss you very much. Promise you will write as often as you can."

"I will, but do not fret. Your sisters will be arriving in Petersbourg soon, and you will have plenty to do, arranging their debuts."

Alex smiled bravely. "Indeed I will."

Randolph regarded his wife with regret, for he was leaving for Vienna as well and must say good-bye to her, too. "The time has come," he said, "but before we leave, Rose, I must have a word with you in private."

Her eyebrows drew together. "Concerning what, exactly?"

He gave her a look that answered the question quite definitively, and she was forced to steel herself against the raw emotion that rose up within her.

"If it concerns the marquess," she replied, "there is no need to keep it from Alexandra. I have told her everything. I would like her to stay."

Alexandra had been a great comfort over the past number of days. She had stayed and listened to Rose express her anger, and had passed her handkerchiefs and embraced her when she wept.

"Very well, then," Randolph said as he reached into his breast pocket and withdrew a letter that bore no seal, which could only mean it had come from the prison.

Oh God. Not another letter. It seemed as if her life were constantly swinging back and forth like a pendulum whenever a letter arrived.

"I am not sure I want to read this," she said. "I've already made up my mind about my future. All I want to do is put all this behind me. I cannot bear for anything to stir up my feelings again."

Alexandra and Randolph looked at each other as if they were discussing the matter with their eyes and wondering how to convince Rose to reconsider.

"Fine," Rose said, taking the letter from her brother. "I will read it if you think I should."

Turning away from them, she unfolded it as she walked to the window.

"Would you prefer to be alone?" Alexandra asked.

"No, I want you both to stay."

Then she began to read.

Dear Rose,

I know there is nothing I can say to excuse what I have done. I was wrong to have kept so many secrets from you. One day soon, however, you will at least know the truth. Everything will be revealed in the trial, but I have learned you will not be here to witness it. This morning I was told you are leaving today.

I write to plead with you not to marry the archduke, for I will go mad if I lose you to another man. That is selfish, I know, and I struggle to cling to what honor I have left and let you go, for you deserve better than to live with what I have become in the eyes of this great nation—a traitor to the crown.

Yet honor means nothing to me if I cannot have you. Please do not marry another. You are mine, and I will not accept the loss of you.

Do not go. Stay. Wait for me. I will find a way to be with you. Whatever it takes.

Always,
Leopold

Rose fought against the tears that flooded her eyes, but they were not tears of woe but of anger. Why had he done this to her a second time? Why did he lead her into a world of passion and hope when he was again hiding something from her? Something that would eventually tear them apart?

"I am so angry with him," she said to Randolph. "He asks me to wait for him and admits he is being selfish. He cannot accept defeat. That is his problem. He has always been ambitious. He wanted your crown." Her eyes shot to Alexandra. "It was only when he lost you to Randolph that he decided he wanted *me* again. Was I just a consolation prize? Or did he truly want to ruin us?" She paused and fought to gather her composure. "At the same time, I am ashamed to admit that it kills me to think of him locked up in prison facing the worst, believing that I despise him, because despite all the lies, I do believe our affair was real. The passion was not a trick. It couldn't have been."

Alexandra approached and laid a sympathetic hand on her shoulder. "I am sure that it was not."

None of them spoke for a long moment while Rose stood at the window, looking out at the white winter cityscape and wrestling with the confusing chaos of her feelings.

At the heart of it, there was sadness.

This was a chapter of her life that would soon be over. She would leave this place—the home that she loved—and abandon all her dreams of a life with Leopold Hunt, supposed hero and gentleman. She must instead try to embrace a new future with a man who deserved her love and fidelity. It was the right thing to do. She knew it in her heart and mind.

Turning to face her brother, she said, "I wish to leave now. Where is Nicholas?"

"He is out front overseeing the loading of the coaches. He is waiting to say good-bye."

A few minutes later, she was standing in the front hall with Nicholas, fighting against all thoughts of not seeing him again for a very long time.

"I want you to do something for me," she said as she opened her reticule and withdrew a small velvet bag. "You must return this to Lord Cavanaugh. These were gifts from him, but I don't feel right keeping them now."

The bag contained the gold medallion that had once belonged to Leopold's ancestors and the diamond and ruby brooch he had given her for Christmas.

"I will return them."

She gazed down at the floor and swallowed hard

over the sorrow that was clenching her heart in a tight fist. "Can you do one more thing for me?"

"Of course."

"Tell him that I read his letter and I thank him for it. Tell him I do not wish him ill, and that I hope his sentence will be fair. Say good-bye for me, and inform him that it is not likely we will ever see each other again."

Still with her gaze lowered, she paused.

"Is that all?" Nicholas said. "You're sure?"

She nodded, then looked up at her brother. "This is difficult. I will miss you terribly."

He gathered her into his arms and held her tightly until her departure could no longer be delayed.

Then she walked out of the palace and did not look back as she climbed into the coach with Randolph and drove away.

PART IV
Love and War

Chapter Twenty-three

For all the future days of his life, Leopold knew he would never forget the harsh and merciless reality of the moment when he learned that Rose had done it. She had walked down the aisle of St. Stephen's Cathedral in Vienna and married Archduke Joseph, eldest son of the Austrian emperor.

Leopold was a cavalry officer in the war against Napoleon. He had charged boldly into murderous enemy lines in Spain and on the battlefields of Leipzig. He had witnessed more horrors than he cared to remember, but nothing struck him so deeply or devastatingly as the knowledge that Rose had given her heart to another and all hope was lost.

She would not change her mind and come home to him now, nor would he be released from this dark hell-hole in the earth, miraculously restore his reputation, and gallop across national borders to reclaim her before it was too late.

She was lost to him now, married to another man, while he was becoming something akin to a caged tiger . . . wounded and ravenous and angry enough to rip a person apart.

Namely the archduke of Austria. If not for him, Rose would still be in Petersbourg, and Leo might still have a chance to repair the damage.

But she was lost to him now, and part of him hated her for abandoning him so quickly, for not trusting him or believing in him.

How could she have married another? Had she already lain with Joseph? *Oh, God in heaven, help me . . .* He couldn't survive the thought . . .

Some days, the jealousy was like a sharp sword in his gut. He felt shackled to these walls. The betrayal burned so searingly in his brain that he cursed Rose for every word she spoke when she came to confront him here. Other days he nearly collapsed with grief at the loss of her and despised himself for such weakness.

He hated the powerlessness, the excruciating torture of this frustrating confinement, interrupted only by the humiliation of standing trial while his father was found guilty, stripped of his title and property, and sentenced to death.

Leopold had never considered himself a vengeful man, but a wretched violence was kindling inside of him and burning very deep in his core. He continued to imagine what he would do if he could escape and meet the archduke again. Perhaps he would grab him by the throat and fling him into the Danube. Or casually elbow him into a well when no one was looking.

They were morbid thoughts, all of them, but somehow they mollified the bitter monster inside of him, which was born from his grief and despair.

And his regrets.

If only he had exposed his father's treason when he first returned from England. If only he had confessed everything to Rose.

He could only blame himself.

All this is my own doing.

With that thought hammering relentlessly in his brain, he woke one morning and smashed his table and chair to bits and pieces. After that, he had only his cot to sit on.

He tried to sleep. It wasn't easy, for he was never at peace.

Days turned to weeks, and by the end of February, the verdict came down. Leopold braced himself for the sentencing.

In the end, the court ruled that he was innocent of the charges of murder, for he had known nothing of it, but was guilty of treason in addition to a number of lesser charges.

He, too, was stripped of his title of marquess, and Cavanaugh Manor was seized by the crown.

His mother was also charged with treason, for she had known of the plot but had never revealed it. However, the court was lenient toward her for she had not spoken to her husband in more than ten years and everyone knew she openly despised him. She was sentenced to time already served in prison, but was stripped of her title of duchess. Naturally the scandal would ruin her socially, but Leo knew she wouldn't care about that.

She never enjoyed moving about in society, and was happiest in the country, and she had her own money.

But Leopold regretted every moment of her suffering. He mourned all that she had lost in her life—her husband, who had never been faithful to her, and her two daughters who had died of typhoid early in life.

Now the disgrace and downfall of her only son.

Leopold had stood at the rail for the reading of his sentence and had borne it bravely—even the final word that he would be spared the hangman's noose but would spend the next twenty years of his life in prison.

If he lived that long. The odds were not good for such longevity at Briggin's.

Hence, he prepared to enter a new chapter in his life, an exceedingly dark one that made him wonder if he might have been better off at the scaffold, for the lonely years ahead of him seemed a much crueler punishment.

But on March 31—less than five weeks into his twenty-year sentence—a royal visitor arrived to convey news of a most shocking turn of events, and an offer he simply could not refuse.

Chapter Twenty-four

Vienna

"You will not believe it," Joseph said to Rose as she entered the palace after her usual morning ride through the park.

Feeling refreshed from the exertion of a fast gallop, she pulled off her riding gloves and hat and handed them to the butler.

"Believe what?" she asked, recognizing the alarm in her husband's expression. "Has something happened?"

"Napoleon has reached Paris," he said. "He has taken back the throne."

Rose halted on the carpet. "Good God. King Louis fled Paris only a week ago. What will it mean for France? For all of Europe?"

Joseph stared at her with uncertainty, then motioned for her to follow him into the library. "There is no question about it . . ." He shut the door behind them. "Bonaparte cannot be trusted to keep the peace. All the allies expect the worst."

"It hardly seems possible," she said. "A month ago he was still sitting on Elba. How could he escape and muster an army so quickly?"

"Speed and recklessness have always been his greatest strengths, but there is more." Joseph paced the room. "Napoleon's former marshal, Murat, who is regrettably still King of Naples, will soon begin an invasion of the Papal States. If that occurs, he will have broken his agreement with my father, and it is very likely that Austria will go to war. I just spoke with Metternich, and he anticipates that we will be sending our troops to Italy very soon."

"Are you certain we should be fighting Murat in Italy, when Napoleon will no doubt be marching north to reclaim what he has lost?"

Joseph nodded. "I share your concerns, Rose, but it is difficult to predict what he will do. What matters is that we are all on the same side. All the great powers here in Vienna have formed a new coalition that will not be broken. We have promised one another not to negotiate separately with Bonaparte. We will present a united front against him."

She collapsed into a chair. "That is good news. Is there any chance that the coalition might march on Paris and simply throw him out before he gathers more forces?"

"He has already gathered an enormous army, I am afraid."

She thought of Leopold that night in the orchard and remembered his prediction that Napoleon would escape from Elba before the year was out. How right he had been . . .

"What about Wellington and the tsar?" she asked. "What are their intentions?"

"Wellington intends to march to the Low Countries where he will be joined by the Prussians. The Russian army is still in Poland and a terrible distance away."

"Have you heard from my brother?" she asked. "I am certain Randolph will commit troops to the campaign." After walking her down the aisle a month ago, Randolph had left Vienna and returned to Petersbourg for the birth of his first child, which could happen any day now. Rose was constantly awaiting news.

"Your foreign minister has already verified a commitment from Petersbourg," Joseph said. "I expect your brother's army will march to Brussels and meet Wellington there as well."

Rose stood up. "I see. That is very good."

But who would command the troops, she wondered, when one of their greatest war heroes was currently rotting away in prison for high treason?

Joseph hurried to the door. "I must go now," he said. "There is much to do and much to discuss with the other foreign ministers. I will see you at dinner and tell you everything I can about what is happening."

She watched him go. "Be careful, Joseph. The world seems suddenly unhinged."

He paused at the door to regard her with both worry and affection.

A moment later he was gone, leaving her alone to think about armies and soldiers—and how life could spin so wildly out of control in the space of a single heartbeat.

Such twists and turns did not surprise her, however, for she had come to expect them in life.

Nevertheless, as she sat down to pour herself a cup of tea, her hands trembled as she brought the cup to her lips.

Leopold paced back and forth in the prison cell and considered all the information that King Randolph had just relayed to him.

Austria was marching to the Rhine to fight Murat, while Russia was still in Poland. British and Prussian forces had gathered in Belgium, and Napoleon was preparing to march.

"He will try to split up their armies and defeat them one at a time," Leopold said. "Divide and conquer. That has always been his strategy."

"This is why we need you in Belgium," Randolph said. "You have fought him before, while Wellington has not yet faced him in battle. At least not until now. We must send our best troops to support the coalition. Wellington will value your experience with Bonaparte."

"Are you forgetting that I am a convicted criminal," Leopold asked, "sentenced to a twenty-year imprisonment?"

Randolph strode to the chair—which had been replaced for the king's visit—and sat down. "No, I have not forgotten, which is why I have come. To offer you a temporary parole for as long as the campaign lasts, in exchange for your loyalty and service as an officer of the crown."

Leopold regarded Randolph shrewdly. "At what rank?"

"General, as before. Cavalry division. In fact, you would be leading many of the same men."

"You believe they would respect my authority, knowing that I have been disgraced?"

"That would be for you to foster their allegiance," Randolph said. "But I would not offer this post if I did not believe you would be as effective as you ever were. You always ran a tight ship and . . ." He paused. "There are many who believe you were wrongly convicted."

Leopold frowned. "How so?"

"Some feel your father was the guilty party, not you. That you could not be held accountable for your upbringing. That your Royalist beliefs were a thing of the past and that as a hero of the war, you should have been awarded some leniency from the court."

Leopold inclined his head. "What do *you* believe?"

Randolph leaned back in the chair—until the front legs lifted off the floor. "I believe I must support the decisions of my magistrates and the jury. I also believe, however, that if you had known of your father's plot to commit murder, you would have come forward and exposed him for what he was. The unfortunate fact of the matter is that there can be no proof of that. It is my own speculation, nothing more, and it is a question that will never be answered, for we cannot turn back the clock."

Leopold sat down on the cot. "But how I wish I could."

They regarded each other intently in the dim candlelight of the cold prison cell until Randolph leaned forward again and rested his elbows on his knees. "Will you do it? Will you accept this commission?"

Leopold was both intrigued and motivated, but he needed further clarification. "It is a parole, not a pardon."

"That is correct, and your time away will count as time served."

Leopold chuckled softly. "I am sure you and your court ministers are well aware that my chances of coming home alive to finish out my sentence are slim. It is going to be a bloody, vicious battle if I know Bonaparte."

"I am sure you are right about that, but I do hope you will return safely, sir, with as few casualties as possible."

"I will do my best."

"Does this mean you will accept?"

Leopold nodded and stood. "I'd be a fool not to, for how could I resist a chance to walk out of this cell, return to the field of battle, and lead a full cavalry charge upon Europe's worst enemy?"

Randolph reached out to shake his hand. "Excellent. I will send a man to release you within the hour. He will escort you to your new post."

"But I have no property," Leopold said. "No home. Where will I stay?"

"At the barracks until it is time to march. That will not be long from now. The sooner you leave Petersbourg the better, for there is little time to spare."

Randolph started for the door.

"Wait . . ." Leopold stepped forward to ask one more question—the question that was still burning like a raging inferno in his brain. "You did not mention Rose. Where is she? *How* is she?"

He needed to know, because if he was going to get out of here . . .

Randolph paused. "She is in Vienna with her husband, and she is very well."

"Joseph is not leading the Austrian army to Naples?"

"No."

"Will she be in Brussels?"

Randolph would give him no more information than that. He turned and walked out of the cell, leaving Leopold to refoster his resolve and prepare himself for one more charge.

Chapter Twenty-five

Brussels

It was with a whisper of uncertainty that the Duchess of Richmond went ahead with her ball on the evening of June 15, when rumors abounded that Napoleon was marching toward the city. An assurance from the Duke of Wellington, however, put her at ease and guaranteed a strong attendance from the illustrious list of invited guests.

Rose and Joseph had arrived in Brussels a few days prior to act as ambassadors. They were to send frequent reports to Joseph's father, Emperor Francis, about the status of the allied armies. Naturally, at the last minute, they had been added to the duchess's guest list and looked forward to an evening of stimulating conversation and merriment.

Rose dressed for the ball with a reliable sense of calm, as if it were any other event on her social calendar, until the unthinkable happened. A knock sounded at her door and her husband—it still felt strange to call him that—entered to request a private moment alone before they departed. She immediately dismissed her maid.

"I am not sure how to tell you this," he said as he sat down on the edge of the bed in their hotel room, "but it is something I felt you should know."

Fastening a dangling sapphire earring to her lobe, Rose swiveled around on the dressing table stool to face him. "Good heavens, it sounds serious. The hotel is not about to be pummeled with grapeshot, is it? Please tell me before I imagine the worst."

He usually chuckled when she spoke in jest, but not so this evening. "There is someone on the guest list whom I doubt you are expecting to see," he said with concern.

Rose raised an eyebrow. "Who is it?"

"Leopold Hunt."

At the mere mention of the name, the hotel might as well have been pummeled with grapeshot after all, for she was stunned to the point of speechlessness.

Leopold? Here? In Brussels?

She drew back in surprise while astonishment fluttered through her. Then immediately she forced herself to feign indifference. "What in the world is he doing here? Has he escaped prison? The last I heard he was sentenced to twenty years. No one has written to tell me otherwise."

"I apologize," Joseph explained. "Perhaps I should not have kept it from you, but I felt it best to let you get on with your life. It's what you said you wanted when we agreed to marry. You said you never wanted to see that man, or hear his name spoken, ever again."

Her stomach was careening. This couldn't be happening. "But you knew he was released?" she asked. "*How* did you know?"

"Your brother Nicholas wrote to me in April and informed me of the situation. He explained that Lord Cavanaugh—" Joseph stopped himself. "Pardon me. He is Mr. Hunt now. Or rather General Hunt. Your brother offered him a temporary parole to serve in the cavalry and lead the Petersbourg troops into battle. He has accepted the commission and is here in Brussels."

Rose stared at her husband in disbelief while her vision clouded over. She never imagined she would ever see Leopold again. She had tried so hard to put all that behind her, but suddenly now she had to prepare to meet him this very night. At a ball.

A part of her wanted to shout at Joseph from across the room—wasn't it customary to shoot the messenger in times of war?—but instead she cleared her throat and reached for her other earring.

"Well, this is certainly unexpected," she coolly said. "I am not sure what I shall say to him if we rub shoulders. To be honest, I am surprised the duchess invited him to her ball. He is disgraced, after all."

"I will be at your side the entire time," Joseph assured her. "Unless you would prefer not to go. I would understand, you know. It is a rather awkward situation, isn't it?"

"That is putting it mildly." She rose from the dressing table stool and tried not to reveal the depths of her anxiety. Joseph had been so good to her, so forgiving for everything. He had come to her rescue when scandal had threatened to ruin her family. He had taken her back even when he knew she had genuinely loved another. And he had been very patient, waiting for her to recover from that heartbreak.

Even on their wedding night.

Now that man she once loved was *here,* threatening everything Joseph wanted from her.

She felt a critical need to reassure him. Her honor demanded it. "I am not thrilled at the notion of seeing the man who once tried to seize my brother's throne," she said. She was intensely aware of Joseph's uneasy gaze watching her as she crossed to the wardrobe and began searching for a different pair of gloves, for she did not like the ones her maid had selected, and she had to do something to appear in control of her emotions. She feared if she stopped and stood still long enough to consider the tidal wave that was about to come crashing over her world that very evening, her true feelings would be exposed.

What were they, exactly? She could barely understand them herself. She cared for Joseph deeply and could never have survived the past few months without his constant devotion and unwavering understanding. He had done everything possible to ease her sorrows and help her feel happy again.

She could not bear to hurt him. No, she would never do that. Not in a thousand years would she throw him over again for the sake of a passionate affair that had been cursed from the beginning.

At the same time, her heart was racing with both terror and uncertainty, for against all odds, she was about to see Leopold Hunt again—when she had expected him to live only in her memories for the rest of her life.

She was pulling on a new set of gloves when she felt a gentle hand on her shoulder and soft words in her ear. "Are you sure you are all right? Perhaps we shouldn't go. I will stay here with you if you prefer."

Rose faced her husband. "That will not be necessary. I am over him, truly. It will be awkward, that is all. We came here to represent Austria, and we must be present at the duchess's ball. Perhaps General Hunt will not even attend."

She felt Joseph's concerned gaze follow her as she strode purposefully to the door.

Rose and Joseph arrived at the ball just as a regiment of Scottish Highlanders took to the floor to dance a reel to the traditional music of the bagpipes.

Afterward, Rose joined her husband in a waltz and tried not to be distracted by all the scarlet uniforms of the British officers and the slightly darker crimson uniforms of the Petersbourg army.

As her husband led her around the room, she resisted every temptation to look left or right when they swirled past the crimson colors, for any one of those brave men could have been Leopold.

When the dance ended, they each enjoyed a glass of champagne while the duchess addressed the rumors that Napoleon had marched his army into Belgium that very night. According to their hostess, they were not rumors, but facts. She was not even certain if Wellington would arrive at the ball, though he had promised to attend.

Tension simmered in the air, as if at any moment cannon fire would erupt in the streets. Each time a

dance came to an end, half the guests expected the officers to draw their swords and dash out the door.

Despite all that—or perhaps because of it—Joseph
was exceedingly attentive the entire night. For that reason, Rose had to sneak any wayward glances in the direction of the officers from Petersbourg. She did not
wish her husband to catch her searching for General
Hunt, but how could it be helped? They were on the
brink of war and many of these brave soldiers would
soon be facing the famous French Imperial Guard and
the terror of oncoming mounted lancers.

Leopold . . . If she encountered him tonight, what
would she say to him?

As the evening wore on, however, she began to relax, for there had been no sign of him. Perhaps he knew
she and Joseph were invited and did not wish to interfere in her new life.

Or perhaps he was busy with his troops preparing
for what lay ahead in the coming days.

It was midnight when the Duke of Wellington finally
strode through the doors, appearing relaxed and confident, as if it were any other evening. His calm presence
helped to alleviate the tension in the room, but the ex-
hale was short-lived, for not long after the guests filed
into the dining room, a messenger arrived to inform the
duke that Bonaparte had advanced on the nearby village of Charleroi and the Prussians had been engaged in
a skirmish.

A number of officers and dignitaries departed the
ball soon afterward. Wellington followed the Duke
of Richmond into his study to inspect a map of the re-
gion.

By that time a low hum of panic had engulfed the ballroom and the guests began to quickly clear out.

Rose found herself comforting Lady Brent, a woman she had just met that night. She was the mother of a young officer who had dashed out of the ballroom in high spirits, eager to meet Napoleon on the battlefield. In his excitement he had forgotten to say good-bye to her.

"He is no doubt a very brave young man," Rose said as she dug into her reticule to offer the woman a hand-kerchief. "You have every reason to be proud."

The woman accepted the handkerchief and dabbed at her eyes, but could not stop weeping.

"There, there, now," Rose gently said, taking her into her arms.

At that moment her eyes lifted and she locked gazes with Leopold. He had just entered the ballroom and was passing by in a hurry, less than ten paces away. He stopped dead in his tracks.

Her heart stood still in her chest as she took in the sight of him in his striking officer's uniform with brass buttons and shiny, polished Hessians. For a blazing few seconds of recognition, he stared at her, then quickly swept his hat off his head, tucked it under his arm and bowed to her. Then he continued on his way in obvious haste to deliver a message to someone.

The woman stopped weeping and stood back to wipe her eyes again. "Thank you so much," she said. "You have been very kind to me tonight."

Rose, who felt as if she had been knocked over by a runaway carriage, fixed all her attention on Lady Brent.

"I am sure everything will be fine. We must be brave and remain hopeful."

"I shall." Lady Brent glanced around the room. "But where is your husband, the archduke?" she asked. "I hope he wasn't called away. Will he be fighting with the allied forces?"

Rose looked around for Joseph but he was nowhere to be seen. Where was he?

"No. We are here only as ambassadors, and I am not sure where he is at the moment. Perhaps he has gone off with Wellington and Richmond to discuss a new strategy."

"But didn't your husband fight at Leipzig?"

"Yes," she replied, "but he has retired his commission."

All at once, Rose sensed a presence behind her. Someone was waiting to speak to her . . .

Lady Brent nodded to acknowledge the person, and thanked Rose again for her kindness before politely taking her leave.

Rose had no choice but to turn around and face the man she had once loved with all her heart and soul. The very man who had taken her innocence, then betrayed her in the worst possible way and gone to prison for life.

Chapter Twenty-six

Rose gazed at Leopold for a blazing hot moment while the room seemed to spin circles all around her. He was unthinkably handsome in his crimson dress uniform, his hat still tucked under his arm. Then all at once she was being dragged by the wrist toward a back room, her heels clicking fast across the floor, following because she had no choice. He was swift and strong and fiercely determined to escape curious eyes, or perhaps to kidnap her, as he had once expressed a wish to do.

Was she afraid? No. And this did not surprise her, for he was the most passionate man she had ever known.

He slung her through the door and up against the wall—as if twirling her through a dance—and kicked the door shut behind him. There was a single candle flickering in a wall sconce, otherwise they would be standing in complete darkness. Not that the darkness would have stopped him. She doubted *anything* would have.

He threw his hat on the floor, braced both palms flat against the wall on either side of her head and looked down at her with wild, panting fury.

"How could you do it, Rose?" he asked. "How could you marry him? You're mine. You'll always be *mine*."

"I am *not* yours!" she replied, fighting to push his arms out of the way, but they were strong, unyielding, and held her captive. "I was *never* your possession, and if I had known about your intention to marry Alexandra, I would not have given myself to you as I did in the orchard. I regret it now. You *lied* to me!"

Suddenly, she was slamming her fists into his chest and slapping at his face with a wild rage that infested her heart and mind like an incurable disease. She swiped at him violently and lashed out with all the pent-up frustration and hurt that had plagued her since that horrendous moment when she watched her brother knock him to the ground beside the reflecting pool at the palace.

Touching him, even like this, was like some sort of spark in a powder keg, and her emotions exploded. Why had he come back to her? Why couldn't he have just stayed away and let her move on with her life? It was not fair, and she hated him for this. For *everything*.

Only then did she realize that he had not tried to defend himself or restrain her. He had weathered her strikes without flinching, as if he knew she needed to get it all out. When she couldn't fight any longer—for she was miserable and too exhausted to continue—he relaxed his shoulders and backed up against the opposite wall. He faced her squarely.

"I'm sorry," he said. "If I could undo it, I would. I would turn back time and confess everything to you."

"But you can't go back," she replied. "None of us can, so we must go forward. I have married Joseph and that is the end of it. The end of *us*."

He shook his head slowly back and forth. "No, I will not accept that."

"You have no choice!" she shouted. "But what am I saying? Of course you wouldn't understand that. You've never lost a battle in your life. You don't know how to accept defeat."

"Not when it comes to you, Rose. I told you before that I would never give up, and I won't."

"But you have to. We both have to, because I am a married woman now. I am wed to a decent man who forgave me for everything I did to him. He came to my rescue, while you were the cause of my downfall. He has been kind and patient and devoted, and he, too, said he would never give me up, and he hasn't. He has fought for me, Leopold, and he has won."

Leopold squeezed his eyes shut, clenched a leather-gloved hand in a fist and pressed it hard up against his forehead. "I cannot hear those words from you, Rose." He opened his eyes, stepped forward and crowded her up against the wall. "Come away with me. We can leave here together. Tonight."

"You don't mean that," she argued in a great rush of sensual awareness. She could not forget the pleasures he aroused in her, and the urge to touch him was deep and penetrating, but she labored hard to cling to her integrity. "You are here to lead the Petersbourg cavalry. You gave your word to my brother."

He bowed his head and nodded. "Afterward, then. When it's over. I'll come back for you."

She shook her head. "No, you cannot. You would be a fugitive. You need to let me go, Leopold, and leave here. If you truly care for me, you will not tempt me like this. You will not try to turn me into an adulteress."

A bugle horn sounded somewhere outside on the street, and his gaze darted to the door.

"You have to go," she pleaded, laying a hand on his cheek. "It's your duty. *Please.*"

For a long moment he stood with his forehead touching hers, his chest heaving with despair. "My duty . . ." he repeated. Then he stepped back and picked up his hat, pressed it onto his head. "Tomorrow I will do my duty for king and country. I will lead the Petersbourg army into battle, and I will fight with all that I am as a man . . . but I will never let you go, Rose. *Never.*"

With that he walked out, leaving her alone to wrestle with her passions and try to recover her composure before she faced her husband.

A moment later she reentered the ballroom just as Joseph bumped shoulders with Leopold on the way out.

"Was that General Hunt?" Joseph asked as he approached.

She swallowed uneasily. "Yes, it was. He stopped to say hello. He is riding out with the troops tomorrow. I wished him luck."

"That is all that was said?"

She was thankful there was no accusation in Joseph's tone, but rather a note of curiosity and a genuine concern for her feelings.

She nodded and hoped her cheeks would not betray her. They felt very flushed. She was still shaken by her encounter with Leopold, but was determined not to reveal it.

"I think I would like to go back to the hotel now," she said.

"I have already sent for the carriage."

Joseph offered his arm, and as they left the ball and climbed into the vehicle, the distant sound of trumpets and drums calling the troops to march did nothing to help Rose relax, for a new war with Bonaparte was now imminent, and she could think of only one thing . . .

Leopold.

Very little news from the front reached Brussels the following day, and there was a strange, almost eerie silence in the town. The previous night, dozens of gun carriages had rumbled through the cobblestone streets, trumpets blared, and thousands of soldiers prepared to march. At the same time, anxious civilians attempted to leave Brussels in fear of a French occupation should the allied forces meet with defeat.

That morning Rose accompanied her husband to the home of a British viscount and diplomat, Lord Rothwell, who was posted to Brussels with his wife and four children. They would wait for news there, but soon found themselves helping to arrange for tents to be set up in the park to house the wounded, who were sure to arrive soon if a battle began, which everyone expected it would.

It was not easy for Rose to keep her emotions concealed as she worked with her husband, loading food and bedding onto carts to be delivered to the hospital. Not an hour went by when she did not think of Leopold and wonder where he was and what he was doing.

Nothing dangerous, perhaps. It had been deathly quiet all day.

If only Bonaparte would lose his courage and retreat. She knew it was an impossible dream, however, for the French emperor was nothing if not fearless to the point of recklessness. His overconfidence defied reason.

But he had never faced Wellington in battle before, she reminded herself—and with her own countrymen, as well as the Dutch-Belgians and Prussians to support Wellington, it would be a fierce battle, no doubt about it.

"You look lost in thought," Joseph said to her shortly after luncheon at the viscount's home when she stood at the open front window looking out at the park.

Startled by her husband's appearance beside her, Rose shook away her worries and pasted on a smile. "I wish we would hear something. It's difficult not knowing what is happening."

Just then the sound of cannon fire rumbled like thunder in the distance. Once . . . twice . . . then another.

"God in heaven," Joseph said. "There it is. A battle has begun."

"Where do you think they are?" she quickly replied. "How far away?"

"A few miles at least."

Lady Rothwell and all her children came running into the front parlor. "We heard something," she said. "Is it what we think it is?"

"Yes, it is." Joseph moved closer to the window and watched the horizon with concern.

* * *

The thunder of the guns continued relentlessly all afternoon, yet still no news arrived.

Rose could barely sit still. She wandered from room to room, restless beneath the terrible weight of her anxieties. Leopold figured prominently in most of them as she remembered how he once described his experiences in the war. Once, his horse had been shot out from under him, and on another occasion, he had been slashed by a bayonet.

Another burst of cannon fire—growing dangerously closer—caused the walls to tremble. The chandelier above her head swung lightly back and forth before a few bits of plaster dropped from the ceiling into her hair. Was the battle encroaching on the city?

Her stomach was in knots.

When, by early evening, there was still no news about the fight, Joseph lost his patience.

"I am a trained cavalry officer," he said, buttoning his coat in a hurry and reaching for his hat. "I cannot sit here knowing nothing. I will follow the sound of the guns and perhaps be of some assistance."

Rose quickly stood. "No! You mustn't go. Please stay here. I am sure we will hear something soon."

It was one thing to imagine Leopold risking his life a few short miles away. It was quite another to allow her husband to walk out the door to join the madness. For surely that's what it must be on that distant battlefield . . .

Just then, a carriage pulled up in front of the viscount's house. They all rushed to the window.

"It is our neighbor, Mr. Brasseur," Lord Rothwell said. "His son marched off with one of the Belgian regiments early this morning. Perhaps he has news."

Rose looked sharply at her husband who returned her uneasy gaze.

She was greatly relieved when he began to remove his coat and hat.

Mr. Brasseur did indeed carry important news. He explained that the Prussians had fought Napoleon's army at the village of Ligny that day, while Wellington and the Petersbourg army fought a separate battle at Quatre Bras.

The Prussians had been soundly defeated and were retreating, possibly back to Germany, while the British allied forces had fared somewhat better, but there were many losses, and they were now marching north to the village of Waterloo to regroup and prepare to meet the French again. This time under the command of Napoleon himself.

"Are the Prussians done for?" Joseph asked as he sat with the viscount and Mr. Brasseur at the table in the dining room. "Is there any chance they will swing around and join with Wellington in time to present a united front?"

"It doesn't look good," Mr. Brasseur said. "I heard that Boney sent one of his field marshals after them to chase them down and finish them off."

Joseph slammed his fist down on the table and caused the wine decanter and all the glasses to jump.

Rose, who was standing at the sideboard listening to the conversation, wished she could ask about the

Petersbourg cavalry. Had they taken part in the battle? Did they charge? Exactly how many losses occurred?

She glanced down at her husband, who was seething with rage. "Damn him! Damn Napoleon's brilliance and speed! We should have been better prepared. We shouldn't have divided our forces."

"No one expected him to march so quickly," Brasseur replied.

Joseph looked up at Rose. His chest was heaving with frustration, but he seemed to grow calmer as he watched her in the candlelight.

What was he thinking? Did he mean to tell her he would join the fight?

Joseph cleared his throat, then turned his attention back to Mr. Brasseur. "As you know, my wife is from Petersbourg," he said. "Do you have any news of the Petersbourg army? Were there many casualties? In particular"—he paused—"we would like to know about the cavalry."

Rose stared at him in shock. Why was he asking the question? Did he know she had been with Leopold in a back room at the ball? Had he seen through her heart that day? Was he aware that her thoughts were with Leopold almost constantly?

"As far as I know," Brasseur replied, "the Petersbourg cavalry did very well. They were instrumental in Wellington's success and lost only a few men."

Rose exhaled with relief and had to bite back the urge to ask specifically about Leopold. Was he one of the few unlucky ones? Then, to her surprise, Joseph fielded the question for her.

"I don't suppose you heard anything about a General

Hunt? He is an old friend of my wife's family. We would like to know if he is safe."

Mr. Brasseur thought about it a moment, then shrugged. "I am sorry. I do not know, but I didn't hear about the death of any generals. The odds are good he is alive and well."

Rose thanked Mr. Brasseur, then excused herself and left the room. She moved into the dimly lit corridor, rested her head against the wall, and shut her eyes.

Thank God.

She swung around quickly, however, when Joseph appeared in the doorway. "You can relax now," he said in a cool voice. "He's probably fine."

She took a step forward to try to explain, to reassure her husband that he was most important to her, but he held up a hand to silence her.

"You don't need to say anything, Rose. *Please.* Let us not speak of it."

All she could do was nod in agreement as he left her alone in the corridor.

Chapter Twenty-seven

Hundreds of wounded soldiers were brought into Brussels the following day. Rose and Lady Rothwell did what they could to assist the doctors and care for all the men who had fought so bravely at Quatre Bras.

By late afternoon she was exhausted and returned to the hotel to change her blood-soaked apron and wash the dirt and grime from her skin.

Joseph had still not returned. Earlier in the day, he had ridden to the Duke of Wellington's headquarters at Waterloo to learn what he could about the situation. He returned to town shortly before seven P.M. in the midst of a terrible downpour of rain that had begun shortly after he left.

He was drenched to the bone when he entered the room. Rose dashed into his arms.

"I am so glad you are back. I was worried about you, afraid you wouldn't return. You must be famished. I will send for a supper tray and arrange a hot bath."

He held her tightly for a moment, tighter than he'd ever held her before, then stepped away and shrugged stiffly out of his sopping-wet coat. "It wasn't easy getting back," he said. "The road is muddy and littered with abandoned wagons and all sorts of things, as if people simply dropped their belongings in a desperate flee to safety."

"I will be glad when this is over," she said. "I hope the coalition is successful and we can end this as swiftly as it has begun." She started toward the door. "I will order that supper tray now."

An hour later they were seated in front of a hot fire sipping wine, thankful for the meal they had just enjoyed while the troops were camped outdoors in the rain.

For a long while they sat in silence until Joseph leaned forward and laid his hand on hers.

"I've made a decision," he said, "and there is no point keeping it from you any longer."

Her heart sank. "What is it?" But she had a feeling she already knew.

Joseph let out a sigh. "I only came back tonight to spend a few hours with you before I return to the duke's headquarters at dawn."

"Why? Do you intend to join the fight?"

His expression was grave. "Yes. You know me, Rose. I am a soldier at heart, and I cannot bear to stand by and watch others do what I should also be doing."

She, too, leaned forward and gripped both his hands in hers. "No. You do not need to do that. You've served your people well on the battlefield in the past. Now you serve them in other ways. You are an important ambassador for Austria. There is much we can do together in that area. I will not let you go."

He gazed at her raptly while the fire illuminated the highlights in his golden hair and caused his eyes to glimmer with regret. Pulling his hands from hers, he leaned back, then stood and walked to the rain-drenched window where the panes were rattling noisily in the wind.

"My mind is made up," he said. "I will fight bravely, and I will return to you when it is over."

Anger coursed through her. She, too, stood up. "This best not have anything to do with General Hunt. I hope you do not feel you must compete with him, because that is completely unnecessary. You are my husband, and I love you. What existed between Leopold and me is dead and buried."

The words ached in her throat, but she managed to get them out.

Joseph finished his wine and set the empty glass down on a table. "There is no need to explain," he said. "I understand how it is, and I am not joining the fight to compete with him. I join it because I feel a duty to fight for what is right. We cannot allow Bonaparte to recapture all of Europe again to satisfy his greed and lust for power. There is strength in numbers. I must offer my services to the coalition."

Rose strode toward him. "Please do not go. I will go mad if I must listen to those guns again tomorrow and think of you in their line of fire."

He cupped her chin in his hand. "At least you will be thinking of *me,* and not another."

Her heart broke at the sound of those words, and she

fought against a sudden violent flood of tears. "I am yours, Joseph," she assured him. "You must believe that."

He pulled her into his embrace, and she knew in that moment there was nothing she could say or do to change his mind. He was a soldier, and he would go to battle, with or without her blessing.

The following morning, when the first light of dawn broke through the opening in the velvet curtains, Joseph was gone. He had galloped back to the village of Waterloo, where two massive opposing armies were preparing to wage a new war.

Chapter
Twenty-eight

On the crest of the hill at the battlefield of Mont-Saint-Jean—a few short miles away from the village of Waterloo—Leopold peered through his spyglass at the French troops on the opposite ridge. The enemy was seventy-two thousand troops strong against the sixty-eight thousand of the British, Petersbourg, and Dutch-Belgian allied forces.

It was just past eleven o'clock in the morning. The sun was high in the sky and the men were quickly growing restless, for they had risen at dawn and taken position, but Bonaparte had yet to fire a single shot.

A young lieutenant of the 22nd Petersbourg Brigade came trotting toward Leopold. "What's he waiting for, General? It's not like Boney to delay."

Leopold lowered the spyglass. "I suspect he's waiting for the ground to dry. All that muck makes it near impossible to move the cannons, and the cannonballs embed in the ground upon impact instead of bouncing and ricocheting through the ranks."

"The mud is in our favor then," the lieutenant replied, "for they outnumber us with their guns. Perhaps we should get things started ourselves. I'd be happy to light a charge and shake those Frenchies up a little."

Leopold chuckled at the lieutenant's impatience. "I am sure you would, Lieutenant, but Wellington is quite content to wait. Anything to delay the start of the battle is also in our favor, for it will give the Prussians more time to reach us, and by God, we need them."

Goliath, Leopold's dependable chestnut charger, tossed his head and nickered. Leo leaned forward to stroke his shiny muscled neck. "It won't be long now, boy. You'll be doing your duty soon enough."

The young lieutenant raised his hand in salute and wheeled his horse around to return to his own regiment, which was sheltered from the enemy fire on the downward slope beyond the crest of the hill.

Just then, another rider approached from the opposite direction. He wore a black coat and fawn breeches, which was not the uniform of any of the participating armies. Leopold watched him for a moment. As he drew closer, Leo recognized the light blond hair and freckled complexion. It was Archduke Joseph.

A knot twisted in Leo's gut, for here was the man who had taken Rose away from him, the man he had dreamed of strangling into a corpse on more than one occasion.

He had been led to believe that Rose's husband would not be fighting today. It was Leo's understanding

that the archduke was in Brussels to perform a diplomatic function only. What the blazes was he doing here
on the battlefield?

A brand-new anger rose up inside him, for he had an
army to lead and an enemy to defeat. He could not afford to become distracted by the heat of his jealousy
and the appalling, devastating failure of his ill-fated
personal life. He must be confident when he called out
his orders. He must be focused.

The archduke trotted up alongside him and reined
in his mount—a handsome white trooper with a shiny
black mane.

"Good morning, General," the archduke said, fin-
gering the brim of his black hat.

Leo clenched both fists tight around the leather
reins to keep from leaping off his horse, dragging
Joseph from the saddle, and swinging a punch that
would start something similar to a drunken taproom
brawl.

"Good morning, Your Royal Highness," he replied,
curious as to why Joseph was here at all. The Austrians
had not brought an army to Belgium. They had marched
south to protect the Rhine.

Joseph glanced to the left to inspect the size and
placement of Leopold's regiments. "Your men look
well," he said. "It wasn't the best of nights, was it?"

Torrential rains had pounded the countryside without
mercy for hours upon hours, while most of the troops
had slept out in the open.

"No, but at least we've been blessed with good
weather this morning."

"Indeed."

Leopold regarded the archduke closely in the late-morning sunshine. He took in the fair color of his hair, his strong jawline, and the freckles on his cheeks. He was tall and muscular and carried himself with pride. A handsome man by any standards, which made Leopold's gut twist sharply with rancor. He was sickened by the sourness of it.

This man had claimed Rose as his own. Her heart belonged to *him* now. He had slipped a ring on her finger a few short months ago and taken her innocence on their wedding night.

God. Oh God . . .

Leo's stomach turned over at the thought of it and the agony was almost debilitating. He couldn't bear it. Why was Joseph here? To torture him with a reminder of all that he had loved and lost?

Leo experienced a sudden, shameful compulsion to break away and gallop into the valley below and challenge those bloody French gunners to bring on their worst. He could give them a fast-moving target to whet their appetites. That would get the battle started, wouldn't it?

He took a deep breath, however, and fought to focus on the men in his care, and the necessity of defeating the true enemy here today, which was Napoleon, not the rival beside him.

The archduke gazed at him for a long moment, probably feeling the same sort of bitter loathing that Leopold had just been wrestling with—for Leopold was Rose's *first* love. No matter that her affection was now extinguished, he would always be that.

"She was worried about you," Joseph said, "when we

could hear the guns at Quatre Bras. I thought you should know."

Leopold frowned in confusion. It was not what he had expected to hear. First off, he was surprised that Rose even cared. But what had she said about it? Did she actually confess such a thing to her husband?

"Why are you telling me this?" he asked.

Joseph glanced back at the troops who were waiting eagerly, some apprehensively, for the bugle call. "I've fought battles before," he said. "I know what it's like to face death. I just thought you would want to know that."

Leopold swallowed uneasily. The bitterness he had felt a moment ago diminished somewhat as he contemplated the fact that he was indeed grateful to know that Rose did not wish him dead, that a part of her still cared for him. Undeserving as he was to receive such a gift.

Another part of him, however, cursed this man for such a selfless act. It was not Joseph's duty to deliver such a message.

Unless . . .

"Did she send you here to tell me this?"

Could it be true? His hopes soared.

Joseph shook his head, however, and looked down at the ground. "No, she didn't want me to come at all. She tried quite heroically to stop me."

"Then why *did* you come?" Leopold asked bitterly, for if he was ever blessed with Rose's love and devotion . . . if she ever pleaded with him to stay with her, he would never leave her side again.

"I am a trained officer of the Austrian army," Joseph explained. "I fought at Leipzig. I couldn't simply stand back and watch thousands of men sacrifice their lives in the name of duty and honor while I did nothing. I had to join the fight. My conscience demanded it."

Leopold regarded him steadily in the blinding sunlight.

While part of him hated Joseph for behaving so honorably—for he had spent the past few months taking a rather perverse pleasure in visions of his cowardice and weakness—another part of Leo was baffled by his selflessness. Not only did Joseph wish to join the fight, he had come here to tell Leopold that Rose still cared for him.

Leo had never seen anything like this before, and he felt a sudden pang of shame for his own selfish desires and violent anger. It was followed quickly by a semblance of reassurance in knowing that Rose would be cared for by a man such as this.

He always knew nothing mattered more to him than Rose's happiness. If he had to, he would lay down his life for her.

He suspected this man would do the same.

Suddenly a shot was fired from the enemy lines. Leopold shared a look with the archduke. Together they galloped farther up the rise. They each withdrew and extended their spyglasses.

Leo saw smoke curling upward from the barrel of one of the French cannons.

"Do you see that?" Joseph asked.

Leo snapped his spyglass shut and slipped it into his pocket. "I do. It appears the French are finally ready to pick a fight."

They glanced at each other for an intense moment of

realization before Joseph wheeled his horse around. "I must return to the 25th. Good luck to you, General!"

"Good luck to you as well, Your Highness."

With an odd sense of bewilderment, Leo watched Joseph gallop off, then returned to his own troops to await Wellington's orders.

After the first shot was fired at approximately 11:30 A.M., the battle began like a series of ocean waves, one after another, each side advancing forward to foam up onto the beach, then retreat back to its position on the plains.

It began with the French forces storming the Hougoumont, a château in the valley between the two opposing armies. It required ten thousand French troops to overtake the twenty-five hundred British defenders that occupied it—but overtake them, they did.

Later in the afternoon Bonaparte laid siege to a second farm in the valley—La Haye Sainte—and captured that as well, causing the situation to look increasingly bleak for Wellington's center.

All day long, Wellington waited for the arrival of the Prussian army, for the battle would be hard won without them, but they remained just out of reach, slowly making their way back from their initial retreat from the lost battle at Ligny.

Again the French advanced across the field, but the British and Petersbourg cavalries, along with the brave Scots Greys, drove them back. The Scots Greys were fearless and passionate in their charge and attacked the French guns, putting an end to the crisis in the British center.

Yet Bonaparte pressed on. The French cuirassiers—a terrifying spectacle of mounted troops with steel helmets and breastplates that reflected the glare of the sun—advanced upon the allied forces, but did so without the support of infantry or cannon and failed to break the well-prepared British squares, which held off the charge of the horses with unbreakable lines of infantry with bayonets at the ready.

At last the Prussians arrived late in the day and captured the village of Plancenoit on the French right flank, just as Wellington's center was beginning to falter.

Recognizing an immediate opportunity for victory, Bonaparte sent his most prized and experienced Imperial Guard forward to break Wellington's back once and for all, but a British brigade of guns rose up on the crest of the hill and fired upon them. Fifteen hundred muskets faced only two hundred French guns, and sent them packing in a staggering array of confusion and broken morale.

With the long-awaited support of the Prussian army, Wellington called out, *"No cheering, my lads, but forward and complete your victory!"*

Leopold heard the command, drew his sword from its scabbard, and called his brave Petersbourg cavalry to action.

"This is it, men! The final charge! Onward in the name of King Randolph!"

His shout echoed through the ranks as every man spurred his horse into a thundering gallop down the slope toward glory, and to conquer and crush Napoleon's famous French Imperial Guard.

The massive charge caused the ground to vibrate beneath the force of thousands of pounding hooves driving forward at an incredible speed.

The allies reached the enemy and fought with raging fury. It was a mad frenzy of violence, which soon became an uncompromising pursuit as the remaining French lines broke and scattered in retreat.

Leopold reined his horse to a skidding halt and paused to look around and gain his bearings.

Violence and madness surrounded him in all directions. Men were shouting and running, driving swords into the bellies of their enemies. Everywhere there was mud and blood and smoke from the guns. The acrid smell of death filled his nostrils, but the allies were winning. Only a few brave French grenadiers remained to fight to the death, while most were escaping in a headlong rush to save themselves.

Leopold could barely see through the shifting smoke from the guns, but that did not stop him from recognizing at a distance that distinctive blond head of hair, hatless now, as the future emperor of Austria galloped into a mob of red-coated English infantry fighting against the blue-uniformed members of the Imperial Guard.

His Highness swung his sword bravely and knocked down four French Guards with expert precision before a bullet struck him in the shoulder. The impact knocked him onto his back in the saddle.

With a red-hot surge of panic and no time to think, Leopold spurred his horse into a gallop and shot like a bullet toward the mob of fighting men. He kept his eyes fixed on the archduke, now rolling off his horse and sliding from the saddle to the ground. His boot twisted in the iron stirrup as he fell.

The archduke's white horse reared up as a cannon-ball whizzed by, then he bolted in a mad dash toward the British right flank.

Leopold shouted *"Yah, yah!"* and galloped faster through the smoke and chaos to chase after Joseph, who was being dragged by the boot along the blood-soaked field.

At last Leo reached the frantic animal and grabbed hold of the bridle to gentle him and pull him to a halt.

A second later, Leo was tossing a leg over Goliath's rear flank and leaping to the ground to free the arch-duke's foot from the stirrup.

He dropped to his knees beside Joseph, who was still breathing but unconscious. Leopold unbuttoned the archduke's coat to assess the damage. His white shirt was drenched in blood.

Leo withdrew his knife and ripped through the fab-ric where the bullet had entered near the shoulder joint. With fast-moving fingers he untied Joseph's cravat and used it to stanch the flow of blood while glancing down at his leg, which was twisted and mangled.

"We need help here!" he shouted, lifting his gaze and looking all around, but his voice was just one more desperate plea among the piercing roar of fighting men and the continuing racket of muskets and cannon.

Joseph moaned. Leopold looked down at him.

"Your Royal Highness," he said. "Can you hear me?"

Joseph's eyes fluttered open. He winced in pain. "My leg . . ."

"I'm quite sure it's broken," Leopold explained to

him, "and you've been shot in the shoulder. Try not to move. An ambulance cart will be here soon."

His heart was racing with fear and dread as he lifted the silk neck cloth to take another look at the wound. It was still bleeding profusely.

Leopold covered it again. *"We need help!"* he shouted, louder this time, feeling more and more powerless with every passing second as the blood continued to pour from the wound. He could do nothing but wait for assistance, which might not come in time.

Joseph's eyes blinked open again and he looked up at Leopold. "Tell me what is happening. Have we won the battle?"

Leo looked around for his men and saw that the battle was nearly won. His mounted regiment was now chasing the Imperial Guard from the field.

"Yes," he replied. "It is a tremendous victory. Napoleon's army is crushed."

The gunfire began to subside. The disturbing roar of the shouting men grew quieter. Leo could hear the sound of trumpets signaling the victory.

"Make sure they are harsher with him this time," Joseph managed to say, though it cost him dearly to breathe deeply enough to get the words out. He grabbed hold of Leopold's arm and pulled him closer. "Don't let them send him back to Elba. He must be imprisoned or sent to St. Helena. That is where they should have sent him the first time."

"I wholeheartedly agree." Leopold gazed desperately about the battlefield, searching for help while the neck cloth soaked up more and more blood.

All the sounds of the battle grew muffled in his ears,

as if he had just plunged his head into a barrel of water. The pop of the musket fire seemed very far away, and the whole world spun to a dizzying halt.

Looking down at the man Rose had married—a good man; an honorable and courageous soldier who was bleeding to death before his very eyes—he cursed this damnable war and prayed that this would be the end of it.

God! Please, God, stop the blood. He pressed firmly against the wound and shouted again, *"Help, goddammit! The archduke of Austria has been shot!"*

Joseph's hand squeezed Leopold's wrist where he held the fabric in place. "Do something for me," he said.

Leo quickly nodded while his heart pounded like a heavy mallet in his chest.

"Tell Rose I love her, and that no woman could ever have made me as happy as she has made me these past few months. Tell her that my world, my life, was not complete until she entered it."

Leopold clenched his jaw against the urge to utter a wrathful oath to curse God for this.

"No," he said. "You will tell her yourself."

Joseph gazed weakly at the sky. "Promise me, if the worst happens . . ."

"I promise," Leopold replied, if only to ease the archduke's mind. "But it won't be necessary, because I am going to get you out of here."

Leo's eyes lifted just as two medics came running toward him with a stretcher.

"Is this the archduke?" one of them asked.

Leopold exhaled with relief. "Yes. He has been shot in the shoulder and his leg is broken."

"Thank you, General. If you would please move aside . . ."

They took charge of the situation and assessed the wound at Joseph's shoulder, then glanced only briefly at his leg, which seemed a lost cause.

"You must take him to the Montgomery Inn in Waterloo and send for the very best surgeon we have," Leopold said. "That is an order. Do you understand?"

"Yes, sir," the medic replied as he eased Joseph onto the stretcher.

Joseph had fallen unconscious by now, which was a blessing as he was awkwardly shifted about.

Leopold watched them go, then took off in a sprint toward his horse and swung up into the saddle. He galloped swiftly back to his regiment and found the first man who was done with the fight and whose horse appeared fresh and strong.

"You there!" he shouted to the young private. "I have an important errand for you!"

The private saluted. "I am at your service, General."

"You must ride back to Brussels immediately and go straight to the hotel on rue Montagne du Parc, where you will deliver an urgent message to Rose, the wife of Archduke Joseph of Austria. Tell her that her husband has been gravely wounded in battle and was taken to the Montgomery Inn in Waterloo. She must go to him, and you must escort her there. Do you understand this? Do you have it?"

"Yes, sir."

"Good. Now go!" The young soldier wheeled his horse around, but Leopold shouted to him again. "Wait!"

The private reined in his mount.

"Tell her we were victorious, and that her husband fought bravely and proved himself to be a great hero."

"I will tell her, sir. Is that all?"

"Yes." With a sinking heart and a painful surge of deep anguish for what Rose was about to endure, Leo watched the rider gallop away.

Chapter
Twenty-nine

It had been an unbearable two-hour carriage ride from Brussels to Waterloo, and by the time Rose arrived, twilight had settled over the town. The streets were teeming with wagonloads of wounded soldiers being taken to God knows where, for the casualties had been enormous. There was an estimated total of fifty thousand dead counting both sides, and many more injured.

Her heart was focused on only one man, however: her husband, who might very well be among the dead by now if she had not reached him in time.

When the coach finally arrived at the inn, she did not wait for a servant to open the door. She opened it herself while the wheels were still turning and leaped onto the street. With a quick glance up at the sign to ensure she was in the correct location, she gathered her skirts in her fists and ran to the door.

Inside, the inn was packed with wounded men lying on the floor of the taproom and along the walls in the center hall. Many were bandaged, bruised, and bloody. Some were weeping for their mothers.

"I am looking for my husband," she said to the first civilian she came to—possibly the innkeeper's wife. "He is Archduke Joseph of Austria. I was told he was taken here."

Let him be alive . . .

The woman's eyes widened. She quickly curtsied. "Yes, Your Royal Highness. We have been expecting you. He is upstairs. Please allow me to take you to him."

They skirted their way through a narrow winding path between the bedrolls laid out on the floor, and climbed the stairs to the top.

The woman led Rose to a room at the end of the corridor and knocked gently with one knuckle upon the door. "The princess is here," she said.

Rose heard the sound of a chair scraping across the floor and heavy footsteps. Then the door quickly opened.

To her utter shock and dismay, there stood Leopold, covered in dirt and grime. His chin was splattered with blood, but he was in one piece, thank God. She sucked in a breath at the sight of him.

Words spilled out of her mouth in a sudden rush of gratitude and relief. "Thank you for sending the message. I will be forever in your debt. How is he?"

Leopold thanked the innkeeper's wife, then invited Rose inside and closed the door behind them. "See for yourself."

She entered the room where a hot fire blazed in the hearth, but stopped dead at the sight of her husband lying unconscious on the bed. She was instantly whisked back to the moment she returned from England to find her father on his deathbed. Her stomach lurched suddenly and threatened to bring up her lunch.

"My God."

"He's lost a lot of blood," Leopold explained as she moved closer to the bed and beheld Joseph's pale countenance. "But we were able to retrieve the bullet. Now it's just a matter of time while we wait and pray that there will be no infection."

She sat down in the chair beside the bed and laid her hand on top of Joseph's. "Has he been awake at all?"

Leopold spoke plainly. "He was briefly conscious on the battlefield after he was shot."

Rose was intensely aware of Leopold moving slowly around the foot of the bed and taking a seat on the opposite side.

"He had a rough time of it, Rose. Do you wish to know all the details? It won't be easy to hear."

She met his gaze directly. "Of course I wish to know them. Surely you know me better than that."

"Forgive me," he replied. "I had to ask."

She fought to bring her breathing under control. "No, Leopold, you are the one who must forgive me. I apologize. It has been a stressful day, but worse for you, no doubt."

The sound of a man downstairs screaming in pain reached them through the floorboards. They both fell silent until the torture came to an end and it was quiet again.

"Tell me everything," she said to him in the warm,

flickering firelight. "I must know exactly what happened. Were you there?"

Leopold hated the fact that he had to describe all the horrific details to Rose, but knew that he must. She deserved no less than the truth, and God knows he owed her that. He drew in a breath.

"I saw him from a distance. It was at the end of the day, and we had finally gained the upper hand. The full force of the allied army charged forward to crush the last French advance, and your husband was as brave as any man I ever saw. He galloped into a mob of French troops and saved the lives of more than a few British infantrymen. Then a bullet struck him and he fell from his horse, but his foot was caught in the stirrup and he was dragged."

"Good heavens."

Leopold paused to give her a moment to digest the information. "I saw it happen, so I pursued him and brought his horse under control. I dismounted and freed his foot from the stirrup, but I could see that his leg was badly broken."

She glanced down at Joseph's leg, but could make out very little of its condition beneath the cover of the sheet. "Then what happened?"

Leopold kept his eyes fixed upon hers. "I opened his coat to inspect the bullet wound. There was a lot of blood so I removed his cravat and used it to apply pressure while I shouted for help."

Her gaze fell upon her husband's ghostly face. She was fighting tears. Leo knew it because he recognized and understood everything about her. He knew that her heart was gentle, vulnerable, and compassionate, but she was also strong. She could—and would—weather any storm.

Her troubled eyes lifted to meet his, and he nearly tumbled headfirst into the extraordinary beauty of those deep blue irises. An ocean of memories came flooding into his head suddenly. His heart broke at the thought of what they had been to each other not so long ago, before all of this madness.

"You told me he was conscious," she said. "Did he speak to you? Was he in pain?"

Leopold cleared his throat. "He was in a lot of pain, yes, but he withstood it and asked me to deliver a message to you. He made me promise."

She lifted her chin as if to prepare herself for something that would no doubt break her heart. "Tell me."

Leopold slowly repeated Joseph's message, word for word, while Rose watched him with frowning, stricken eyes. When he finished, she gave no reply. All she could do was stare at him in silence while he nearly broke down, for they were words he wished were his own.

Tell her I love her . . . that she made my life complete . . .

He could not speak of such things, however. Not now, not ever again. He had to accept it, no matter how difficult it was. She was another man's wife, and he would no longer insult her honor by imagining there was hope.

Rose leaned forward and kissed her husband's hand. She took a moment to gather her composure. "What about his leg? You said it was broken."

"Yes, the doctor found three breaks, but he was able

to set the bones back into place. By God's grace, your husband was not conscious for that."

She wet her lips. "It will heal?"

Leopold swallowed uneasily. "We cannot yet be sure. At the very best, he will require months of convalescence and will likely use a cane."

"And the worst?"

He hesitated. "It was a bad break, Rose, and the shinbone penetrated the skin. It is wrapped as well as it can be, but again, we must pray that there will be no infection."

"If there is, could he lose his leg?"

Leopold nodded somberly.

For a long time they sat without speaking in the dimly lit chamber while the fire blazed and crackled in the hearth, and Joseph lay as white and still as death.

"Perhaps I should leave you now," Leopold said, knowing his duty was done. He had ensured Joseph received the very best medical care and had arranged the reunion of husband and wife. Rose was here with him now, and it felt wrong for Leo to remain at the bedside when he knew damn well it was a selfish act, for how many times had he dreamed of seeing Rose again, one last time? Imagined hearing the sound of her voice and breathing in the intoxicating fragrance of her perfume?

Her eyes held his.

He could barely move.

"Please do not go," she softly said. "I am sure you are needed elsewhere and you've already done so much for us, but I want very much for you to stay."

She said it as if it were a burden she was placing

upon his shoulders, which was ridiculous, for he cared for no duties outside of this room.

The truth was . . . he would do anything—he would sacrifice every moment of his entire future—for one more hour in her presence. Even if they did not speak a single word to each other, he would be content.

"I would be happy to stay," he replied. "I just wasn't sure . . ."

He wasn't sure if she wanted him here. He feared she was still angry with him. That she hated him.

Rose shook her head, as if he were a complete and utter fool for doubting his welcome.

"If you think I bear any ill will toward you, Leopold, then you are wrong, for you were my guardian angel today. What would have happened to Joseph if you had not been there? I cannot bear to think of it, and I am so grateful for what you did."

His aching heart rejoiced at the sound of those words upon her lips. Perhaps he had redeemed himself just a little in her eyes, which was a task he had considered impossible a few short days ago.

Though it was not why he had done it. When he galloped after Joseph's runaway horse, he had already considered his reputation a lost cause—in her eyes and everyone else's. What he'd done today was a matter of honor, and above all, an act of love.

Rose cared for her husband. Leopold was therefore compelled to save his life and bring him home to her.

He could not say any of that, however. "It's what any dutiful soldier would have done," he replied.

"No," she argued. "You are too modest. I believe your actions went beyond duty. I also believe . . ." She paused. "I beg your pardon, Leopold, but I must speak from my heart. I believe you might have been thinking of *me,* for you left your regiment and abandoned the fight to save him, did you not?"

Leopold cleared his throat. "I did abandon it, yes, because I am always thinking of you, Rose. You are in my heart at all times. You were in it when I was riding after your husband."

Her eyes filled with tears, and color rushed to her cheeks as she fought against the emotion she was trying so hard to conceal.

God, how he loved her. Too much to do this to her.

"But I really had no choice," he continued. "Your husband is the future emperor of Austria. Let us leave it at that."

Being the noble princess that she was, she respected his wishes and did not argue the point or press him to admit more of his feelings. For that he was grateful.

"Well," she said, quickly wiping at a tear that spilled from her eye. "You were a hero today from any and all perspectives. I suspect you will be awarded more medals of honor from Petersbourg, as well as Austria. My new home country thanks you."

He didn't want medals. He had enough of those. All he wanted was Rose, but it was long past time for him to accept that it was not to be.

"No thanks are necessary," he replied. "As I said before, it is what any soldier would have done."

She accepted his words without argument this time and regarded him with a weary sorrow that made him wish he could stand up, circle around this bed, and take her into his arms.

If he could have done just that, he would have never asked for anything else as long as he lived. But he resisted the urge and remained in his seat.

The night was not an easy one. Rose sat devotedly at her husband's side, and for many hours he did not move. As a result, she grew increasingly fretful, for it seemed a very deep sleep, a state too close to death. Often she touched his cheek to ensure he was still warm, or she placed her fingers under his nose to feel the soft beat of his breath.

Joseph fought his own private battle through the night, and she assisted the only way she could—by kneeling on the floor beside the bed and praying for his life to be spared.

And Leopold. Dear, wonderful Leopold. He, too, remained at Joseph's side and watched over him whenever Rose needed to rest her eyes. When she grew frantic, fearing that a fever had set in, Leopold was there, laying the back of his hand on Joseph's forehead and ensuring her that all was well.

When at last the morning light found its way into the room, and the fire was nothing but a dry pile of ash and embers, Joseph stirred.

"Rose?" he whispered.

She woke from an uncomfortable slumber in the chair, sat forward and clasped his hand. "I am here, darling. I've been here all night."

He turned his head on the pillow to look at her. His eyes were bloodshot and filled with pain and confusion. "My leg hurts," he said. "I cannot move it."

Rose glanced across at Leopold, who quickly stood. "I will fetch the doctor."

He left them alone. Rose had maintained her composure all night long, but she could no longer suppress her feelings. She broke down and wept over Joseph's arm. "Thank God you have come back to us. I was so worried."

"My love," he whispered as he cupped her cheek in a hand and waited for her to collect herself. "Nothing could keep me from you, not even a bullet from Boney's infamous Imperial Guard. It was pure dumb luck they hit me, you know. They were probably aiming at the Prussians but found themselves shooting in the wrong direction."

Suddenly Rose was laughing, then weeping the most wonderful tears of joy. Joseph was alive. All her prayers had been answered.

Well, perhaps not all of them, for she had been forced to sacrifice something else. Sometimes she wished she could live two parallel lives. But this would be enough.

It would have to be.

A few minutes later, a knock sounded at the door. "Come in!"

Rose was relieved to see Leopold, but her belly turned over at the sight of the doctor who entered behind him, for he wore a blood-soaked apron and carried a leather case that clanked with steel instruments inside when he set it down on the table.

"This is Dr. Harris," Leopold said.

"I am told the patient has regained consciousness.

That is wonderful news." The doctor bowed. "Your Royal Highness, I am honored to serve you. Now let us have a look, shall we?"

Rose backed away to give the doctor room to examine Joseph. He began by listening to his heart and consulting his pocket watch to time the pulse beats.

He lifted Joseph's eyelids to examine his pupils and asked a number of questions about how he was feeling, then removed the bandage at his shoulder to assess the bullet wound.

"Everything looks fine here," he said. "You were very lucky, sir. Inches to the left and . . . Well, let us simply say that your star was shining yesterday."

He replaced the bandage with a fresh one.

"Now let us have a look at that break." He tossed the covers aside.

Rose looked warily upon her husband's broken leg, which was wrapped in a bloodied bandage and held in place by a splint.

Carefully, the doctor removed the bandage to examine the area where the bone had cut through the skin. Upon looking at it, he promised Joseph laudanum to numb the pain for as long as he needed it.

Joseph tried to sit up, but he couldn't rise on his injured shoulder. Rose quickly moved around the bed to fetch an extra pillow, which she placed under his head.

All the while, Leopold remained a silent observer. He had sat down in a chair by the window on the opposite side of the room and was watching vigilantly.

Rose knew him too well. There was a hint of displeasure in his expression. Something was wrong. She could sense it.

He met her gaze just then, and she felt her eyebrows pull together as she frowned. *What is it?* she wanted to ask, but the doctor interrupted her thoughts by saying, "Tsk-tsk-tsk. That leg should have come off."

Rose shot him a horrified look. How could he say such a thing in front of Joseph, who had just woken up and needed encouragement, not this sudden reproachful diagnosis without at least saying something to prepare him if the news was grave.

"Doctor," she snapped. "You have barely looked at it. My understanding is that it was set in place last night and had a good chance of healing. Isn't that right, General Hunt?"

Leopold stood up. "Yes, the princess is correct. You should speak to Dr. Samson."

The doctor scoffed arrogantly. "Samson? He is a mere pup. He knows next to nothing about military medicine, while I've been serving this campaign for fifteen years. He was no doubt frazzled during the procedure and couldn't bring himself to confess the truth."

Leopold glanced down at Joseph briefly, then addressed the doctor again. "With all due respect, sir, Dr. Samson was not frazzled. I assisted him myself in removing the bullet from His Highness's shoulder. Samson was highly skilled, and I would have him back now if it can be arranged."

Rose felt suddenly caught in an angry crossfire. Leopold and the doctor were facing each other squarely, while Joseph could do nothing but watch and listen with dire concern.

"It certainly cannot be arranged," Dr. Harris replied.

"Samson has gone to Brussels to tend to the wounded there, while I have been assigned to the wounded here. The archduke is now my responsibility, General, and I will not permit that wound to fester and kill the heir to the throne of Austria."

"It's not festering," Leopold stated plainly. "It is just badly bruised."

"How would you know anything about it? You are a soldier, not a surgeon."

"I've seen my share of festering wounds, sir, and this wound is not among them."

Joseph tried again to sit up. "Are you sure, General Hunt? Clearly my leg will be of little use to me regardless. Perhaps it's not worth the risk."

Leopold spoke firmly. "Your leg is fine, Your Highness, and you will walk again."

Rose didn't know what to think. She trusted Leopold with all her heart, but this doctor claimed to have fifteen years' experience in military medicine. What if he was right? Perhaps it wasn't worth the risk. Either way, Joseph would need a cane to walk . . .

"We disagree, General," the doctor said, "and it is not up to you, is it? The decision lies with the archduke and his wife."

He looked to them for a final verdict.

Leopold said nothing. He simply waited.

With as calm a demeanor as possible, Rose approached the bed to look more closely at the wound. She was not an expert in medicine, but it looked quite ghastly. Whether or not it was infected, she had no clue. Bruised, yes, definitely, and terribly swollen, but did that mean his life was at risk?

"I don't know, Joseph," she whispered. "I am not qualified to make such a decision, but I do not like risks."

"Nor do I," he replied. "And as I said before, my leg will be of little use to me. Perhaps the doctor is right."

"Of course I am right," Harris said haughtily. "I know a thing or two. Now if you will give me your permission, sir, I will send for a nurse and begin right away. There is no time to lose."

The sound of a pistol hammer cocking caused them all to look toward the window, where Leopold stood aiming his weapon at the doctor's face. "There will be no such surgeries in this room today, Dr. Harris. I suggest you leave now."

The doctor gasped. "You mean to threaten me, General?"

"Is it not clear that I am already doing so?"

Rose stood frozen in shock while Leopold held the gun steady.

"If that wound festers," the doctor warned, "it will be on your head, General. Not mine."

"If it festers, we will consider surgery at that time," Leo replied. "Until then, we will follow Dr. Samson's orders and the archduke will keep his leg."

The doctor turned to Joseph. "And *you*, sir? What do *you* say?"

Joseph—who was clearly in excruciating pain at the present moment—spoke through gritted teeth. "I must agree with General Hunt. Let us wait and see. Now please put a fresh bandage on this wound and return in twelve hours to assess it again."

The doctor reluctantly obeyed and set to work, while

Joseph clenched his jaw in a valiant effort to withstand the pain.

When the doctor finished and was packing up his supplies, Rose disliked the fact that she had to remind him of what he had promised earlier.

"The laudanum now, Doctor, if you please."

He let out a huff as if it were a great inconvenience to open up his bag again. He withdrew a small bottle and handed it to her, explained the dosage, bowed to them, then turned and left the room.

Rose followed him out into the corridor and closed the door behind her. "Dr. Harris, please wait." He paused. "I trust you will not reveal to anyone what just occurred. You were *not* threatened with a pistol. If you suggest such a thing to anyone, both the archduke and I will deny it. Do you understand?"

He stared at her for a blistering second, then bowed again. "Yes, madam."

When she returned to the bedchamber a moment later, she found Leopold, unaware of her presence, helping Joseph to sit up and take the laudanum. After administering the dosage, he gently set her husband's weary head down on the pillow and inserted the cork back into the small bottle.

"There now," he softly said. "That should ease some of the pain, Your Highness." Only then did he turn and acknowledge Rose in the open doorway.

"Thank you," she said. "I am quite sure you are right about Joseph's leg, and the doctor was wrong."

Joseph reached out and clasped Leopold's forearm. "Yes, thank you. I don't think I could have borne an amputation at the present moment. Not quite at my best, you know?"

Leopold regarded him with understanding. "A day or two will make all the difference."

Joseph closed his eyes and fell back to sleep, leaving Rose alone with Leopold.

Heaven help her, there was so much to say.

Chapter Thirty

"You shouldn't have drawn your pistol," Rose whispered to Leopold as they stood at the open window. "You may be a general who just saved the life of a very important man, but you are also a convicted criminal on parole. I do not wish to see you get into any more trouble."

He chuckled. "How much more trouble can I possibly get into, Rose? I am already sentenced to twenty years in prison. Honestly, I didn't think I had much to lose. Your husband on the other hand . . ."

"That is very self-sacrificing," she said.

"Call it what you want. It matters not. I simply couldn't allow that quack doctor to take your husband's leg."

She breathed deeply the cool, fresh air blowing in through the window. "Are you certain about everything? You truly believe it is just bruised?"

"I am positive," he said, "and there is no doubt in my

mind that it would do more harm than good to remove the leg. Joseph said himself that he is very weak. He would be at an even greater risk of infection if the doctor took such measures."

"I hope you are right," she said.

"I hope so, too," he replied, "because certain people might accuse me of murder if things take an unfortunate turn. It wouldn't be difficult to prove a motive."

He was joking of course, and she took it as such, then found herself resting her forehead on his shoulder. "Oh, Leopold. I am so glad you are here. What would I have done without you?"

He put his arm around her and kissed the top of her head, but gave no reply.

Later that morning, when Joseph woke again and seemed to be feeling better, Leopold left him and Rose alone and did not return for several hours. When at last he knocked on the door, it was nearing twilight. Rose stood quickly from her chair.

"Where were you?" she asked as she invited him in to see her husband sitting up in bed and taking some broth and tea.

Joseph seemed pleased to see him as well. "General Hunt, have you eaten?"

Leopold entered the room and removed his hat. "Not yet, Your Highness, but I have come with a visitor. I rode to Brussels today to bring back Dr. Samson, who treated you last night."

Joseph set down his spoon with a clunk. "My word, you don't say. And what have you done with Dr. Harris? I hesitate to ask."

Rose laughed, while Leopold looked down and turned his hat over in his hands. "I apologize for my conduct earlier. Lack of sleep makes me irritable."

"Thank heavens for that," Joseph replied good-naturedly. "I am more than certain that you saved me from a horrendous ordeal."

"Let us hope so. Now, if you would permit Dr. Samson to examine you, he will give us a better idea of the state of things. He is a brilliant surgeon, and I trust his opinion."

"If you trust him, then I trust him as well," Joseph said. "Where is he? Bring him in."

Leopold turned to go and fetch him.

Rose stopped Leopold at the door. "What about Dr. Harris?" she asked. "Where is he? I hope they are not clashing swords in the taproom."

Leopold turned back and gave her a dazzling smile. "Now *that* I would like to see. I regret to say, however, that Dr. Harris was called away rather suddenly. There was a request for his services in Ligny."

"And whose request was it?" Joseph inquired with a chuckle. "Yours, I presume?"

Leopold shrugged innocently and went to fetch the doctor.

A quarter of an hour later, Dr. Samson was rewrapping Joseph's leg. "The wound looks excellent," he said. "I am very pleased, and I see you are taking some broth. That is excellent as well." He glanced at Rose. "Many victories in Belgium recently, Your Highness. Have you all heard the latest news about Napoleon? He dashed off the field so fast yesterday, someone said they saw sparks beneath the carriage wheels."

Joseph laughed, but winced in pain. Rose rushed to his side. "No laughing for you, dear. You'll hurt yourself."

"At least I will do so on two legs instead of one," he replied.

She laughed and kissed him on the forehead, then glanced at Leopold and smiled.

Rose's smile left Leopold spellbound. Seconds later he was heartsick, for he knew he must leave her soon, when all he wanted to do was stay with her forever.

Dr. Samson packed up his instruments and promised to check back later that night. As soon as he was gone, Leopold cleared his throat and forced himself to begin the difficult process of saying good-bye.

"Clearly you are in good hands now," he said.

The color drained from Rose's face. She regarded him unhappily. "You are leaving us?"

She spoke in a tone that suggested he was betraying her all over again, but it was quite the opposite. It would be wrong for him to stay and dream of things that could never be. To the contrary, it would be best to put some distance between them—and quite a substantial amount of it. Surely she understood that.

Why, then, did he feel an overwhelming compulsion to close the distance between them now and pull her into his arms and kiss her passionately with every spark of fire left in his soul?

For a few pounding heartbeats it felt as if Joseph had simply vanished into thin air and it was just the two of them alone . . . as lovers, as they had once been.

God, how he wanted her. This was agony—heart-wrenching, merciless agony.

Joseph spoke up in that moment. The sound of his voice was like a glass of water in Leo's face.

"I am sure General Hunt has more important things to do than watch over a wounded man," he said. "The battle is over now. You have a proud army to lead back to Petersbourg, I can well imagine."

"Indeed I do." Leopold was surprisingly thankful for Joseph's casual remark to bring him back from the brink.

Rose was not quite so casual, however, at least not in Leo's eyes, for he could see she did not want him to go.

Part of him reveled in the evidence of her lingering affection, while another part of him wished she would treat him with indifference or even disdain. That would make all of this so much easier to bear.

"I see," she said. "You have been so helpful. We will never forget what you did for us. You saved Joseph's life."

The archduke clasped Rose's hand and squeezed it. "We both thank you, General, from the bottom of our hearts. I give you my word that I will make sure your heroic efforts are recognized. Perhaps there is something I could do to influence your sentencing in Petersbourg. Honestly, sir, I owe you my life."

Leopold regarded them as they sat close together, then quickly dropped his gaze to his hat, which he held in his hands. "Thank you, but I require nothing in return. I am pleased you are well." He swallowed with some difficulty, then bowed to them. "I shall bid you farewell and say a prayer that none of us have to fight Bonaparte ever again."

"Quite right," Joseph replied as Leopold moved to the door. "Please wait, General."

Leopold halted and shut his eyes. How close he had been to an honorable discharge . . .

"Rose, you must walk the general to his horse."

"Yes, of course," she graciously replied, rising to her feet. "I would be happy to."

Leopold couldn't bring himself to turn around, but could not escape the sound of a quick kiss—perhaps on a hand or a cheek. All at once Rose was following him out of the room and down the stairs to the reception room.

Together they walked out the door.

Neither of them spoke as they crossed the stable yard toward Leopold's handsome chestnut charger, who was tethered to a rail in the shade of the inn.

Rose stroked Goliath's shiny mane and neck. "You two have been through a lot together," she said. "You will ride him all the way home to Petersbourg, I presume?"

There was a hint of melancholy in her voice when she mentioned going home.

Leopold waved quickly to dismiss a groom who came running to assist him. The groom immediately retreated.

"Eventually," Leo replied, "but for now, he will take me only as far as Brussels. It will be some time before we can leave Belgium. We must first account for all the dead and wounded and organize ourselves for the march."

The setting sun cast a glistening glow upon the golden hues of Rose's hair, and her eyes shimmered like gemstones when she looked at him. "How long before you must leave?" she asked.

"I cannot say for sure. A fortnight, perhaps."

She sighed heavily. "I don't suppose you could return to visit us again? I doubt we will be moving Joseph for at least that long."

He considered it for a moment, but felt as if he were fighting against a current that threatened to sweep him downriver to a place where he imagined himself sliding over the top of a giant waterfall, plunging headlong into the swirling white pool below—and taking Rose with him.

No. He had to grab hold of something. He could not pull her over the edge. He must not return to see her again.

"I suspect I will be kept very busy in Brussels," he said.

She inclined her head at him. "That's not the real reason, is it? Surely, Leopold, we know each other well enough by now to speak the truth."

He paused a moment, then shook his head at this impossible situation. "Sometimes I don't know what the truth is. All I know is that I have to find a way to stop loving you, Rose, and I don't know if I can do it."

Before he had a chance to prepare himself, she asked the burning question that would plague him forever. "What happened to us in Petersbourg? How could there have been any secrets? Why didn't you tell me about your family?"

"I was ashamed," he replied. "Ashamed of my past and how I was so greatly influenced by my father for all those years. When you and I danced at the Coronation Ball, I thought he had given up his foolish ambitions. I just wanted it all to disappear."

A terrible sorrow filled her eyes. If only he could take her by the hand and run away with her.

But she was a princess, wed to the future emperor of Austria. She would most certainly be missed.

"I wish you had told me about it," she said. "We could have warned Randolph, and you would never have been arrested."

He nodded. "Believe me, I've thought about it a thousand times and I torture myself when I imagine what could have been. But as you said, we cannot turn back time. We can only go forward. At least I will be content knowing that you are happy and living a wonderful life."

She looked up at him with stricken eyes that were on the verge of spilling forth a flood of tears.

"But *I* won't be content," she replied, "for I will not be able to think of *your* happiness, not if you are locked away for the next twenty years. Tell me what to do, Leopold, and I will do it."

He stared at her closely. Did she mean she would run away with him? Would she do it if he asked? Would she leave with him right now, this very instant?

She was breathing hard, waiting for him to say something.

He looked up at the inn where her husband lay recovering.

"You *will* be content," he said, closing his eyes as he spoke the words, "knowing that you have allowed me to reclaim my honor. It will have to be enough."

She moved closer, laid her forehead on his chest,

and wept quietly. He forced himself to keep his hands at his sides, to resist the urge to hold her.

"I will ask Joseph to insist that you receive a full pardon," she said. "Then at least I will know that you have your freedom. Perhaps you could write to me sometimes. I must know how you are."

He took hold of her shoulders and gently pushed her away. "That wouldn't be wise," he said, feeling as if he had just been pierced through the heart by a lance on the battlefield.

"So this is it, then?" she whispered. "Good-bye for the last time?"

"Yes. That is how it must be."

She bowed her head and nodded, while he struggled with the desire to pull her into his arms, taste her sweet lips, and know the ecstasy of her heart, body, and soul—freely given to him, and him alone.

But she was no longer free. Destiny had other plans for her. She would be a great empress one day, and he would always be her secret champion in all causes from afar.

Turning away, he put his foot into the stirrup and mounted his horse.

Rose stepped out of the way and lifted a hand to shade her eyes from the blinding glare of the setting sun.

"Travel safely," she said.

"And you as well. Give my best to Joseph and tell him . . ." He paused.

"Tell him what?"

He shouldn't say the words, for there was too much meaning in them, but he did so nonetheless. "Tell him I said he is a very lucky man, and that Dr. Harris was right about one thing at least. Your husband stands under a shining star."

With that he galloped off, knowing that for once in his life, he had done the right thing. As he reached the outskirts of the village, however, he found he could not go on. He reined in his horse under a giant oak tree, dismounted and sat down under it, where he sat alone and wept for a very long time.

Chapter Thirty-one

Three weeks later, Rose stood in the stable yard at the inn, upon the very spot where she and Leopold had said their final good-byes.

Since that day, Joseph had made significant progress and his wounds were healing well. Dr. Samson had served them devotedly and agreed to accompany them all the way back to Austria, for it would be an arduous journey and Joseph would require continued medical attention. There was some talk of appointing Dr. Samson to the office of palace physician at the Hofburg, for he was highly skilled and brilliant in his field.

All that would be decided later, of course. For now, Rose must let go of all hope that Leopold might come to visit them at the inn one last time. She didn't even know if he was still in Belgium. He could already be on his way back to Petersbourg.

At any rate, it was time to leave the village of Waterloo. Joseph had already been assisted into the coach, and she mustn't keep him waiting.

But oh, it was not easy to leave. She found herself gazing up the road, imagining that Leopold might somehow know she was leaving today and would come galloping on his magnificent chestnut charger to bid her a final farewell. In her heart she had called to him and stared out the window for many hours over the past few weeks.

But he did not come.

Now it was time to leave.

With a brave but aching heart, she walked to the coach and climbed inside.

Joseph was stretched out on the opposite seat with his leg propped up on a pile of thick brocade pillows to cushion against the swaying movements of the coach. It was going to be a long journey, but he wanted desperately to return home.

"I am happy to see you," he said, gazing at her with affection. "For a moment I was worried you might decide to stay behind."

She stared at him for a tender moment while the servants placed one last trunk on the rooftop. "How could you ever think such a thing?" Reaching forward, she took his hand in hers and kissed the back of it. "From now on, there shall be no more foolish talk. We are going home, Joseph, and the war is over."

Breathing deeply with relief, he leaned back in the seat and closed his eyes, while Rose gazed out the window and said her own private farewell to Waterloo.

Chapter Thirty-two

Cavanaugh Manor, Petersbourg
Three months later

As the coach rumbled to a halt before the front steps of the home Leo never imagined he would ever see again, he clasped his hands together and thanked God for this one small mercy among so many painful sacrifices.

The coach door opened suddenly, and he looked out at the butler who was lowering the iron step in the early autumn sunshine.

"Good afternoon, Johnson," Leopold said as he climbed out and gazed up at the front of the house.

"Good afternoon, my lord," Johnson replied, as if not a single day had passed since Leopold's terrible fall from grace.

And how odd to be addressed that way again after eight months without a title, other than "general."

It had all been returned to him now. His service at Waterloo—in particular his actions that saved the life of the future Austrian emperor—had been rewarded.

He had been given a full pardon, and his property and title of marquess had been restored.

He suspected Rose had something to do with it, but he would never know, for he would not permit himself to ask.

"Leopold . . ." His mother hurried out the front door. "Welcome home." She took both his hands in hers and kissed them. "I am so happy to see you. The servants have been positively brimming with excitement all day."

"I am pleased to hear it," he replied as he offered his arm to escort her up the front steps. "Were we fortunate enough to hire most of them back?"

"Yes, every single one, even those who found positions elsewhere after we lost the house. As soon as they learned you would be returning, they gave their notice and dashed back here as fast as their legs could carry them."

As they walked through the door, Leopold stopped and drew back in surprise when the entire staff—lined up in the hall to greet him—broke into an enthusiastic round of applause and cheering.

He had not expected such a homecoming, nor had he imagined how it would affect him. A wave of emotion rose up within him, and he had to fight to keep his composure in check as he shook hands with all of them.

"This is unexpected," Leo said.

"Lord Cavanaugh," Johnson said, "please permit me to say, for all of us, that you have been dearly missed these past eight months. We are all exceedingly pleased to have you home. Your heroism at Waterloo has thrilled and inspired us, and we are honored to serve you again."

Leo thanked him then turned to continue shaking hands with each servant.

A short while later, after the staff dispersed to resume their duties, Leopold accompanied his mother to the drawing room for tea, where they sat together on the sofa.

As she poured him a cup, she said, "We are all so proud of you. I hope you know that."

The entire country seemed to have gone to great lengths to show him he was no longer disgraced. King Randolph had been more than generous in his praise.

"I feel very blessed."

She handed him the cup and saucer. "But how are you otherwise? I do not wish to pry, but I suspect you know what I am referring to."

He took a sip of the tea. "I am as well as can be expected. It wasn't easy, of course, seeing Rose in Brussels, but I have made my peace with it. Now I must get on with my life and put the past behind me."

"I am sorry it didn't turn out the way you wanted," she gently replied.

"So am I." He took another sip of tea, and was grateful for the silence as his mother let the subject go.

He listened to the clock ticking on the mantelpiece.

A bird chirped outside the window.

Since the battle at Waterloo, he had become very aware and very grateful for how blessedly quiet the world could be sometimes. He supposed he'd heard enough noise that one day to last the rest of his life.

"It's probably too early to speak of such things," his mother said, "but have you given any thought to the idea of marrying one day?"

He gave his mother a warm, forgiving look. "You are right about one thing. It is too early to speak of it. I will require some time for my wounds to heal."

He knew, however, that he would have to think of it eventually, for the title "Marquess of Cavanaugh" was originally bestowed upon him for his past service in the campaign against Napoleon. He was the first Cavanaugh, so there were no other heirs. Similarly, all his father's titles had been dissolved, therefore if Leopold died without issue, this title and property would revert back to the crown.

It wouldn't be the end of the world, he supposed, as long as his mother was taken care of—and she would be, for she had her own money.

Nevertheless, he felt a responsibility to uphold the title, for the king had been most generous in bestowing it upon him a second time. Such gifts should not be squandered.

His mother set down her cup and folded her hands on her lap. "Very well. I won't push you, Leopold. I only bring it up because I feel it necessary to warn you that you may have to fight the young women off with a rather large stick. In particular Lady Elise. You remember her, don't you? She and her mother came to visit us last year during those few weeks when it was so unbearably hot."

Leopold chuckled softly as he recalled the flying fruit basket and the young lady's desperate attempts to attract his attention when he was blind to all women but one.

"I do remember her," he said. "She was rather giddy if I recall."

"Yes. She was too young for you last year, but she has matured. As it happens, when she failed to catch your eye, she set her cap for Prince Nicholas. I am not sure what happened between them exactly, but she was most decidedly disappointed."

"I cannot say I am surprised," Leopold said. "Nicholas is not the sort of man who will wish to settle down any time soon."

"That is true. More tea?"

He passed her his cup. She refilled it and handed it back.

"At any rate," she said, "Lady Elise and her mother will be passing through here on their way to visit relatives in the north over Christmas. They will only stay one night. Perhaps it would cheer you a little to enjoy some female company."

"I shall endeavor to be charming," he graciously replied.

They chatted about other things for a while, then Leopold stood up to cross the room and look out the window.

The leaves were glorious in their rich autumn colors, and the sky was a clear October blue. In the distance, the lake shimmered magnificently in the late afternoon sunlight.

By God, it was good to be alive, and doubly good to be home in one piece.

He felt very blessed all of a sudden, and was determined to make the most of this second chance at a life of honor. Perhaps, in the pursuit of it, he would find some measure of happiness.

PART V
Peace

Chapter
Thirty-three

Five years later

The summer of 1820 was an exceedingly hot one in Petersbourg. Rose was quite certain she had not known its equivalent since that memorable year when her father passed away and she had mourned him so deeply.

Yet it had also been a summer of love.

Though in the end she had mourned that, too.

Now she was home again for the first time in five years and felt quite jubilant at the prospect. Everything looked much the same—the streets, the buildings, the people, and the palace where she grew up. Very little had changed in the city, though she now looked upon it with different eyes. More worldly eyes, for she was not the same young woman she had been when she left here.

Since that time, she had been through a war; she had enjoyed a happy marriage and was a mother now to a beautiful daughter who was the center of her world.

Marie was four and precocious, and very blond like

her parents. Rose was charmed and beguiled by her every moment of every day.

On this particular day, however, her daughter was being well entertained and no doubt indulged by her uncles at the palace, while Rose and her sister-in-law, Queen Alexandra, were scheduled to attend an outdoor concert in the park, given by one of Petersbourg's leading composers.

It was a most superb afternoon of entertainment. The only complaint from anyone concerned the heat. The fans fluttered constantly during the performance and the poor hapless conductor was dripping with perspiration by the end of it.

Afterward, Rose and Alexandra waved to the crowds lining the streets on their return procession to the palace, which took them through the shopping district in Elmsdale and past the new hospital on Sycamore Street.

Fanning herself in the warm interior of the coach, Rose leaned forward to admire the stunning Baroque architecture of the hospital and the sculpted fountain out front. As they drove past it, the shiny brass plaque on the outer gate caused her belly to flip over in response.

"Wait, can we stop?" she said to Alexandra.

Alexandra did not pause to ask why. She slid across the seat, leaned out the open window, and called to the driver, "Stop here, please!"

The coach immediately pulled to a halt, which jostled Rose forward in her seat. "I apologize," she said to Alexandra, "but I saw something back there. Can we turn around?"

"What did you see?"

"The new hospital," she replied. "I couldn't help but notice the plaque at the gate. Did it say 'Cavanaugh'?"

Alexandra regarded her carefully in the thick and humid summer heat. "Yes, and now that you are home, I suppose you should know everything there is to know about what has changed since you left." She leaned out the window again. "Take us through the gate at All Saints' Hospital, please."

The coach lumbered forward on the wide street and turned around, while Rose's heart began to beat very fast. She had not experienced anything like it in years, and it made her feel rather young and foolish.

"Are you going to tell me about the changes, or am I required to guess?"

Alexandra crossed to sit beside Rose and laid a gloved hand on her knee. "When you left Petersbourg all those years ago, I remember how difficult it was for you. I knew that you were in love with Lord Cavanaugh. What happened between you was most unfortunate."

Surprised by her sister-in-law's blunt confession, Rose inclined her head with curiosity. "For him more than anyone."

"Yes, indeed, but everything changed for him after Waterloo. Thanks to you and your husband, his honor was restored, as well as his title and property."

Rose had known about that, naturally, for she had made inquiries not long afterward, but it had been many years since she asked any questions about Leopold. She had felt it best to let go of the past and live the life she had chosen.

"Ever since then," Alexandra continued, "he has devoted himself to the service of this country. He is greatly loved by the people."

The coach drove through the open gates at the entrance. The hospital, at the end of a long circular drive, was situated on a wide expanse of grassy parkland overlooking the meadows on the south side of the city. It was the park where Rose—in what seemed like another lifetime—went riding each morning.

"This is all his doing?" she asked, admiring the ornate stonework outside the front entrance.

"Yes. It took him three years to raise the funds, which he accomplished through various charity events and . . . well, mostly by asking every influential aristocrat in the country to donate something. All their names are engraved on the wall on the east side of the building, so they are recognized and feel quite heroic for their contributions."

"Can we go inside?" Rose asked. "I would like to see it."

Alexandra glanced at the front of the building, its white walls gleaming in the bright summer sunshine. "The staff will have a fit. Perhaps we should make arrangements to come another day."

"Oh, no, that will not do," Rose replied. "I must see it now. There is no need to make a big fuss about it. We will just stroll into the reception hall and take a quick look around. I don't require a formal tour. Perhaps while we are there we can make arrangements for that."

Alexandra hesitated and stared at her uncertainly.

"What's wrong?" Rose asked.

Alexandra laid a hand on her knee again. "He won't be there, you know. He spends most of his time in the country."

Rose wasn't sure if she was relieved or disappointed . . .

Relieved. Yes, of course she was relieved—for it was difficult to imagine what she would say if she encountered Leopold unexpectedly. It had been such a long time . . .

She looked out the window at the gardens as they passed by. "Is he married?"

Alexandra shook her head. "No, he never took a wife."

The bells chimed at the nearby cathedral to indicate the hour, and Rose leaned her head back against the soft, plum-colored velvet upholstery. She closed her eyes. "How I missed the sound of those bells." She waited for them to finish, then opened her eyes and lifted her head. "I admit I am surprised to hear that Leopold never married. Surely he could have any woman he wanted."

"He certainly could, and he has had no shortage of female suitors. That's probably why he spends so much time in the country—to escape the hunt. Poor man . . . like a fox in a hole with the dogs constantly yapping at his heels."

The coach pulled to a halt at the front of the hospital, and a servant opened the door.

"Well, then," Rose said. "Let us venture inside and see the place, shall we?"

Gathering up her reticule and slipping her fan into it, she slid across the seat. A footman quickly appeared to assist her and Alexandra out. Together they strolled up the stone walk to the main entrance.

"What a lovely hospital," Rose said to Alexandra an hour later after enjoying a full tour of the building from top to bottom, and making arrangements to return another day to visit the children in the east wing. They would organize some form of entertainment. A puppet show perhaps.

Though Rose had been very interested in the tour, she often found herself preoccupied, for it was as if the walls were alive with Leopold's presence. Every step she took over the smooth marble floors made her feel connected to him again, for this was his project, his creation.

She was so very proud of him and could not deny that still—after all these years—he held a special place in her heart and always would.

As she and Alexandra entered the coach, she found herself wishing that fate had intervened and brought Leopold to the hospital that day while they were taking their tour. She would have congratulated him for his achievements since the last time she saw him.

She had been a married woman then.

Oh . . . dear, sweet Joseph. He had been the best husband a woman could ask for. It had been more than a year since his passing, and she still missed him every day.

Rose was accustomed to such feelings, however, for she had lived with them most of her adult life.

"Is there anywhere else you would like to visit?" Alexandra asked as they settled into their seats, facing each other.

Rose withdrew her fan from her reticule and opened

it with a slow flick of her wrist. "No, I would prefer to go home now. It has been a long day."

The coach lurched forward, and they headed back to the palace.

The breeze was cool on Rose's cheeks as she galloped fast and hard across the rolling green meadow with her groom a short distance behind.

Indeed, it was glorious to be home again, to bask in the familiar surroundings that were so much a part of her identity. How many times had she ridden across these gorgeous green pastures? Hundreds of times, to be sure, and now, after having been away for five years, she cherished them more than ever. She cherished *everything* about Petersbourg, and felt suddenly euphoric as Zeus leaped over a low stone wall and carried her toward the sweet-smelling forest, where it would be cool in the shade of the leaves.

Slowing Zeus to a trot, she entered the wood and patted him on the neck. "Good boy. Let's walk for a while and catch our breath, shall we?"

She closed her eyes and breathed in the fresh pine-scented air while the canopy of branches overhead reigned majestically over the path that would take her to the top of the ridge.

Again, her thoughts drifted to another time when she had ridden this path with the expectation of meeting her first love. He had come, as promised, and that day would always remain one of the most magical, romantic memories of her life.

How could she not help but dream about encountering him here again? What would she do if he came cantering down the bridle path, exactly as before? She would smile, of course. Her heart would delight in the happiness.

She did not encounter Leopold, however, as she slowly climbed the ridge. There were no others in the forest except for her groom, who followed at a discreet distance.

At last, she reached the clearing at the top and dismounted. She handed Zeus to her groom who tethered both animals to a tree and waited patiently while she strolled to the edge of the rise to look out over the city.

Sitting down on a fallen tree that had not been there before, she untied the ribbons of her bonnet, carefully removed it, and set it down beside her while she cooled off in the gentle mountain breezes.

A short while later, the sound of voices caused her to turn quickly, for she thought she was alone here.

Her heart nearly beat out of her chest when she saw Lord Cavanaugh—*Leopold*—sitting high in his saddle carrying on a casual conversation with her groom, who held Leo's horse steady while he dismounted.

Wondering if this was yet another fantasy, Rose stood up and stared.

Oh, how handsome he looked, dressed in a dark green riding jacket and tawny breeches with polished boots and an elegant top hat. Muscular and fit, he still possessed an inconceivable power to knock her over with his unparalleled charisma and confidence.

Slowly he approached and removed his hat. "Your Royal Highness," he said with a bow.

She needed a moment to collect herself, for her heart was on fire at the shock and pleasure of seeing him again. It was like staring into the sun.

At last, she managed to find her voice. "Leopold."

It was wrong to address him by his given name, but it spilled from her lips before she had a chance to think it through.

"I thought I might find you here," he said. "I heard you had returned to Petersbourg. Yesterday I was informed of your visit to the hospital."

Her eyebrows lifted. "Oh, yes! It is very beautiful. I was most impressed. I was going to send you a note to congratulate you."

He gazed into her eyes for a moment, then spoke in a gentle tone. "I was sorry to hear about your husband. He was a good man. Please accept my condolences."

"Thank you."

They each lowered their gazes while a light breeze whispered through the treetops.

Feeling a sudden reckless impulse she could not resist, Rose looked up and said, "Will you excuse me for a moment?"

"Of course."

She picked up her skirts and crossed the clearing to speak to her groom. A few seconds later, he was mounting his horse and riding back to the palace alone.

"I told him he could leave us," she explained to Leopold as she returned to him. "Perhaps you would be kind enough to escort me back?"

"I would be honored."

She smiled at him and motioned toward the fallen tree, which served as a comfortable bench to look out over the city. They sat down beside each other.

"I must confess it is wonderful to see you," Leopold said. "I can hardly believe we are sitting here."

"Nor can I," she replied.

"There is so much to talk about, isn't there. I don't know where to begin. How much time do we have?"

She laughed. "I am feeling the same way, as if we will be forced to part ways before we are finished."

He laid a hand on his chest. "My heart is pounding."

"Mine, too."

In the distance, the bells chimed in the cathedral tower. Rose closed her eyes, again relishing the sound.

"You have a daughter," Leopold said. "Will you tell me about her?"

Naturally, Rose was delighted to talk about her beautiful Marie and how she was so confident and smart for her age. Leopold listened intently with genuine interest and fascination.

She then asked about the hospital and his other charitable endeavors, and he described a number of worthy causes that inspired him. She was inspired as well, and offered to help in any way she could.

Next they chatted about how the world had changed for the better since the war, and Leopold told her that his mother had recently remarried. She was now Lady Bosworth, wife of a kindhearted viscount who shared her love of flowers and country living.

Before Rose realized it, more than an hour had passed. She glanced with some concern at the horses. "They are probably getting thirsty," she mentioned, though she didn't want to leave just yet. She wanted to continue the conversation.

"Shall we walk them to the creek?" Leopold suggested.

"An excellent idea." Rose stood and picked up her bonnet, which she tied quickly under her chin.

They untethered the two animals, led them into the woods, and began the gradual descent down the east side of the ridge.

It was shady and cool beneath the shelter of the tall pines, and Rose was highly attuned to the sound of their footsteps, and the tap of the horses' hooves upon the packed ground as they walked.

"It's so peaceful here," she said on a wistful sigh as she looked up at the sky.

"It's like heaven," he replied. "Not a day goes by that I don't appreciate the peace of our country and the simple fact that I am here on this earth, alive and well enough to enjoy the beauty of it." He slanted a look at her. "Forgive me, Rose. I shouldn't have said that."

"Why not?" she asked. "I feel the same way."

He squinted into a sun-dappled clearing along the side of the path. "Yes, but you lost your husband recently. That was insensitive of me."

"Not at all," she assured him. "It's important that we embrace life and never take it for granted. Joseph believed that, and he made the most of the time he had after Waterloo. He often said that what happened to him was a blessing because it taught him to appreciate life so much more."

Leopold was quiet for a moment. "What happened in the end?" he asked. "I often think of those days in Waterloo and the decision I forced upon you."

"You didn't force us," she said. "We agreed with you."

"I held a gun to the doctor's head," he reminded her with a half chuckle. "It wasn't my finest moment, I assure you."

She couldn't help but laugh along with him. "I must disagree with you there, Leopold. What you did was very fine indeed. And if you are wondering about Joseph's leg, it healed remarkably well. He walked with a limp that was barely noticeable, and he only required a cane in the last year, when it began to ache more than usual on rainy days. He lived a full and healthy life, and we had you to thank for that. It was something else entirely that claimed him in the end. A severe fever. It happened quickly."

They reached the creek and led the horses for a drink.

Leopold turned to her. "Are you home to stay now, Rose, or will you return to Austria?"

"Oh, I am most definitely home to stay," she replied. "Did you not know that?"

He shook his head. "I thought perhaps Emperor Francis might not wish to part with his grandchild."

She stroked Zeus's shoulder. "I am sure things would be different if I'd had a son, but my daughter has no claim to the throne. That will go to Ferdinand. Francis has always been sympathetic to my attachment to Petersbourg. He wanted me to be happy. He let me go with his blessing."

The horses finished drinking, so they led them back to the path.

"Then I am very glad you are home," Leopold said, pausing before they mounted to ride the rest of the way.

"I am glad, too," she replied. "I never said this to

anyone before, but I always felt rather displaced in Austria."

"I felt displaced, too," he softly said, "even though I was here the entire time."

They faced each other in the cool shade of the forest, and all at once, an unsettling wave of emotion washed over Rose. She felt exuberant and excited as she admired Leopold's arresting blue eyes and handsome face, yet melancholy at the same time, for she wasn't sure if it was too late for this mad love they had once shared. So much had happened to tear them apart, and she knew very well that no one could ever turn back the hands of time. She was no longer the young, inexperienced virgin she had once been. She was a widow now, with a young daughter . . .

Leopold squinted in a blinding shaft of sunlight that broke through the treetops and illuminated his face. He was still the most handsome man she had ever known. That would never change.

"I've missed you," he said, gazing at her with intense affection and an obvious vulnerability that curled around her heart like a sweet caress.

"I missed you, too," she replied. "It hurts sometimes when I think of how we lost touch, and how I never knew what was happening in your life. There is still so much I want to ask you."

"Ask me now," he said.

She glanced down at her feet and smiled. "I fear that if I start heading down that path, Leopold, we could be here all night, for I would like to know every detail of every moment of your life since we parted in the stable yard that last day in Waterloo."

He nodded as if he felt the same way. They turned and started walking again.

"You never married," she mentioned in a casual tone.

"No, though I considered it a few times. My mother has certainly done her part to wrangle me into matrimony, but I could never go ahead with it, despite everyone's best efforts."

"Why not?"

The horses plodded along behind them, their heads bobbing as they walked.

"Because I could never love anyone but you, Rose, and I am quite sure my heart will be yours until the end of time."

Another deep wave of emotion rolled over her and she stopped abruptly, for they were the sweetest words she'd ever heard in her life.

Oh God . . . how she loved this man.

Leopold stopped, too, and faced her.

"I always told you that I'd never give you up," he said. "That I'd wait forever, and it has felt like forever since I let you go. But now you're here before me, and all I want to do is hold you in my arms. I don't know how I've managed not to."

"Then hold me," she breathlessly replied. "*Please,* for I've waited a long time as well."

He needed no further encouragement. He stepped forward and pulled her into his loving embrace. The forest all around them seemed to explode into a stunning rainbow of color.

His touch was pure heaven. Rose wrapped her arms around his shoulders and clung tightly to his strength.

She couldn't seem to get enough of him. How long she had waited for this. Everything felt right and no longer displaced. She was where she was meant to be—with the man who had always possessed her heart.

He drew back and took her face in his hands, searching the depths of her eyes with joyful disbelief. "Is this really happening?" he asked. "Is it possible you could be mine? Am I dreaming?"

She shook her head and laughed through a flood of happy tears. "It's real," she replied, "and yes, I am yours, Leopold. I was always yours, despite everything, and I am still waiting for you to kiss me."

In the very next instant, his lips covered hers with exquisite, unrestrained passion, and the world shifted beneath her feet. His mouth was moist and hot and the taste of him pleasured her to the very depths of her soul.

Running her fingers through his hair, Rose sighed with enchantment and clung to his shoulders. Soon he was sweeping her off her feet and into his arms like a groom on a wedding night. He carried her into the woods.

Kissing her along the way, while stepping over ferns and pushing through the underbrush, he finally reached a small, private clearing surrounded by sycamores.

There, with the sun raining down upon them, he dropped to his knees and set her down in the grass. Rose held her arms out to him, inviting him closer, and he covered her body with his own.

"Tell me it won't end this time," he whispered huskily in her ear while he stroked her body with roving, desperate hands.

"I promise it won't," she replied. "I am yours forever. Nothing will ever come between us again. I won't let it."

Not even Napoleon's army could separate them now, for she had waited too long for this. Leopold Hunt was the man she loved more than life itself, and she would not lose him again.

"Marry me," he said, "with or without the king's permission. I don't care who approves, nor will I ever again make the mistake of placing duty above my love for you. I will steal you away if I have to."

Overcome with happiness, her body on fire, Rose kissed him deeply. "Oh, Leopold. Freedom was a luxury I rarely ever dreamed of. Perhaps I should have rebelled when I had the chance, but I, too, chose duty over love, and I am so sorry."

"No," he said, leaning back. "There shall be no regrets. Though it was painful, I believe everything was meant to be exactly as it was. You have a beautiful daughter now, and I found my dignity again. I reclaimed my honor."

She laid her open palm on his cheek and smiled. "Yes, you did. I knew it the moment you sent word to me in Brussels, when I learned you saved Joseph's life, and I vow that I will never doubt you again."

He brushed his lips over hers. "Let us move forward now, Rose, for it is the only direction I wish to go."

"It is a fine direction," she replied with a smile. "And I don't care who approves, either. Yes, I will marry you. All that matters is that we are together."

His expression turned serious. "Yes, but I will still seek your brother's blessing."

Feeling cheeky all of a sudden, Rose flipped him over to straddle his hips and pin him down. "I am quite sure he will give it to you, Leopold. All you have to do is ask."

"How can you be so sure?" he asked, his eyes narrowing with curiosity.

"Because I already asked him, and he said yes."

Leopold regarded her with both admiration and desire. "When?"

"Yesterday," she explained, "when I returned from the hospital, because I knew I had to have you. Nothing was going to stop me this time."

"You were that confident?"

"Yes, because you promised me you would wait forever, and you did. Now, there will be no more waiting."

He sat up and kissed her deeply while hugging her body close.

"I love you, Rose," he whispered, "more than anything in this world."

"And I love you, too," she replied, "until forever and beyond."

The horses nickered to each other on the path, and a tiny sparrow fluttered out of the sycamores and soared high up to the sky as they held each other tightly.

This time, they would never let go. This time, it would be just as it was meant to be.

Epilogue

Cavanaugh Manor
Summer 1821

"Congratulations, my lord. You have a son."

Leopold stood quickly from the chair in the corridor and barely managed to thank the doctor as he brushed past him, for it had not been an easy task over the past two hours, listening to his wife's screams during the delivery. The butler had suggested he wait in the library where he would be spared the discomfort, but he needed to remain close by. If Rose had to endure it, then so would he.

But it was over now, and she was well.

He burst into the room and stopped just inside the door to behold his beautiful wife sitting up against the pillows with her flaxen hair loose and wild about her shoulders. There was a noticeable pallor to her complexion, but a sparkle in her eyes. She flashed him a brilliant smile and a rush of awe flowed through him.

In her arms she held their first child—a tiny person

he could barely comprehend as he stared at the small white bundle.

"You can come closer," she said with a light chuckle. "Come and see your son."

Slowly, he moved to the side of the bed and let his gaze fall upon the babe's face. He was quiet and content . . . so very tiny. His little fingers were flexing.

"Isn't he beautiful?" Rose said.

"He's a miracle," Leopold replied. "*You* are a miracle. This *life* is a miracle."

Carefully, trying not to disturb the sense of peace that seemed so very precious at this moment, Leopold climbed onto the bed beside Rose. She snuggled closer to rest her head on his shoulder.

"I am so happy," she said.

"I've been happy since the moment you returned to me," he replied, "but I had no idea this was before us. I never imagined it could be better than it already was. How is this much joy possible?"

"You've earned it, my darling."

He shook his head in disbelief. "If that is so, I am very grateful, for I cannot help but look back at the despair I suffered at the loss of you." He paused. "When I left you in Waterloo that day, it was the first time I ever accepted defeat, but now that we are here, I believe that was how it was meant to be, and this was worth waiting for. I was not worthy of you in those early days. I needed to be taught a lesson."

"What lesson?" she asked, looking up at him with those wise and luminous blue eyes.

He gently touched her cheek. "I needed to learn how to temper my ambition. My selfish greed for you.

You—and Joseph—showed me how to live for something other than myself. It was a gift I cannot put a value upon. And now you have given me a son. A son!"

The precious newborn reached out a small hand. Leopold put his finger into that miniature palm and felt a momentous surge of love and happiness envelop him when all five little fingers curled around his one big one.

"What shall we name him?" Rose asked with a smile.

"What about Frederick, after your father?"

The warmth of her smile filled her whole face and echoed in the silky tone of her voice. "That would make me very happy."

"Then it is decided—because you know I live for your happiness."

A knock sounded at the open door, and they both looked up.

The housekeeper entered the room. "I beg your pardon, Lord Cavanaugh, but you asked me to send for Marie. She is here now and very anxious to see her new brother. May I bring her in?"

"Of course!" Rose and Leopold both replied in unison.

Seconds later, Marie came dashing into the room. Leopold was quick to hold out an arm and invite her up onto his side of the bed. "Are you ready to see your new brother?" he asked. "But you must be gentle and quiet, for he is very small."

"I'm always gentle and quiet," Marie replied as she climbed up beside him. "But I shall be even more so today." She sat on her knees and inspected her new brother. "You're right, Papa, he is very small. When will he be able to walk?"

"Not for a while," Leopold replied. "Perhaps a year. And when that time comes, we will need you to hold his hand, sweetheart. Will you be able to do that?"

"Yes. I will be very good, and if he falls, I will pick him up and give him a kiss, just like you did for me yesterday when we were running too fast down to the swimming hole."

Rose laid her head on Leopold's shoulder again, and he felt even more love than he ever imagined possible.

"You were very brave," he said to Marie. "How is your knee today?"

"It's better, but I don't want to take the bandage off yet. I think tomorrow will be the right day."

"Yes," Leo agreed. "Tomorrow will be a very good day for that." Peace and wonder flowed through him when Marie snuggled into his arms to watch her little brother fall asleep.

Rose smiled up at him with love, and the whole world seemed to glow in the morning light as Leopold leaned closer and touched his lips to hers.

Don't miss the next novel in this
spectacular series from bestselling author
JULIANNE MACLEAN

The Prince's Bride

Available in May 2013 from St. Martin's Paperbacks